Thissel glanced bitterly across the esplanade toward the mask-maker's shop, "No one will tell me anything; I doubt if they care that a murderer is walking their docks," he complained. Kershaul surveyed him gravely. "It's true that they dislike interference. And should you locate Angmark, what will you do then?" Thissell looked grim and replied, "My duty."

The Forest Goblin's music became irritated and he sang, "He asserts that I am an outworlder? Let him prove his case."

Thissell said, "Very well, I will. Let's see your face, that'll demonstrate your identity!" The Forest Goblin sprang back in amazement. He reached to the nape of his neck, jerked the cord to his duel gong, and with his other hand snatched his scimitar.

"Run!" screamed Kershaul.

JACK VANCE

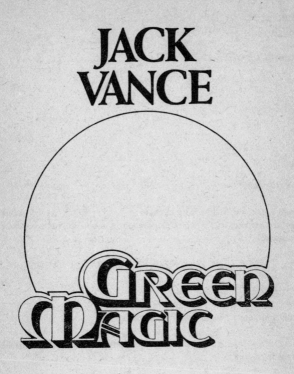

GREEN MAGIC

A TOM DOHERTY ASSOCIATES BOOK

A limited edition hardcover was previously published by Underwood/Miller

GREEN MAGIC: THE FANTASY REALMS OF JACK VANCE

A TOR Book
Published by Tom Doherty Associates, Inc.
49 West 24 Street
New York, NY 10010

Cover art by Rodney Matthews

ISBN: 0-812-55702-6   Can. ISBN: 0-812-55703-4

First edition: August 1988

Printed in the United States of America

0 9 8 7 6 5 4 3 2 1

ACKNOWLEDGMENTS

"Green Magic," copyright © 1963 by Mercury Press, Inc. *The Magazine of Fantasy and Science Fiction*, June, 1963.

"The Miracle Workers," copyright © 1958 by Street & Smith Publications, Inc. *Astounding Science Fiction*, July, 1958.

"The Moon Moth," copyright © 1961 by Galaxy Publishing Corporation. *Galaxy*, August, 1961.

"The Mitr," copyright © 1953 by Specific Fiction Corporation. *Vortex Science Fiction*, 1953.

"The Men Return," copyright © 1957 by Royal Publications, Inc. *Infinity Science Fiction*, July, 1957.

"The Narrow Land," copyright © 1967 by Ziff Davis Publishing Co. *Fantastic Science Fiction*, July, 1967.

"The Pilgrims," copyright © 1966 by Mercury Press, Inc. *The Magazine of Fantasy and Science Fiction*, June, 1966.

"The Secret," copyright © 1966 by Impulse. *Impulse*, March 1966.

"Liane the Wayfarer," copyright © 1950 by Hillman Periodicals, Inc. *The Dying Earth*, 1950.

Contents

FOREWORD
by Poul Anderson

It is a pleasure as well as an honor to write about Jack Vance —not nearly as great a pleasure as to read him or meet him, but nevertheless real, what the late Anthony Boucher used to call "the noble pleasure of praising."

Science fiction readers are as prone to fashion as everybody else. For many years, most of them seemed to take Jack Vance pretty much for granted. They glorified newcomer after newcomer for brilliance of style, depth of insight, sweep of narration, and so on, but seldom noticed that all the while a possessor of all these virtues was quietly at work enriching the field. As one of those who did admire (and, in my case, envy) his gifts, I was puzzled at such blindness. I am happy to see it coming to an end at last, and he starting to get the honor that is overdue him.

Among the reasons for this delay is, doubtless, that he himself is a quiet fellow, who doesn't blow his own horn— except occasionally in a jazz combo—and declines to become a plastic celebrity as too many with far less talent are busy being. He doesn't talk about his art, he practices it. He won't tell you how totally consecrated to it he is, when in fact he is not; he is, instead, a whole man, with a tremendous range of interests, skills, and experience of life. That shows in his work, to which he does give an overflowing measure of devotion when he is engaged in it.

What memories cluster around his name! *Big Planet*, the Demon Princes series, *The Dragon Masters*, *The Last Castle*, *The Moon Moth*—on and on. He is endlessly inventive, but his inventions (worlds, peoples, societies, institutions, individuals, artifacts, incidents), no matter how gorgeously exotic, are so well planned and executed that one instantly believes they could in fact come to be. He is as great a master of the English language as was Lord Dunsany, whom in certain respects he recalls though he does not imitate. He can be exciting, satirical, funny, stark, tender, sensuous, thoughtful, and all in the same story. Elsewhere I have called him a maker of epics, not grandiose but nevertheless of Homeric scope and power. Furthermore, his detective and crime novels, published semi-pseudonymously as by John Holbrook Vance, are marvelous portrayals of real mileus, anywhere from the South Seas to rural California. Do look them up if you haven't already.

In person, Jack Vance is an amiable, unassuming sort, though he can get mighty salty when he wants to. I've mentioned that he is a musician. He is a master carpenter as well, who has of late been converting his house into a mansion; a sailor, who is currently planning a Pacific cruise; a gourmet cook; a world traveler; a husband and father; a steadfast friend—and, germane to this occasion, the best of company. Meet him here for the first time, or renew acquaintance, and enjoy.

INTRODUCTION

It seems fairly evident that we draw inspiration from the "other" dimensions of reality which exist in the subconscious. We absorb the world, we digest, we formulate, we revise, we elaborate, we weave, we produce.

So where and how is Jack Vance doing his absorbing, digesting, formulating, revising, elaborating, weaving, and producing?

I wonder at this only distantly. I suspect, in some remote part of my mind, that he is utilizing his background as a world-traveler, to a certain extent; his eclectic comprehension of the various arts—many schools of music, painting, crafts, philosophy, literature. He has been a carpenter and an able-bodied seaman and at the same time he has been a man of academic depth and witty converse and poetic sensibilities; hence he is comfortable in several cultural classes of humanity. He can converse comfortably with the longshoreman or the professor of history. This gives him a cutting edge of comparative perspective, and a fundamental experience of the relativity of values. It might be instrumental in freeing him to conceptualize seemingly alien viewpoints.

On the other hand, all the foregoing might well be pure balderdash. Bunkum.

How can we know? And, more importantly, *should* we know? Should we squander our valuable time trying to analyze something we should be savoring? I think we should analyze the art of a great fantasist (if that is what Jack is) only insofar as our probing enhances our entertainment-value appreciation of the work subjectively—oh, professional writers have a need to examine the plumbing and skeleton and internal anatomy of other writers, so that they may learn. But that is another matter, really. This business of imputing psychological profundities to a writer too subtle and tasteful to utilize them is distasteful to me. And as for the writer's sources and unconscious motivations—none of the reader's business, in my opinion. Jack has likened this excessive scrutiny of the substructure of fiction to a disclosure of a stage magician's techniques for obtaining effects; obviously, it spoils everything.

If there is an implied morality in much of Vance's writing, so be it. It will find its place in our minds without our gouging it forth.

Now, satire—ah! Vance's writing is rich with satire and irony and it is there displayed for all to see without too much camouflage. His parables, however, are not gawky and out-at-elbows like so many self-conscious writings. They are elegantly devised, and shimmering with ramifications. His humor shows, perhaps, the influence of P.G. Wodehouse and James Branch Cabell—but he is imitating no one. His is one of the more distinctive stylistic voices of the twentieth century.

Whether describing the homely circumstances of a village inn, the picturesque but familiar spread of a seascape, the peculiar rituals of an otherworldly tribe, or a magnificent city of eccentric architectures and eccentric denizens, his writing is musical, painterly-visual, pointed, and wry. His is a peculiar combination of lyrical expansiveness and an economy of language that gives us lucid visual imagery with a handful of deft color-strokes . . . Color is a winning element of Jack's Universe.

If you are unfamiliar with Vance, and if you conceive of science-fiction and fantasy as sketchy space opera with little in the way of plausible background, then you had best steady yourself for a shock—you are about to enter realms which are astonishingly well-realized, even in the short stories, and which are rich in flavor of verisimilitude as well as being joyfully phantasmagoric. Once you've got a feel for his style, and you hear clearly his idiosyncratic "voice," you will be absorbed into unfolding adventure. Stylish Vance is, but for the careful reader he is never—or scarcely ever—self-indulgent. His fictions are carefully crafted machineries, whirring contrivances which, when given their due attention, deliver an extra dimension beyond the fascination of jeweled distractions—the whole that is more than the sum of the parts is a powerful subcurrent which will carry you through a rainbow valency of moods and story revelations.

Excuse me if I'm carried away—but I've just re-read the stories in this book and I'm dazzled, though I've read them all before. My friends regard me dolefully and shake their heads, muttering, "It must be that he's gotten himself into drugs— note the dilated eyes, the stunned look. It's as if he's seen into another world." Indeed I have, with a means less diminishing and more instructive than drugs. I've been reading *Green Magic*.

Green Magic is an unusual anthology in that it encompasses the sheer fantasy and the inarguably science-fictional reaches of Vance's facility. "Liane the Wayfarer" is a picaresque fantasy from *The Dying Earth*—"The Miracle Workers" is pure science fiction.

I was pleased to see "The Men Return" included, as it was an important story in the field I think, which exerted a great deal of influence on our ways of thinking—certainly, on mine. "The Men Return" is somewhere between fantasy and science fiction, though its substance has a speculative core—that causality, cause and effect, the reasonable concatenation establishing an orderly and predictable Universe, might be finite in its extent. That there might, at least, be a "pocket of noncausality" into which the earth could drift, freeing madmen to order the world as they please by psychokinesis, destroying all but a handful of "sane" men who are lost in a world of chaos and capriciousness, a world gone mad without consistent physical laws. How are we to say for sure that such a state does not exist, that it could not happen to us? Charles Forte understood. This story might well be the ultimate literary statement of the relativity of Being. But in the end of the story, "The Men Return." And the tough ones, the survivors, take advantage of the new orderliness. In many of Vance's stories a protagonist finds himself in bizarre, dangerous, alien, or otherwise testing surroundings only to triumph in the end by dint of cunning, common sense, persistence and constructive innovation. Perhaps this is one of the more consistent themes, if that's what it is, running through Vance's work. It is a simple theme, a proud one, rich in potential, and just plain good advice for us all.

Introduction

You are about to meet quirky characters who are nicely-shaded parodies of cupidity and self-absorption; you will meet Heroes, too, of surprising depth and humanity behind their basic nobility; you will smile at wry dialogue as, through the characters' viewpoints, you "dicker with avaricious shopkeepers, tavern-owners, salt-of-the-earth salesmen of every variety . . . These commonfolk seem to speak with an uncommon formality, in a style rococo and polysyllabic and universal from planet to planet . . . But break down these speeches—and I am including the remarks of aborigines and mountain-bandits of other Vance books who spout philosophy lamenting their existential dilemma and determinism—into more ordinary vernacular and you will find that the shopkeeper, bandit, whomever, is saying just what might be expected in the given situation . . . Vance chooses to elaborate a simple statement into a series of ironic convolutions . . . perhaps he is saying that the wisdom of the simple man is as great or greater than the wisdom of the complex man . . ." (I'm quoting from a certain brilliant reviewer writing in *Science Fiction Review* No. 31.)

In "The Mitr" we see that Vance is capable of writing a literary lament, a lovely parable as cutting and singingly downbeat as any in modern mainstream literature . . . It's a departure from his usual pattern of straightforward visionary-adventure.

The "Moon Moth" is a classic study of an alien culture and one man's adaptation to it.

The title story made me wonder if perhaps, as a foolish young man, I hadn't been right about a fantasist's source of inspiration in spiritworld benevolence. Never have I read a story with more atmosphere of realms inhuman. One almost concludes that Vance stumbled onto something real, beyond the ken of—

My friends are shaking me, asking me if I'm all right. I'll awaken in a moment, my friends. In a moment.

But first I want to savor a panoply of exquisite dreams.

JOHN SHIRLEY
PORTLAND, OREGON, 1979

Green Magic

OWARD FAIR, looking over the relics of his great-uncle Gerald McIntyre, found a large ledger entitled:

WORKBOOK AND JOURNAL
Open at Peril!

Fair read the journal with interest, although his own work went far beyond ideas treated only gingerly by Gerald McIntyre.

"The existence of disciplines concentric to the elementary magics must now be admitted without further controversy," wrote McIntyre. "Guided by a set of analogies from the white and black magics (to be detailed in due course), I have delineated the basic extension of purple magic, as well as its corollary, Dynamic Nomism."

Fair read on, remarking the careful charts, the projections and expansions, the transpolations and transformations by which Gerald McIntyre had conceived his systemology. So swiftly had the technical arts advanced that McIntyre's expositions, highly controversial sixty years before, now seemed pedantic and overly rigorous.

"Whereas benign creatures: angels, white sprites, merrihews, sandestins—are typical of the white cycle; whereas demons, magners, trolls and warlocks are evinced by black

magic; so do the purple and green cycles sponsor their own
particulars, but these are neither good nor evil, bearing, rather, the same relation to the black and white provinces that
these latter do to our own basic realm."

Fair re-read the passage. The "green cycle"? Had Gerald
McIntyre wandered into regions overlooked by modern
workers?

He reviewed the journal in the light of this suspicion, and
discovered additional hints and references. Especially provoc-
ative was a bit of scribbled marginalia: "More concerning my
latest researches I may not state, having been promised an
infinite reward for this forbearance."

The passage was dated a day before Gerald McIntyre's
death which had occurred on March 21, 1898, the first day
of spring. McIntyre had enjoyed very little of his "infinite
reward," whatever had been its nature . . . Fair returned to a
consideration of the journal, which, in a sentence or two, had
opened a chink on an entire new panorama. McIntyre provided
no further illumination, and Fair set out to make a fuller
investigation.

His first steps were routine. He performed two divinations,
searched the standard indexes, concordances, handbooks and
formularies, evoked a demon whom he had previously found
knowledgeable: all without success. He found no direct reference to cycles beyond the purple; the demon refused even to
speculate.

Fair was by no means discouraged; if anything, the intensity of his interest increased. He re-read the journal, with
particular care to the justification for purple magic, reasoning
that McIntyre, groping for a lore beyond the purple, might
well have used the methods which had yielded results before.
Applying stains and ultraviolet light to the pages, Fair made
legible a number of notes McIntyre had jotted down, then
erased.

Fair was immensely stimulated. The notes assured him
that he was on the right track, and further indicated a number

of blind alleys which Fair profited by avoiding. He applied himself so successfully that before the week was out he had evoked a sprite of the green cycle.

It appeared in the semblance of a man with green glass eyes and a thatch of young eucalyptus leaves in the place of hair. It greeted Fair with cool courtesy, would not seat itself, and ignored Fair's proffer of coffee.

After wandering around the apartment inspecting Fair's books and curios with an air of negligent amusement, it agreed to respond to Fair's questions.

Fair asked permission to use his tape-recorder, which the sprite allowed, and Fair set the apparatus in motion. (When subsequently he replayed the interview, no sound could be heard.)

"What realms of magic lie beyond the green?" asked Fair.

"I can't give you an exact answer," replied the sprite, "because I don't know. There are at least two more, corresponding to the colors we call rawn and pallow, and very likely others."

Fair arranged the microphone where it would more directly intercept the voice of the sprite.

"What," he asked, "is the green cycle like? What is its physical semblance?"

The sprite paused to consider. Glistening mother-of-pearl films wandered across its face, reflecting the tinge of its thoughts. "I'm rather severely restricted by your use of the word 'physical.' And 'semblance' involves a subjective interpretation, which changes with the rise and fall of the seconds."

"By all means," Fair said hastily, "describe it in your own words."

"Well—we have four different regions, two of which floresce from the basic skeleton of the universe, and so subsede the others. The first of these is compressed and isthiated, but is notable for its wide pools of mottle which we use sometimes for deranging stations. We've transplanted club-mosses from Earth's Devonian and a few ice-fires from Perdition.

They climb among the rods which we call devil-hair—" he
went on for several minutes but the meaning almost entirely
escaped Fair. And it seemed as if the question by which he
had hoped to break the ice might run away with the entire
interview. He introduced another idea.

" 'Can we freely manipulate the physical extensions of
Earth?' " The sprite seemed amused. "You refer, so I assume,
to the various aspects of space, time, mass, energy, life,
thought and recollection."

"Exactly."

The sprite raised its green cornsilk eyebrows. "I might as
sensibly ask can you break an egg by striking it with a club?
The response is on a similar level of seriousness."

Fair had expected a certain amount of condescension and
impatience, and was not abashed. "How may I learn these
techniques?"

"In the usual manner: through diligent study."

"Ah, indeed—but where could I study? Who would teach
me?"

The sprite made an easy gesture, and whorls of green
smoke trailed from his fingers to spin through the air. "I could
arrange the matter, but since I bear you no particular animos-
ity, I'll do nothing of the sort. And now, I must be gone."

"Where do you go?" Fair asked in wonder and longing.
"May I go with you?"

The sprite, swirling a drape of bright green dust over
its shoulders, shook his head. "You would be less than
comfortable."

"Other men have explored the worlds of magic!"

"True: your uncle Gerald McIntyre, for instance."

"My uncle Gerald learned green magic?"

"To the limit of his capabilities. He found no pleasure in
his learning. You would do well to profit by his experience
and modify your ambitions." The sprite turned and walked
away.

Fair watched it depart. The sprite receded in space and

dimension, but never reached the wall of Fair's room. At a distance which might have been fifty yards, the sprite glanced back, as if to make sure that Fair was not following, then stepped off at another angle and disappeared.

Fair's first impulse was to take heed and limit his explorations. He was an adept in white magic, and had mastered the black art—occasionally he evoked a demon to liven a social gathering which otherwise threatened to become dull—but he had by no means illuminated every mystery of purple magic, which is the realm of Incarnate Symbols.

Howard Fair might have turned away from the green cycle except for three factors.

First was his physical appearance. He stood rather under medium height, with a swarthy face, sparse black hair, a gnarled nose, a small heavy mouth. He felt no great sensitivity about his appearance, but realized that it might be improved. In his mind's eye he pictured the personified ideal of himself: he was taller by six inches, his nose thin and keen, his skin cleared of its muddy undertone. A striking figure, but still recognizable as Howard Fair. He wanted the love of women, but he wanted it without the interposition of his craft. Many times he had brought beautiful girls to his bed, lips wet and eyes shining; but purple magic had seduced them rather than Howard Fair, and he took limited satisfaction in such conquests.

Here was the first factor which drew Howard Fair back to the green lore; the second was his yearning for extended, perhaps eternal, life; the third was simple thirst for knowledge.

The fact of Gerald McIntyre's death, or dissolution, or disappearance—whatever had happened to him—was naturally a matter of concern. If he had won to a goal so precious, why had he died so quickly? Was the "infinite reward" so miraculous, so exquisite, that the mind failed under its possession? (If such were the case, the reward was hardly a reward.)

Fair could not restrain himself, and by degrees returned to a study of green magic. Rather than again invoke the sprite whose air of indulgent contempt he had found exasperating, he decided to seek knowledge by an indirect method, employing the most advanced concepts of technical and cabalistic science.

He obtained a portable television transmitter which he loaded into his panel truck along with a receiver. On a Monday night in early May, he drove to an abandoned graveyard far out in the wooded hills, and there, by the light of a waning moon, he buried the television camera in graveyard clay until only the lens protruded from the soil.

With a sharp alder twig he scratched on the ground a monstrous outline. The television lens served for one eye, a beer bottle pushed neck-first into the soil the other.

During the middle hours, while the moon died behind wisps of pale cloud, he carved a word on the dark forehead; then recited the activating incantation.

The ground rumbled and moaned, the golem heaved up to blot out the stars.

The glass eyes stared down at Fair, secure in his pentagram.

"Speak!" called out Fair. "*Enteresthes, Akmai Adonai Bidemgir! Elohim, pa rahulli! Enteresthes, HVOI!* Speak!"

"Return me to earth, return my clay to the quiet clay from whence you roused me."

"First you must serve."

The golem stumbled forward to crush Fair, but was halted by the pang of protective magic.

"Serve you I will, if serve you I must."

Fair stepped boldly forth from the pentagon, strung forty yards of green ribbon down the road in the shape of a narrow V. "Go forth into the realm of green magic," he told the monster. "The ribbons reach forty miles; walk to the end, turn about, return, and then fall back, return to the earth from which you rose."

The golem turned, shuffled into the V of green ribbon, shaking off clods of mold, jarring the ground with its ponderous tread.

Fair watched the squat shape dwindle, recede, yet never reach the angle of the magic V. He returned to his panel truck, tuned the television receiver to the golem's eye, and surveyed the fantastic vistas of the green realm.

Two elementals of the green realm met on a spun-silver landscape. They were Jaadian and Misthemar, and they fell to discussing the earthen monster which had stalked forty miles through the region known as Cil; which then, turning in its tracks, had retraced its steps, gradually increasing its pace until at the end it moved in a shambling rush, leaving a trail of clods on the fragile moth-wing mosaics.

"Events, events, events," Misthemar fretted, "they crowd the chute of time till the bounds bulge. Or then again, the course is as lean and spare as a stretched tendon . . ." He paused for a period of reflection, and silver clouds moved over his head and under his feet.

Jaadian remarked, "You are aware that I conversed with Howard Fair; he is so obsessed to escape the squalor of his world that he acts with recklessness."

"The man Gerald McIntyre was his uncle," mused Misthemar. "McIntyre besought, we yielded; as perhaps now we must yield to Howard Fair."

Jaadian uneasily opened his hand, shook off a spray of emerald fire. "Events press, both in and out. I find myself unable to act in this regard."

"I likewise do not care to be the agent of tragedy."

A Meaning came fluttering up from below: "A disturbance among the spiral towers! A caterpillar of glass and metal has come clinking; it has thrust electric eyes into the Portinone and broken open the Egg of Innocence. Howard Fair is the fault."

Jaadian and Misthemar consulted each other with wry disinclination. "Very well, both of us will go; such a duty needs two souls in support."

They impinged upon Earth and found Howard Fair in a

wall booth at a cocktail bar. He looked up at the two strangers and one of them asked, "May we join you?"

Fair examined the two men. Both wore conservative suits
and carried cashmere topcoats over their arms. Fair noticed
that the left thumb-nail of each man glistened green.

Fair rose politely to his feet. "Will you sit down?"

The green sprites hung up their overcoats and slid into
the booth. Fair looked from one to the other. He addressed
Jaadian. "Aren't you he whom I interviewed several weeks
ago?"

Jaadian assented. "You have not accepted my advice."

Fair shrugged. "You asked me to remain ignorant, to
accept my stupidity and ineptitude."

"And why should you not?" asked Jaadian gently. "You
are a primitive in a primitive realm; nevertheless not one man
in a thousand can match your achievements."

Fair agreed, smiling faintly. "But knowledge creates a crav-
ing for further knowledge. Where is the harm in knowledge?"

Mithemar, the more mercurial of the sprites, spoke angrily. "Where is the harm? Consider your earthen monster! It
befouled forty miles of delicacy, the record of ten million
years. Consider your caterpillar! It trampled our pillars of
carved milk, our dreaming towers, damaged the nerve-skeins
which extrude and waft us our Meanings."

"I'm dreadfully sorry," said Fair. "I meant no destruction."

The sprites nodded. "But your apology conveys no guarantee of restraint."

Fair toyed with his glass. A waiter approached the table,
addressed the two sprites. "Something for you two gentle-
men?"

Jaadian ordered a glass of charged water, as did Misthemar. Fair called for another highball.

"What do you hope to gain from this activity?" inquired
Misthemar. "Destructive forays teach you nothing!"

Fair agreed. "I have learned little. But I have seen miraculous sights. I am more than ever anxious to learn."

The green sprites glumly watched the bubbles rising in their glasses. Jaadian at last drew a deep sigh. "Perhaps we can obviate toil on your part and disturbance on ours. Explicitly, what gains or advantages do you hope to derive from green magic?"

Fair, smiling, leaned back into the red imitation-leather cushions. "I want many things. Extended life—mobility in time—comprehensive memory—augmented perception, with vision across the whole spectrum. I want physical charm and magnetism, the semblance of youth, muscular endurance . . . Then there are qualities more or less speculative, such as—"

Jaadian interrupted. "These qualities and characteristics we will confer upon you. In return you will undertake never again to disturb the green realm. You will evade centuries of toil; we will be spared the nuisance of your presence, and the inevitable tragedy."

"Tragedy?" inquired Fair in wonder. "Why tragedy?"

Jaadian spoke in a deep reverberating voice. "You are a man of Earth. Your goals are not our goals. Green magic makes you aware of our goals."

Fair thoughtfully sipped his highball. "I can't see that this is a disadvantage. I am willing to submit to the discipline of instruction. Surely a knowledge of green magic will not change me into a different entity?"

"No. And this is the basic tragedy!"

Misthemar spoke in exasperation. "We are forbidden to harm lesser creatures, and so you are fortunate; for to dissolve you into air would end all the annoyance."

Fair laughed. "I apologize again for making such a nuisance of myself. But surely you understand how important this is to me?"

Jaadian asked hopefully, "Then you agree to our offer?"

Fair shook his head. "How could I live, forever young, capable of extended learning, but limited to knowledge which I already see bounds to? I would be bored, restless, miserable."

"That well may be," said Jaadian. "But not so bored, restless and miserable as if you were learned in green magic."

Fair drew himself erect. "I must learn green magic. It is an opportunity which only a person both torpid and stupid could refuse."

Jaadian sighed. "In your place I would make the same response." The sprites rose to their feet. "Come then, we will teach you."

"Don't say we didn't warn you," said Misthemar.

Time passed. Sunset waned and twilight darkened. A man walked up the stairs, entered Howard Fair's apartment. He was tall, unobtrusively muscular. His face was sensitive, keen, humorous; his left thumb-nail glistened green.

Time is a function of vital processes. The people of Earth had perceived the motion of their clocks. On this understanding, two hours had elapsed since Howard Fair had followed the green sprites from the bar.

Howard Fair had perceived other criteria. For him the interval had been seven hundred years, during which he had lived in the green realm, learning to the utmost capacity of his brain.

He had occupied two years training his senses to the new conditions. Gradually he learned to walk in the six basic three-dimensional directions, and accustomed himself to the fourth-dimensional short-cuts. By easy stages the blinds over his eyes were removed, so that the dazzling over-human intricacy of the landscape never completely confounded him.

Another year was spent training him to the use of a code-language—an intermediate step between the vocalizations of Earth and the meaning-patterns of the green realm, where a hundred symbol-flakes (each a flitting spot of delicate iridescence) might be displayed in a single swirl of import. During this time Howard Fair's eyes and brain were altered, to allow him the use of the many new colors, without which the meaning-flakes could not be recognized.

These were preliminary steps. For forty years he studied the flakes, of which there were almost a million. Another forty years was given to elementary permutations and shifts, and another forty to parallels, attenuation, diminishments and extensions; and during this time he was introduced to flake patterns, and certain of the more obvious displays.

Now he was able to study without recourse to the code-language, and his progress became more marked. Another twenty years found him able to recognize more complicated Meanings, and he was introduced to a more varied program. He floated over the field of moth-wing mosaics, which still showed the footprints of the golem. He sweated in embarrassment, the extent of his wicked willfulness now clear to him.

So passed the years. Howard Fair learned as much green magic as his brain could encompass.

He explored much of the green realm, finding so much beauty that he feared his brain might burst. He tasted, he heard, he felt, he sensed, and each one of his senses was a hundred times more discriminating than before. Nourishment came in a thousand different forms: from pink eggs which burst into a hot sweet gas, suffusing his entire body; from passing through a rain of stinging metal crystals; from simple contemplation of the proper symbol.

Homesickness for Earth waxed and waned. Sometimes it was insupportable and he was ready to forsake all he had learned and abandon his hopes for the future. At other times the magnificence of the green realm permeated him, and the thought of departure seemed like the threat of death itself.

By stages so gradual he never realized them he learned green magic.

But the new faculty gave him no pride: between his crude ineptitudes and the poetic elegance of the sprites remained a tremendous gap—and he felt his innate inferiority much more keenly than he ever had in his old state. Worse, his most earnest efforts failed to improve his technique, and sometimes, observing the singing joy of an improvised manifestation by one of the sprites, and contrasting it to his own labored constructions, he felt futility and shame.

The longer he remained in the green realm, the stronger grew the sense of his own maladroitness, and he began to long for the easy environment of Earth, where each of his acts would not shout aloud of vulgarity and crassness. At times he would watch the sprites (in the gossamer forms natural to them) at play among the pearl-petals, or twining like quick flashes of music through the forest of pink spirals. The contrast between their verve and his brutish fumbling could not be borne and he would turn away. His self-respect dwindled with each passing hour, and instead of pride in his learning, he felt a sullen ache for what he was not and could never become. The first few hundred years he worked with the enthusiasm of ignorance, for the next few he was buoyed by hope. During the last part of his time, only dogged obstinacy kept him plodding through what now he knew for infantile exercises.

In one terrible bitter-sweet spasm, he gave up. He found Jaadian weaving tinkling fragments of various magics into a warp of shining long splines. With grave courtesy, Jaadian gave Fair his attention, and Fair laboriously set forth his meaning.

Jaadian returned a message. "I recognize your discomfort, and extend my sympathy. It is best that you now return to your native home."

He put aside his weaving and conveyed Fair down through the requisite vortices. Along the way they passed Misthemar. No flicker of meaning was expressed or exchanged, but Howard Fair thought to feel a tinge of faintly malicious amusement.

Howard Fair sat in his apartment. His perceptions, augmented and sharpened by his sojourn in the green realm, took note of the surroundings. Only two hours before, by the clocks of Earth, he had found them both restful and stimulating; now they were neither. His books: superstition, spuriousness, earnest nonsense. His private journals and workbooks: a pathetic scrawl of infantilisms. Gravity tugged at his feet, held him rigid. The shoddy construction of the house, which heretofore he had never noticed, oppressed him. Everywhere he looked he saw slipshod disorder, primitive filth. The thought of the food he must now eat revolted him.

He went out on his little balcony which overlooked the street. The air was impregnated with organic smells. Across the street he could look into windows where his fellow humans lived in stupid squalor.

Fair smiled sadly. He had tried to prepare himself for these reactions, but now was surprised by their intensity. He returned into his apartment. He must accustom himself to the old environment. And after all there were compensations. The most desirable commodities of the world were now his to enjoy.

Howard Fair plunged into the enjoyment of these pleasures. He forced himself to drink quantities of expensive wines, brandies, liqueurs, even though they offended his palate. Hunger overcame his nausea, he forced himself to the consumption of what he thought of as fried animal tissue, the hypertrophied sexual organs of plants. He experimented with erotic sensations, but found that beautiful women no longer seemed different from the plain ones, and that he could barely steel himself to the untidy contacts. He bought libraries of erudite books, glanced through them with contempt. He tried to amuse himself with his old magics; they seemed ridiculous.

He forced himself to enjoy these pleasures for a month; then he fled the city and established a crystal bubble on a crag in the Andes. To nourish himself, he contrived a thick liquid, which, while by no means as exhilarating as the substances of the green realm, was innocent of organic contamination.

After a certain degree of improvisation and make-shift, he arranged his life to its minimum discomfort. The view was one of austere grandeur; not even the condors came to disturb him. He sat back to ponder the chain of events which had started with his discovery of Gerald McIntyre's workbook. He frowned. Gerald McIntyre? He jumped to his feet, looked far off over the crags.

He found Gerald McIntyre at a wayside service station in the heart of the South Dakota prairie. McIntyre was sitting in an old wooden chair, tilted back against the peeling yellow paint of the service station, a straw hat shading his eyes from the sun.

He was a magnetically handsome man, blond of hair, brown of eyes whose gaze stung like the touch of icicles. His left thumb-nail glistened green.

Fair greeted him casually; the two men surveyed each other with wry curiosity.

"I see you have adapted yourself," said Howard Fair.

McIntyre shrugged. "As well as possible. I try to maintain a balance between solitude and the pressure of humanity." He looked into the bright blue sky where crows flapped and called. "For many years I lived in isolation. I began to detest the sound of my own breathing."

Along the highway came a glittering automobile, rococo as a hybrid goldfish. With the perceptions now available to them, Fair and McIntyre could see the driver to be red-faced and truculent, his companion a peevish woman in expensive clothes.

"There are other advantages to residence here," said McIntyre. "For instance, I am able to enrich the lives of passers-by with trifles of novel adventure." He made a small gesture; two dozen crows swooped down and flew beside the automobile. They settled on the fenders, strutted back and forth along the hood, fouled the windshield.

The automobile squealed to a halt, the driver jumped out, put the birds to flight. He threw an ineffectual rock, waved his arms in outrage, returned to his car, proceeded.

"A paltry affair," said McIntyre with a sigh. "The truth of the matter is that I am bored." He pursed his mouth and blew forth three bright puffs of smoke: first red, then yellow, then blazing blue. "I have arrived at the estate of foolishness, as you can see."

Fair surveyed his great-uncle with a trace of uneasiness. McIntyre laughed. "No more pranks. I predict, however, that you will presently share my malaise."

"I share it already," said Fair. "Sometimes I wish I could abandon all my magic and return to my former innocence."

"I have toyed with the idea," McIntyre replied thoughtfully. "In fact I have made all the necessary arrangements. It is really a simple matter." He led Fair to a small room behind the station. Although the door was open, the interior showed a thick darkness.

McIntyre, standing well back, surveyed the darkness with a quizzical curl to his lip. "You need only enter. All your magic, all your recollections of the green realm will depart. You will be no wiser than the next man you meet. And with your knowledge will go your boredom, your melancholy, your dissatisfaction."

Fair contemplated the dark doorway. A single step would resolve his discomfort.

He glanced at McIntyre; the two surveyed each other with sardonic amusement. They returned to the front of the building.

"Sometimes I stand by the door and look into the darkness," said McIntyre. "Then I am reminded how dearly I cherish my boredom, and what a precious commodity is so much misery."

Fair made himself ready for departure. "I thank you for this new wisdom, which a hundred more years in the green realm would not have taught me. And now—for a time, at least—I go back to my crag in the Andes."

McIntyre tilted his chair against the wall of the service

station. "And I—for a time, at least—will wait for the next passer-by."

"Goodby then, Uncle Gerald."

"Goodby, Howard."

The Miracle Workers

HE WAR PARTY from Faide Keep moved eastward across the downs; a column of a hundred armored knights, five hundred foot soldiers, a train of wagons. In the lead rode Lord Faide, a tall man in his early maturity, spare and catlike, with a sallow dyspeptic face. He sat in the ancestral car of the Faides, a boat-shaped vehicle floating two feet above the moss, and carried, in addition to his sword and dagger, his ancestral side weapons.

An hour before sunset a pair of scouts came racing back to the column, their club-headed horses loping like dogs. Lord Faide braked the motion of his car. Behind him the Faide kinsmen, the lesser knights, the leather-capped foot soldiers halted; to the rear the baggage train and the high-wheeled wagons of the jinxmen creaked to a stop.

The scouts approached at breakneck speed, at the last instant flinging their horses sidewise. Long shaggy legs kicked out, padlike hooves plowed through the moss. The scouts jumped to the ground, ran forward. "The way to Ballant Keep is blocked!"

Lord Faide rose in his seat, stood staring eastward over the gray-green downs. "How many knights? How many men?"

"No knights, no men, Lord Faide. The First Folk have planted a forest between North and South Wildwood."

Lord Faide stood a moment in reflection, then seated himself, pushed the control knob. The car wheezed, jerked, moved forward. The knights touched up their horses; the foot soldiers resumed their slouching gait. At the rear the baggage train creaked into motion, together with the six wagons of the jinxmen.

The sun, large, pale and faintly pink, sank in the west. North Wildwood loomed down from the left, separated from South Wildwood by an area of stony ground, only sparsely patched with moss. As the sun passed behind the horizon, the new planting became visible: a frail new growth connecting the tracts of woodland like a canal between two seas.

Lord Faide halted his car, stepped down to the moss. He appraised the landscape, then gave the signal to make camp. The wagons were ranged in a circle, the gear unloaded. Lord Faide watched the activity for a moment, eyes sharp and critical, then turned and walked out across the downs through the lavender and green twilight. Fifteen miles to the east his last enemy awaited him: Lord Ballant of Ballant Keep. Contemplating tomorrow's battle, Lord Faide felt reasonably confident of the outcome. His troops had been tempered by a dozen campaigns; his kinsmen were loyal and single-hearted. Head Jinxman to Faide Keep was Hein Huss, and associated with him were three of the most powerful jinxmen of Pangborn: Isak Comandore, Adam McAdam and the remarkable Enterlin, together with their separate troupes of cabalmen, spell-binders and apprentices. Altogether, an impressive assemblage. Certainly there were obstacles to be overcome: Ballant Keep was strong; Lord Ballant would fight obstinately; Anderson Grimes, the Ballant jinxman, was efficient and highly respected. There was also this nuisance of the First Folk and the new planting which closed the gap between North and South Wildwood. The First Folk were a pale and feeble race, no match for human beings in single combat, but they guarded their forests with traps and deadfalls. Lord Faide cursed softly under his breath. To circle either North or South Wildwood meant a delay of three days, which could not be tolerated.

Lord Faide returned to the camp. Fires were alight, pots bubbled, orderly rows of sleep-holes had been dug into the moss. The knights groomed their horses within the corral of wagons; Lord Faide's own tent had been erected on a hummock, beside the ancient car.

Lord Faide made a quick round of inspection, noting every detail, speaking no word. The jinxmen were encamped a little distance apart from the troops. The apprentices and lesser spell-binders prepared food, while the jinxmen and cabalmen worked inside their tents, arranging cabinets and cases, correcting whatever disorder had been caused by the jolting of the wagons.

Lord Faide entered the tent of his Head Jinxman. Hein Huss was an enormous man, with arms and legs heavy as tree trunks, a torso like a barrel. His face was pink and placid, his eyes were water-clear; a stiff gray brush rose from his head, which was innocent of the cap jinxmen customarily wore against the loss of hair. Hein Huss disdained such precautions; it was his habit, showing his teeth in a face-splitting grin, to rumble, "Why should anyone hoodoo me, old Hein Huss? I am so inoffensive. Whoever tried would surely die, of shame and remorse."

Lord Faide found Huss busy at his cabinet. The doors stood wide, revealing hundreds of mannikins, each tied with a lock of hair, a bit of cloth, a fingernail clipping, daubed with grease, sputum, excrement, blood. Lord Faide knew well that one of these mannikins represented himself. He also knew that should he request it Hein Huss would deliver it without hesitation. Part of Huss' *mana* derived from his enormous confidence, the effortless ease of his power. He glanced at Lord Faide and read the question in his mind. "Lord Ballant did not know of the new planting. Anderson Grimes has now informed him, and Lord Ballant expects that you will be

delayed. Grimes has communicated with Gisborne Keep and
Castle Cloud. Three hundred men march tonight to reinforce
Ballant Keep. They will arrive in two days. Lord Ballant is
much elated."

Lord Faide paced back and forth across the tent. "Can
we cross this planting?"

Hein Huss made a heavy sound of disapproval. "There are
many futures. In certain of these futures you pass. In others
you do not pass. I cannot ordain these futures."

Lord Faide had long learned to control his impatience at
what sometimes seemed to be pedantic obfuscation. He
grumbled, "They are either very stupid or very bold, planting
across the downs in this fashion. I cannot imagine what they
intend."

Hein Huss considered, then grudgingly volunteered an
idea. "What if they plant west from North Wildwood to Sarrow Copse? What if they plant west from South Wildwood to
Old Forest?

Lord Faide stood stock-still, his eyes narrow and thoughtful. "Faide Keep would be surrounded by forest. We would
be imprisoned . . . These plantings, do they proceed?"

"They proceed, so I have been told."

"What do they hope to gain?"

"I do not know. Perhaps they hope to isolate the keeps,
to rid the planet of men. Perhaps they merely want secure
avenues between the forests."

Lord Faide considered. Huss' final suggestion was reasonable enough. During the first centuries of human settlement,
sportive young men had hunted the First Folk with clubs and
lances, eventually had driven them from their native downs
into the forests. "Evidently they are more clever than we
realize. Adam McAdam asserts that they do not think, but it
seems that he is mistaken."

Hein Huss shrugged. "Adam McAdam equates thought to
the human cerebral process. He cannot telepathize with the
First Folk, hence he deduced that they do not 'think.' But I

have watched them at Forest Market, and they trade intelli-
gently enough." He raised his head, appeared to listen, then
reached into his cabinet, delicately tightened a noose around
the neck of one of the mannikins. From outside the tent
came a sudden cough and a whooping gasp for air. Huss grinned, twitched open the noose. "That is Isak Comandore's
apprentice. He hopes to complete a Hein Huss mannikin. I
must say he works diligently, going so far as to touch its feet
into my footprints whenever possible."

Lord Faide went to the flap of the tent. "We break camp
early. Be alert, I may require your help." Lord Faide departed
the tent.

Hein Huss continued the ordering of the cabinet. Presently he sensed the approach of his rival, Jinxman Isak Comandore, who coveted the office of Head Jinxman with all-con-
suming passion. Huss closed the cabinet and hoisted himself
to his feet.

Comandore entered the tent, a man tall, crooked and
spindly. His wedge-shaped head was covered with coarse
russet ringlets; hot red-brown eyes peered from under his red
eyebrows. "I offer my complete rights to Keyril, and will include the masks, the headdress, and amulets. Of all the
demons ever contrived he has won the widest public acceptance. To utter the name Keyril is to complete half the work
of a possession. Keyril is a valuable property. I can give no
more."

But Huss shook his head. Comandore's desire was the full
simulacrum of Tharon Faide, Lord Faide's oldest son, complete with clothes, hair, skin, eyelashes, tears, excreta, sweat
and sputum—the only one in existence, for Lord Faide guarded his son much more jealously than he did himself. "You
offer convincingly," said Huss, "but my own demons suffice.
The name Dant conveys fully as much terror as Keyril."

"I will add five hairs from the head of Jinxman Clarence
Sears; they are the last, for he is now stark bald."

"Let us drop the matter; I will keep the simulacrum."

"As you please," said Comandore with asperity. He glanced out the flap of the tent. "That blundering apprentice. He puts the feet of the mannikin backwards into your prints."

Huss opened his cabinet, thumped a mannikin with his finger. From outside the tent came a grunt of surprise. Huss grinned. "He is young and earnest, and perhaps he is clever, who knows?" He went to the flap of the tent, called outside. "Hey, Sam Salazar, what do you do? Come inside."

Apprentice Sam Salazar came blinking into the tent, a thick-set youth with a round florid face, overhung with a rather untidy mass of straw-colored hair. In one hand he carried a crude pot-bellied mannikin, evidently intended to represent Hein Huss.

"You puzzle both your master and myself," said Huss. "There must be method in your folly, but we fail to perceive it. For instance, this moment you place my simulacrum backwards into my track. I feel a tug on my foot, and you pay for your clumsiness."

Sam Salazar showed small evidence of abashment. "Jinxman Comandore has warned that we must expect to suffer for our ambitions."

"If your ambition is jinxmanship," Comandore declared sharply, "you had best mend your ways."

"The lad is craftier than you know," said Hein Huss. "Look now." He took the mannikin, spit into its mouth, plucked a hair from his head, thrust it into a convenient crevice. "He has a Hein Huss mannikin, achieved at very small cost. Now, Apprentice Salazar, how will you hoodoo me?"

"Naturally I would never dare. I merely want to fill the bare spaces in my cabinet."

Hein Huss nodded his approval. "As good a reason as any. Of course you own a simulacrum of Isak Comandore?"

Sam Salazar glanced uneasily sidewise at Isak Comandore. "He leaves none of his traces. If there is so much as an open bottle in the room, he breathes behind his hand."

"Ridiculous!" exclaimed Hein Huss. "Comandore, what do you fear?"

"I am conservative," said Comandore drily. "You make a fine gesture, but some day an enemy may own that simulacrum; then you will regret your bravado."

"Bah. My enemies are all dead, save one or two who dare not reveal themselves." He clapped Sam Salazar a great buffet on the shoulder. "Tomorrow, Apprentice Salazar, great things are in store for you."

"What manner of great things?"

"Honor, noble self-sacrifice. Lord Faide must beg permission to pass Wildwood from the First Folk, which galls him. But beg he must. Tomorrow, Sam Salazar, I will elect you to lead the way to the parley, to deflect deadfalls, scythes and nettle-traps from the more important person who follows."

Sam Salazar shook his head and drew back. "There must be others more worthy; I prefer to ride in the rear with the wagons."

Comandore waved him from the tent. "You will do as ordered. Leave us; we have had enough apprentice talk."

Sam Salazar departed. Comandore turned back to Hein Huss. "In connection with tomorrow's battle, Anderson Grimes is especially adept with demons. As I recall, he has developed and successfully publicized Font, who spreads sleep; Everid, a being of wrath, Deigne, a force of fear. We must take care that in countering these effects we do not neutralize each other."

"True," rumbled Huss. "I have long maintained to Lord Faide that a single jinxman—the Head Jinxman in fact—is more effective than a group at cross-purposes. But he is consumed by ambition and does not listen."

"Perhaps he wants to be sure that should advancing years overtake the Head Jinxman other equally effective jinxmen are at hand."

"The future has many paths," agreed Hein Huss. "Lord Faide is well-advised to seek early for my successor, so that I

may train him over the years. I plan to assess all the subsidiary jinxmen, and select the most promising. Tomorrow I
relegate to you the demons of Anderson Grimes."

Isak Comandore nodded politely. "You are wise to give
over responsibility. When I feel the weight of my years I hope
I may act with similar forethought. Good night, Hein Huss. I
go to arrange my demon masks. Tomorrow Keyril must walk
like a giant."

"Good night, Isak Comandore."

Comandore swept from the tent, and Huss settled himself
on his stool. Sam Salazar scratched at the flap. "Well, lad?"
growled Huss. "Why do you loiter?"

Sam Salazar placed the Hein Huss mannikin on the table.
"I have no wish to keep this doll."

"Throw it in a ditch, then," Hein Huss spoke gruffly.
"You must stop annoying me with stupid tricks. You efficiently obtrude yourself upon my attention, but you cannot trans-
fer from Comandore's troupe without his express consent."

"If I gain his consent?"

"You will incur his enmity, he will open his cabinet
against you. Unlike myself, you are vulnerable to a hoodoo. I
advise you to be content. Isak Comandore is highly skilled
and can teach you much."

Sam Salazar still hestiated. "Jinxman Comandore, though
skilled, is intolerant of new thoughts."

Hein Huss shifted ponderously on his stool, examined
Sam Salazar with his water-clear eyes. "What new thoughts
are these? Your own?"

"The thoughts are new to me, and for all I know new to
Isak Comandore. But he will say neither yes nor no."

Hein Huss sighed, settled his monumental bulk more
comfortably. "Speak then, describe these thoughts, and I will
assess their novelty."

"First, I have wondered about trees. They are sensitive to
light, to moisture, to wind, to pressure. Sensitivity implies

sensation. Might a man feel into the soul of a tree for these sensations? If a tree were capable of awareness, this faculty might prove useful. A man might select trees as sentinels in strategic sites, and enter into them as he chose."

Hein Huss was skeptical. "An amusing notion, but practically not feasible. The reading of minds, the act of possession, televoyance, similar interplay requires psychic congruence as a basic condition. The minds must be able to become identities at some particular stratum. Unless there is sympathy, there is no linkage. A tree is at opposite poles from a man; the images of tree and man are incommensurable. Hence, anything more than the most trifling flicker of comprehension must be a true miracle of jinxmanship."

Sam Salazar nodded mournfully "I realize this, and at one time hoped to equip myself with the necessary identification."

"To do this you must become a vegetable. Certainly the tree will never become a man."

"So I reasoned," said Sam Salazar. "I went alone into a grove of trees, where I chose a tall conifer. I buried my feet in the mold, I stood silent and naked—in the sunlight, in the rain; at dawn, noon, dusk, midnight. I closed my mind to man-thoughts, I closed my eyes to vision, my ears to sound. I took no nourishment except from rain and sun. I sent roots forth from my feet and branches from my torso. Thirty hours I stood, and two days later, another thirty hours, and after two days another thirty hours. I made myself a tree, as nearly as possible to one of flesh and blood."

Hein Huss gave the great inward gurgle which signalized his amusement. "And you achieved sympathy?"

"Nothing useful," Sam Salazar admitted. "I felt something of the tree's sensations—the activity of light, the peace of dark, the coolness of rain. But visual and auditory experience—nothing. However, I do not regret the trial. It was a useful discipline."

"An interesting effort, even if inconclusive. The idea is by no means of startling originality, but the empiricism—to use

an archaic word—of your method is bold, and no doubt an-
tagonized Isak Comandore, who has no patience with the
superstitions of our ancestors. I suspect that he harangued
you against frivolity, metaphysics, and inspirationalism."

"True," said Sam Salazar. "He spoke at length."

"You should take the lesson to heart. Isak Comandore is
sometimes unable to make the most obvious truth seem cred-
ible. However, I cite you the example of Lord Faide who
considers himself an enlightened man, free from superstition.
Still, he rides in the feeble car, he carries a pistol sixteen hundred years old, he relies on Hellmouth to protect Faide Keep."

"Perhaps—unconsciously—he longs for the old magical
times," suggested Sam Salazar thoughtfully.

"Perhaps," agreed Hein Huss. "And you do likewise?"

Sam Salazar hesitated. "There is an aura of romance, a
kind of wild grandeur to the old days—but of course," he
added quickly, "mysticism is no substitute for orthodox logic."

"Naturally not," agreed Hein Huss. "Now go; I must consider the events of tomorrow."

Sam Salazar departed, and Hein Huss, rumbling and
groaning, hoisted himself to his feet. He went to the flap of
his tent, surveyed the camp. All now was quiet. The fires
were embers, the warriors lay in the pits they had cut into
the moss. To the north and south spread the woodlands.
Among the trees and out on the downs were faint flickering
luminosities, where the First Folk gathered spore-pods from
the moss.

Hein Huss became aware of a nearby personality. He
turned his head and saw approaching the shrouded form of
Jinxman Enterlin, who concealed his face, who spoke only in
whispers, who disguised his natural gait with a stiff stiltlike
motion. By this means he hoped to reduce his vulnerability
to hostile jinxmanship. The admission carelessly let fall of
failing eyesight, of stiff joints, forgetfulness, melancholy,
nausea might be of critical significance in controversy by
hoodoo. Jinxmen therefore maintained the pose of absolute

health and virility, even though they must grope blindly or limp doubled up from cramps.

Hein Huss called out to Enterlin, lifted back the flap to the tent. Enterlin entered; Huss went to the cabinet, brought forth a flask, poured liquor into a pair of stone cups. "A cordial only, free of covert significance."

"Good," whispered Enterlin, selecting the cup farthest from him. "After all, we jinxmen must relax into the guise of men from time to time." Turning his back on Huss, he introduced the cup through the folds of his hood, drank. "Refreshing," he whispered. "We need refreshment: tomorrow we must work."

Huss issued his reverberating chuckle. "Tomorrow Isak Comandore matches demons with Anderson Grimes. We others perform only subsidiary duties."

Enterlin seemed to make a quizzical inspection of Hein Huss through the black gauze before his eyes. "Comandore will relish this opportunity. His vehemence oppresses me, and his is a power which feeds on success. He is a man of fire, you are a man of ice."

"Ice quenches fire."

"Fire sometimes melts ice."

Hein Huss shrugged. "No matter. I grow weary. Time has passed all of us by. Only a moment ago a young apprentice showed me to myself."

"As a powerful jinxman, as Head Jinxman to the Faides, you have cause for pride."

Hein Huss drained the stone cup, set it aside. "No. I see myself at the top of my profession, with nowhere else to go. Only Sam Salazar the apprentice thinks to search for more universal lore: he comes to me for counsel, and I do not know what to tell him."

"Strange talk, strange talk!" whispered Enterlin. He moved to the flap of the tent. "I go now," he whispered. "I go to walk on the downs. Perhaps I will see the future."

"There are many futures."

Enterlin rustled away and was lost in the dark. Hein Huss groaned and grumbled, then took himself to his couch, where he instantly fell asleep.

II

The night passed. The sun, flickering with films of pink and green, lifted over the horizon. The new planting of the First Folk was silhouetted, a sparse stubble of saplings, against the green and lavender sky. The troops broke camp with practiced efficiency. Lord Faide marched to his car, leaped within; the machine sagged under his weight. He pushed a button, the car drifted forward, heavy as a waterlogged timber.

A mile from the new planting he halted, sent a messenger back to the wagons of the jinxmen. Hein Huss walked ponderously forward, followed by Isak Comandore, Adam McAdam, and Enterlin; Lord Faide spoke to Hein Huss. "Send someone to speak to the First Folk. Inform them we wish to pass, offering them no harm, but that we will react savagely to any hostility."

"I will go myself," said Hein Huss. He turned to Comandore. "Lend me, if you will, your brash young apprentice. I can put him to good use."

"If he unmasks a nettle trap by blundering into it, his first useful deed will be done," said Comandore. He signaled to Sam Salazar, who came reluctantly forward. "Walk in front of Head Jinxman Hein Huss that he may encounter no traps or scythes. Take a staff to probe the moss."

Without enthusiasm Sam Salazar borrowed a lance from one of the foot soldiers. He and Huss set forth, along the low rise that previously had separated North from South Wildwood. Occasionally outcroppings of stone penetrated the cover of moss; here and there grew bayberry trees, clumps of tarplant, ginger-tea, and rosewort.

A half mile from the planting Huss halted. "Now take care, for here the traps will begin. Walk clear of hummocks, these often conceal swing-scythes; avoid moss which shows a pale blue; it is dying or sickly and may cover a deadfall or a nettle trap."

"Why cannot you locate the traps by clairvoyance?" asked Sam Salazar in a rather sullen voice. "It appears an excellent occasion for the use of these faculties."

"The question is natural," said Hein Huss with composure. "However you must know that when a jinxman's own profit or security is at stake his emotions play tricks on him. I would see traps everywhere and would never know whether clairvoyance or fear prompted me. In this case, that lance is a more reliable instrument than my mind."

Sam Salazar made a salute of understanding and set forth, with Hein Huss stumping behind him. At first he prodded with care, uncovering two traps, then advanced more jauntily; so swiftly indeed that Huss called out in exasperation, "Caution, unless you court death!"

Sam Salazar obligingly slowed his pace. "There are traps all around us, but I detect the pattern, or so I believe."

"Ah, ha, you do? Reveal it to me, if you will. I am only Head Jinxman, and ignorant."

"Notice. If we walk where the spore-pods have recently been harvested, then we are secure."

Hein Huss grunted. "Forward then. Why do you dally? We must do battle at Ballant Keep today."

Two hundred yards farther, Sam Salazar stopped short. "Go on, boy, go on!" grumbled Hein Huss.

"The savages threaten us. You can see them just inside the planting. They hold tubes which they point toward us."

Hein Huss peered, then raised his head and called out in the sibilant language of the First Folk.

A moment or two passed, then one of the creatures came forth, a naked humanoid figure, ugly as a demonmask. Foam-sacs bulged under its arms, orange-lipped foam-vents pointed forward. Its back was wrinkled and loose, the skin serving as a bellows to blow air through the foam-sacs. The fingers of

the enormous hands ended in chisel-shaped blades, the head
was sheathed in chitin. Billion-faceted eyes swelled from
either side of the head, glowing like black opals, merging
without definite limit into the chitin. This was a representative of the original inhabitants of the planet, who until the
coming of man had inhabited the downs, burrowing in the
moss, protecting themselves behind masses of foam exuded
from the underarm sacs.

The creature wandered close, halted. "I speak for Lord
Faide of Faide Keep," said Huss. "Your planting bars his
way. He wishes that you guide him through, so that his men
do not damage the trees, or spring the traps you have set
against your enemies."

"Men are our enemies," responded the autochthon. "You
may spring as many traps as you care to; that is their purpose."
It backed away.

"One moment," said Hein Huss sternly. "Lord Faide
must pass. He goes to battle Lord Ballant. He does not wish
to battle the First Folk. Therefore it is wise to guide him
across the planting without hindrance."

The creature considered a second or two. "I will guide
him." He stalked across the moss toward the war party.

Behind followed Hein Huss and Sam Salazar. The autochthon, legs articulated more flexibly than a man's, seemed to
weave and wander, occasionally pausing to study the ground
ahead.

"I am puzzled," Sam Salazar told Hein Huss. "I cannot
understand the creature's actions."

"Small wonder," grunted Hein Huss. "He is one of the
First Folk, you are human. There is no basis for understanding."

"I disagree," said Sam Salazar seriously.

"Eh?" Hein Huss inspected the apprentice with vast disapproval. "You engage in contention with me, Head Jinxman
Hein Huss?"

"Only in a limited sense," said Sam Salazar. "I see a basis

for understanding with the First Folk in our common ambition to survive."

"A truism," grumbled Hein Huss. "Granting this community of interests with the First Folk, what is your perplexity?"

"The fact that it first refused, then agreed to conduct us across the planting."

Hein Huss nodded. "Evidently the information which intervened, that we go to fight at Ballant Keep, occasioned the change."

"This is clear," said Sam Salazar. "But think—"

"You exhort me to think?" roared Hein Huss.

"—here is one of the First Folk, apparently without distinction, who makes an important decision instantly. Is he one of their leaders? Do they live in anarchy?"

"It is easy to put questions," Hein Huss said gruffly. "It is not as easy to answer them."

"In short—"

"In short, I do not know. In any event, they are pleased to see us killing one another."

III

The passage through the planting was made without incident. A mile to the east the autochthon stepped aside and without formality returned to the forest. The war party, which had been marching in single file, regrouped into its usual formation. Lord Faide called Hein Huss and made the unusual gesture of inviting him up into the seat beside him. The ancient car dipped and sagged; the power-mechanism whined and chattered. Lord Faide, in high good spirits, ignored the noise. "I feared that we might be forced into a time-consuming wrangle. What of Lord Ballant? Can you read his thoughts?"

Hein Huss cast his mind forth. "Not clearly. He knows of our passage. He is disturbed."

Lord Faide laughed sardonically. "For excellent reason!

Listen now, I will explain the plan of battle so that all may coordinate their efforts."

"Very well."

"We approach in a wide line. Ballant's great weapon is of course Volcano. A decoy must wear my armor and ride in the lead. The yellow-haired apprentice is perhaps the most expendable member of the party. In this way we will learn the potentialities of Volcano. Like our own Hellmouth, it was built to repel vessels from space and cannot command the ground immediately under the keep. Therefore we will advance in dispersed formation, to regroup two hundred yards from the keep. At this point the jinxmen will impel Lord Ballant forth from the keep. You no doubt have made plans to this end."

Hein Huss gruffly admitted that such was the case. Like other jinxmen, he enjoyed the pose that his power sufficed for extemporaneous control of any situation.

Lord Faide was in no mood for niceties and pressed for further information. Grudging each word, Hein Huss disclosed his arrangements. "I have prepared certain influences to discomfit the Ballant defenders and drive them forth. Jinxman Enterlin will sit at his cabinet, ready to retaliate if Lord Ballant orders a spell against you. Anderson Grimes undoubtedly will cast a demon—probably Everid—into the Ballant warriors; in return, Jinxman Comandore will possess an equal or a greater number of Faide warriors with the demon Keyril, who is even more ghastly and horrifying."

"Good. What more?"

"There is need for no more, if your men fight well."

"Can you see the future? How does today end?"

"There are many futures. Certain jinxmen—Enterlin for instance—profess to see the thread which leads through the maze; they are seldom correct."

"Call Enterlin here."

Hein Huss rumbled his disapproval. "Unwise, if you desire victory over Ballant Keep."

Lord Faide inspected the massive jinxman from under his black saturnine brows. "Why do you say this?"

"If Enterlin foretells defeat, you will be dispirited and fight poorly. If he predicts victory, you become overconfident and likewise fight poorly."

Lord Faide made a petulant gesture. "The jinxmen are loud in their boasts until the test is made. Then they always find reasons to retract, to qualify."

"Ha, ha!" barked Hein Huss. "You expect miracles, not honest jinxmanship. I spit—" he spat. "I predict that the spittle will strike the moss. The probabilities are high. But an insect might fly in the way. One of the First Folk might raise through the moss. The chances are slight. In the next instant there is only one future. A minute hence there are four futures. Five minutes hence, twenty futures. A billion futures could not express all the possibilities of tomorrow. Of these billion, certain are more probable than others. It is true that these probable futures sometimes send a delicate influence into the jinxman's brain. But unless he is completely impersonal and disinterested, his own desires overwhelm this influence. Enterlin is a strange man. He hides himself, he has no appetites. Occasionally his auguries are exact. Nevertheless, I advise against consulting him. You do better to rely on the practical and real uses of jinxmanship."

Lord Faide said nothing. The column had been marching along the bottom of a low swale; the car had been sliding easily downslope. Now they came to a rise, and the power-mechanism complained so vigorously that Lord Faide was compelled to stop the car. He considered. "Once over the crest we will be in view of Ballant Keep. Now we must disperse. Send the least valuable man in your troupe forward— the apprentice who tested out the moss. He must wear my helmet and corselet and ride in the car."

Hein Huss alighted, returned to the wagons, and presently Sam Salazar came forward. Lord Faide eyed the round, florid face with distaste. "Come close," he said crisply. Sam Salazar obeyed. "You will now ride in my place," said Lord Faide. "Notice carefully. This rod impels a forward motion. This arm steers—to right, to left. To stop, return the rod to its first position."

Sam Salazar pointed to some of the other arms, toggles, switches, and buttons. "What of these?"

"They are never used."

"And these dials, what is their meaning?"

Lord Faide curled his lip, on the brink of one of his quick furies. "Since their use is unimportant to me, it is twenty times unimportant to you. Now. Put this cap on your head, and this helmet. See to it that you do not sweat."

Sam Salazar gingerly settled the magnificent black and green crest of Faide on his head, with a cloth cap underneath.

"Now this corselet."

The corselet was constructed of green and black metal sequins, with a pair of scarlet dragon-heads at either side of the breast.

"Now the cloak." Lord Faide flung the black cloak over Sam Salazar's shoulders. "Do not venture too close to Ballant Keep. Your purpose is to attract the fire of Volcano. Maintain a lateral motion around the keep, outside of dart range. If you are killed by a dart, the whole purpose of the deception is thwarted."

"You prefer me to be killed by Volcano?" inquired Sam Salazar.

"No. I wish to preserve the car and the crest. These are relics of great value. Evade destruction by all means possible. The ruse probably will deceive no one; but if it does, and if it draws the fire of Volcano, I must sacrifice the Faide car. Now—sit in my place."

Sam Salazar climbed into the car, settled himself on the seat.

"Sit straight," roared Lord Faide. "Hold your head up! You are simulating Lord Faide! You must not appear to slink!"

Sam Salazar heaved himself erect in the seat. "To simulate

Lord Faide most effectively, I should walk among the warriors, with someone else riding in the car."

Lord Faide glared, then grinned sourly. "No matter. Do as I have commanded."

IV

Sixteen hundred years before, with war raging through space, a group of space captains, their home bases destroyed, had taken refuge on Pangborn. To protect themselves against vengeful enemies, they built great forts armed with weapons from the dismantled spaceships.

The wars receded, Pangborn was forgotten. The newcomers drove the First Folk into the forests, planted and harvested the river valleys. Ballant Keep, like Faide Keep, Castle Cloud, Boghoten, and the rest, overlooked one of these valleys. Four squat towers of a dense black substance supported an enormous parasol roof, and were joined by walls two-thirds as high as the towers. At the peak of the roof a cupola housed Volcano, the weapon corresponding to Faide's Hellmouth.

The Faide war party advancing over the rise found the great gates already secure, the parapets between the towers thronged with bowmen. According to Lord Faide's strategy, the war party advanced on a broad front. At the center rode Sam Salazar, resplendent in Lord Faide's armor. He made, however, small effort to simulate Lord Faide. Rather than sitting proudly erect, he crouched at the side of the seat, the crest canted at an angle. Lord Faide watched with disgust. Apprentice Salazar's reluctance to be demolished was understandable: if his impersonation failed to convince Lord Ballant, at least the Faide ancestral car might be spared. For a certainty Volcano was being manned; the Ballant weapon-tender could be seen in the cupola, and the snout protruded at a menacing angle.

Apparently the tactic of dispersal, offering no single tempting target, was effective. The Faide war party advanced

quickly to a point two hundred yards from the keep, below
Volcano's effective field, without drawing fire; first the
knights, then the foot soldiers, then the rumbling wagons of
the magicians. The slow-moving Faide car was far outdis-
tanced; any doubt as to the nature of the ruse must now be
extinguished.

Apprentice Salazar, disliking the isolation, and hoping to
increase the speed of the car, twisted one of the other switches,
then another. From under the floor came a thin screeching
sound; the car quivered and began to rise. Sam Salazar peered
over the side, threw out a leg to jump. Lord Faide ran forward, gesturing and shouting. Sam Salazar hastily drew back
his leg, returned the switches to their previous condition. The
car dropped like a rock. He snapped the switches up again,
cushioning the fall.

"Get out of that car!" roared Lord Faide. He snatched
away the helmet, dealt Sam Salazar a buffet which toppled
him head over heels. "Out of the armor; back to your duties!"

Sam Salazar hurried to the jinxmen's wagons where he
helped erect Isak Comandore's black tent. Inside the tent a
black carpet with red and yellow patterns was laid; Comandore's cabinet, his chair, and his chest were carried in, and
incense set burning in a censer. Directly in front of the main
gate Hein Huss superintended the assembly of a rolling stage,
forty feet tall and sixty feet long, the surface concealed from
Ballant Keep by a tarpaulin.

Meanwhile, Lord Faide had dispatched an emissary, enjoining Lord Ballant to surrender. Lord Ballant delayed his
response, hoping to delay the attack as long as possible. If he
could maintain himself a day and a half, reinforcements from
Gisborne Keep and Castle Cloud might force Lord Faide to
retreat.

Lord Faide waited only until the jinxmen had completed
their preparations, then sent another messenger, offering two
more minutes in which to surrender.

One minute passed, two minutes. The envoys turned on their heels, marched back to the camp.

Lord Faide spoke to Hein Huss. "You are prepared?"

"I am prepared," rumbled Hein Huss.

"Drive them forth."

Huss raised his arm; the tarpaulin dropped from the face of his great display, to reveal a painted representation of Ballant Keep.

Huss retired to his tent, and pulled the flaps together. Braziers burnt fiercely, illuminating the faces of Adam McAdam, eight cabalmen, and six of the most advanced spellbinders. Each worked at a bench supporting several dozen dolls and a small glowing brazier. The cabalmen and spellbinders worked with dolls representing Ballant men-at-arms; Huss and Adam McAdam employed simulacra of the Ballant knights. Lord Ballant would not be hoodooed unless he ordered a jinx against Lord Faide—a courtesy the keep-lords extended each other.

Huss called out: "Sebastian!"

Sebastian, one of Huss's spellbinders, waiting at the flap to the tent, replied, "Ready, sir."

"Begin the display."

Sebastian ran to the stage, struck fire to a fuse. Watchers inside Ballant Keep saw the depicted keep take fire. Flame erupted from the windows, the roof glowed and crumbled. Inside the tent the two jinxmen, the cabalmen, and the spellbinders methodically took dolls, dipped them into the heat of the braziers, concentrating, reaching out for the mind of the man whose doll they burnt. Within the keep men became uneasy. Many began to imagine burning sensations, which became more severe as their minds grew more sensitive to the idea of fire. Lord Ballant noted the uneasiness. He signaled to his chief jinxman Anderson Grimes. "Begin the counterspell."

Down the front of the keep unrolled a display even larger than Hein Huss's, depicting a hideous beast. It stood on four legs and was shown picking up two men in a pair of hands, biting off their heads. Grime's cabalmen meanwhile took up dolls representing the Faide warriors, inserted them into models of the depicted beast, and closed the hinged jaws, all the while projecting ideas of fear and disgust. And the Faide warriors, staring at the depicted monster, felt a sense of horror and weakness.

Inside Huss's tent, censers and braziers reeked and dolls smoked. Eyes stared, brows glistened. From time to time one of the workers gasped—signaling the entry of his projection into an enemy mind. Within the keep warriors began to mutter, to slap at burning skin, to eye each other fearfully, noting each other's symptoms. Finally one cried out, and tore at his armor. "I burn! The cursed witches burn me!" His pain aggravated the discomfort of the others; there was a growing sound throughout the keep.

Lord Ballant's oldest son, his mind penetrated by Hein Huss himself, struck his shield with his mailed fist. "They burn me! They burn us all! Better to fight than burn!"

"Fight! Fight!" came the voices of the tormented men.

Lord Ballant looked around at the twisted faces, some displaying blisters, scaldmarks. "Our own spell terrifies them; wait yet a moment!" he pleaded.

His brother called hoarsely, "It is not your belly that Hein Huss toasts in the flames, it is mine! We cannot win a battle of hoodoos; we must win a battle of arms!"

Lord Ballant cried desperately, "Wait, our own effects are working! They will flee in terror; wait, wait!"

His cousin tore off his corselet. "It's Hein Huss! I feel him! My leg's in the fire, the devil laughs at me. Next my head, he says. Fight, or I go forth to fight alone!"

"Very well," said Lord Ballant in a fateful voice. "We go forth to fight. First—the beast goes forth. Then we follow and smite them in their terror."

The gates to the keep swung suddenly wide. Out sprang what appeared to be the depicted monster; legs moving, arms waving, eyes rolling, issuing evil sounds. Normally the Faide warriors would have seen the monster for what it was; a model carried on the backs of three horses. But their minds had been influenced: they had been infected with horror; they drew back with arms hanging flaccid. From behind the monster the Ballant knights galloped, followed by the Ballant foot soldiers. The charge gathered momentum, tore into the Faide center. Lord Faide bellowed orders; discipline asserted itself. The Faide knights disengaged, divided into three platoons, and engulfed the Ballant charge, while the foot soldiers poured darts into the advancing ranks.

There was the clatter and surge of battle; Lord Ballant, seeing that his sally had failed to overwhelm the Faide forces, and thinking to conserve his own forces, ordered a retreat. In good order the Ballant warriors began to back up toward the keep. The Faide knights held close contact, hoping to win to the courtyard. Close behind came a heavily loaded wagon pushed by armored horses, to be wedged against the gate.

Lord Faide called an order; a reserve platoon of ten knights charged from the side, thrust behind the main body of Ballant horsemen, rode through the foot soldiers, fought into the keep, cut down the gate-tenders.

Lord Ballant bellowed to Anderson Grimes, "They have won inside; quick with your cursed demon! If he can help us, let him do so now!"

"Demon-possession is not a matter of an instant," muttered the jinxman. "I need time."

"You have no time! Ten minutes and we're all dead!"

"I will do my best. Everid, Everid, come swift!"

He hastened into his workroom, donned his demonmask, tossed handful after handful of incense into the brazier. Against one wall stood a great form: black, slit-eyed, noseless. Great white fangs hung from its upper palate; it stood on heavy bent legs, arms reached forward to grasp. Anderson Grimes swallowed a cup of syrup, paced slowly back and forth. A moment passed.

"Grimes!" came Ballant's call from outside. "Grimes!" A voice spoke. "Enter without fear."

Lord Ballant, carrying his ancestral side arm, entered. He drew back with an involuntary sound. "Grimes!" he whispered.

"Grimes is not here," said the voice. "I am here. Enter."

Lord Ballant came forward stiff-legged. The room was dark except for the feeble glimmer of the brazier. Anderson Grimes crouched in a corner, head bowed under his demon-mask. The shadows twisted and pulsed with shapes and faces, forms struggling to become solid. The black image seemed to vibrate with life.

"Bring in your warriors," said the voice. "Bring them in five at a time, bid them look only at the floor until commanded to raise their eyes."

Lord Ballant retreated; there was no sound in the room.

A moment passed; then five limp and exhausted warriors filed into the room, eyes low.

"Look slowly up," said the voice. "Look at the orange fire. Breathe deeply. Then look at me. I am Everid, Demon of Hate. Look at me. Who am I?"

"You are Everid, Demon of Hate," quavered the warriors.

"I stand all around you, in a dozen forms . . . I come closer. Where am I?"

"You are close."

"Now I am you. We are together."

There was a sudden quiver of motion. The warriors stood straighter, their faces distorted.

"Go forth," said the voice. "Go quietly into the court. In a few minutes we march forth to slay."

The five stalked forth. Five more entered.

Outside the wall the Ballant knights had retreated as far as the gate; within, seven Faide knights still survived, and with their backs to the wall held the Ballant warriors away from the gate mechanism.

In the Faide camp Huss called to Commandore, "Everid is walking. Bring forth Keyril."

"Send the men," came Comandore's voice, low and harsh. "Send the men to me. I am Keyril."

Within the keep twenty warriors came marching into the courtyard. Their steps were cautious, tentative, slow. Their faces had lost individuality, they were twisted and distorted, curiously alike.

"Bewitched!" whispered the Ballant soldiers, drawing back. The seven Faide knights watched with sudden fright. But the twenty warriors, paying them no heed, marched out the gate. The Ballant knights parted; for an instant there was a lull in the fighting. The twenty sprang like tigers. Their swords glistened, twinkling in water-bright arcs. They crouched, jerked, jumped; Faide arms, legs, heads were hewed off. The twenty were cut and battered, but the blows seemed to have no effect.

The Faide attack faltered, collapsed. The knights, whose armor was no protection against the demoniac swords, retreated. The twenty possessed warriors raced out into the open toward the foot soldiers, running with great strides, slashing and rending. The Faide foot soldiers fought for a moment, then they too gave way and turned to flee.

From behind Comandore's tent appeared thirty Faide warriors, marching stiffly, slowly. Like the Ballant twenty their faces were alike—but between the Everid-possessed and the Keyril-possessed was the difference between the face of Everid and the face of Keyril.

Keyril and Everid fought, using the men as weapons, without fear, retreat, or mercy. Hack, chop, cut. Arms, legs, sundered torsos. Bodies fought headless for moments before collapsing. Only when a body was minced, hacked to bits, did the demoniac vitality depart. Presently there were no more men of Everid, and only fifteen men of Keyril. These hopped and limped and tumbled toward the keep where Faide knights still held the gate. The Ballant knights met them in despair, knowing that now was the decisive moment. Leaping, leering from chopped faces, slashing from tireless arms, the warriors cut a hole into the iron. The Faide knights, roaring victory cries, plunged after. Into the courtyard surged the battle, and now there was no longer doubt of the outcome. Ballant Keep was taken.

Back in his tent Isak Comandore took a deep breath, shuddered, flung down his demonmask. In the courtyard the twelve remaining warriors dropped in their tracks, twitched, gasped, gushed blood and died.

Lord Ballant, in the last gallant act of a gallant life, marched forth brandishing his ancestral side arm. He aimed across the bloody field at Lord Faide, pulled the trigger. The weapon spewed a brief gout of light; Lord Faide's skin prickled and hair rose from his head. The weapon crackled, turned cherry-red, and melted. Lord Ballant threw down the weapon, drew his sword, marched forth to challenge Lord Faide.

Lord Faide, disinclined to unnecessary combat, signaled to his soldiers. A flight of darts ended Lord Ballant's life, saving him the discomfort of formal execution.

There was no further resistance. The Ballant defenders threw down their arms and marched grimly out to kneel before Lord Faide, while inside the keep the Ballant women gave themselves to mourning and grief.

V

Lord Faide had no wish to linger at Ballant Keep, for he took no relish in his victories. Inevitably, a thousand decisions had to be made. Six of the closest Ballant kinsmen were summarily stabbed and the title declared defunct. Others of the clan were offered a choice: an oath of lifelong fealty together with a moderate ransom, or death. Eyes blazing hate, two chose death and were stabbed.

Lord Faide had now achieved his ambition. For over a thousand years the keep-lords had struggled for power; now one, now another gaining ascendancy. None before had ever extended his authority across the entire continent—which meant control of the planet, since all other land was either sun-parched rock or eternal ice. Ballant Keep had long thwarted Lord Faide's drive to power; now—success, total and absolute. It still remained to chastise the lords of Castle Cloud and Gisborne, both of whom, seeing opportunity to overwhelm Lord Faide, had ranged themselves behind Lord Ballant. But these were matters that might well be assigned to Hein Huss.

Lord Faide, for the first time in his life, felt a trace of uncertainty. Now what? No real adversaries remained. The First Folk must be whipped back, but here was no great problem: they were numerous, but no more than savages. He knew that dissatisfaction and controversy would ultimately arise among his kinsmen and allies. Inaction and boredom would breed irritability; idle minds would calculate the pros and cons of mischief. Even the most loyal would remember the campaigns with nostalgia and long for the excitement, the release, the license, of warfare. Somehow he must find means to absorb the energy of so many active and keyed-up men. How and where, this was the problem. The construction of roads? New farmland claimed from the downs? Yearly tournaments-at-arms? Lord Faide frowned at the inadequacy of his solutions, but his imagination was impoverished by the lack of tradition. The original settlers of Pangborn had been warriors, and had brought with them a certain amount of practical rule-of-thumb knowledge, but little else. The tales they passed down the generations described the great spaceships which moved with magic speed and certainty, the miraculous weapons, the wars in the void, but told nothing of human history or civilized achievement. And so Lord Faide, full of power and success, but with no goal toward which to turn his strength, felt more morose and saturnine than ever.

He gloomily inspected the spoils from Ballant Keep. They were of no great interest to him. Ballant's ancestral car was no longer used, but displayed behind a glass case. He inspected the weapon Volcano, but this could not be moved. In any

event it was useless, its magic lost forever. Lord Faide now
knew that Lord Ballant had ordered it turned against the
Faide car, but that it had refused to spew its vaunted fire.
Lord Faide saw with disdainful amusement that Volcano had
been sadly neglected. Corrosion had pitted the metal, careless
cleaning had twisted the exterior tubing, undoubtedly diminishing the potency of the magic. No such neglect at Faide
Keep! Jambart the weapon-tender cherished Hellmouth with
absolute devotion. Elsewhere were other ancient devices,
interesting but useless—the same sort of curios that cluttered
shelves and cases at Faide Keep. (Peculiar, these ancient men!
thought Lord Faide: at once so clever, yet so primitive and
impractical. Conditions had changed: there had been enormous advances since the dark ages sixteen hundred years ago.
For instance, the ancients had used intricate fetishes of metal
and glass to communicate with each other. Lord Faide need
merely voice his needs; Hein Huss could project his mind a
hundred miles to see, to hear, to relay Lord Faide's words.)
The ancients had contrived dozens of such objects, but the
old magic had worn away and they never seemed to function.
Lord Ballant's side arm had melted, after merely stinging
Lord Faide. Imagine a troop armed thus trying to cope with
a platoon of demon-possessed warriors! Slaughter of the
innocents!

Among the Ballant trove Lord Faide noted a dozen old
books and several reels of microfilm. The books were worth-
less, page after page of incomprehensible jargon; the microfilm was equally undecipherable. Again Lord Faide wondered
skeptically about the ancients. Clever of course, but to look
at the hard facts, they were little more advanced than the
First Folk: neither had facility with telepathy or voyance or
demon-command. And the magic of the ancients: might there
not be a great deal of exaggeration in the legends? Volcano,
for instance. A joke. Lord Faide wondered about his own
Hellmouth. But no—surely Hellmouth was more trustworthy;

Jambart cleaned and polished the weapon daily and washed the entire cupola with vintage wine every month. If human care could induce faithfulness, then Hellmouth was ready to defend Faide Keep!

Now there was no longer need for defense. Faide was supreme. Considering the future, Lord Faide made a decision. There should no longer be keep-lords on Pangborn; he would abolish the appellation. Habitancy of the keeps would gradually be transferred to trusted bailiffs on a yearly basis. The former lords would be moved to comfortable but indefensible manor houses, with the maintenance of private troops forbidden. Naturally they must be allowed jinxmen, but these would be made accountable to himself—perhaps through some sort of licensing provision. He must discuss the matter with Hein Huss. A matter for the future, however. Now he merely wished to settle affairs and return to Faide Keep.

There was little more to be done. The surviving Ballant kinsmen he sent to their homes after Huss had impregnated fresh dolls with their essences. Should they default on their ransoms, a twinge of fire, a few stomach cramps would more than set them right. Ballant Keep itself Lord Faide would have liked to burn—but the material of the ancients was proof to fire. But in order to discourage any new pretenders to the Ballant heritage Lord Faide ordered all the heirlooms and relics brought forth into the courtyard, and then, one at a time, in order of rank, he bade his men choose. Thus the Ballant wealth was distributed. Even the jinxmen were invited to choose, but they despised the ancient trinkets as works of witless superstition. The lesser spellbinders and apprentices rummaged through the leavings, occasionally finding an overlooked bauble or some anomalous implement. Isak Comandore was irritated to find Sam Salazar staggering under a load of the ancient books. "And what is your purpose with these?" he barked. "Why do you burden yourself with rubbish?"

Sam Salazar hung his head. "I have no definite purpose.

Undoubtedly there was wisdom—or at least knowledge—among the ancients: perhaps I can use these symbols of knowledge to sharpen my own understanding."

Comandore threw up his hands in disgust. He turned to Hein Huss who stood nearby. "First he fancies himself a tree and stands in the mud; now he thinks to learn jinxmanship through a study of ancient symbols."

Huss shrugged. "They were men like ourselves, and, though limited, they were not entirely obtuse. A certain simian cleverness is required to fabricate these objects."

"Simian cleverness is no substitute for sound jinxmanship." retorted Isak Comandore. "This is a point hard to overemphasize; I have drummed it into Salazar's head a hundred times. And now, look at him."

Huss grunted noncommitally. "I fail to understand what he hopes to achieve."

Sam Salazar tried to explain, fumbling for words to express an idea that did not exist. "I thought perhaps to decipher the writing, if only to understand what the ancients thought, and perhaps to learn how to perform one or two of their tricks."

Comandore rolled up his eyes. "What enemy bewitched me when I consented to take you as apprentice? I can cast twenty hoodoos in an hour, more than any of the ancients could achieve in a lifetime."

"Nevertheless," said Sam Salazar, "I notice that Lord Faide rides in his ancestral car, and that Lord Ballant sought to kill us all with Volcano."

"I notice," said Comandore with feral softness, "that my demon Keyril conquered Lord Ballant's Volcano, and that riding on my wagon I can outdistance Lord Faide in his car."

Sam Salazar though better of arguing further. "True, Jinxman Comandore, very true. I stand corrected."

"Then discard that rubbish and make yourself useful. We return to Faide Keep in the morning."

"As you wish, Jinxman Comandore." Sam Salazar threw the books back into the trash.

VI

The Ballant clan had been dispersed, Ballant Keep was despoiled. Lord Faide and his men banqueted somberly in the great hall, tended by silent Ballant servitors.

Ballant Keep had been built on the same splendid scale as Faide Keep. The great hall was a hundred feet long, fifty feet wide, fifty feet high, paneled in planks sawn from pale native hardwood, rubbed and waxed to a rich honey color. Enormous black beams supported the ceiling; from these hung candelabra, intricate contrivances of green, purple, and blue glass, knotted with ancient but still bright light-motes. On the far wall hung portraits of all the lords of Ballant Keep —105 grave faces in a variety of costumes. Below, a genealogical chart ten feet high detailed the descent of the Ballants and their connections with the other noble clans. Now there was a desolate air to the hall, and the 105 dead faces were meaningless and empty.

Lord Faide dined without joy, and cast dour side glances at those of his kinsmen who revelled too gladly. Lord Ballant, he thought, had conducted himself only as he himself might have done under the same circumstances; coarse exultation seemed in poor taste, almost as if it were disrespect for Lord Faide himself. His followers were quick to catch his mood, and the banquet proceeded with greater decorum.

The jinxmen sat apart in a smaller room to the side. Anderson Grimes, erstwhile Ballant Head Jinxman, sat beside Hein Huss, trying to put a good face on his defeat. After all, he had performed creditably against four powerful adversaries, and there was no cause to feel a diminution of *mana*. The five jinxmen discussed the battle, while the cabalmen and spellbinders listened respectfully. The conduct of the demon-possessed troops occasioned the most discussion. Anderson Grimes readily admitted that his conception of Everid was a force absolutely brutal and blunt, terrifying in its indomitable vigor. The other jinxmen agreed that he undoubtedly succeeded in projecting these qualities; Hein Huss however pointed out that Isak Comandore's Keyril, as cruel and vigorous as Everid, also combined a measure of crafty malice, which tended to make the possessed soldier a more effective weapon.

Anderson Grimes allowed that this might well be the case, and that in fact he had been considering such an augmentation of Everid's characteristics.

"To my mind," said Huss, "the most effective demon should be swift enough to avoid the strokes of the brute demons, such as Keyril and Everid. I cite my own Dant as example. A Dant-possessed warrior can easily destroy a Keyril or an Everid, simply through his agility. In an encounter of this sort the Keyrils and Everids presently lose their capacity to terrify, and thus half the effect is lost."

Isak Comandore pierced Huss with a hot russet glance. "You state a presumption as if it were fact. I have formulated Keyril with sufficient craft to counter any such displays of speed. I firmly believe Keyril to be the most fearsome of all demons."

"It may well be," rumbled Hein Huss thoughtfully. He beckoned to a steward, gave instructions. The steward reduced the light a trifle. "Behold," said Hein Huss. "There is Dant. He comes to join the banquet." At the side of the room loomed the tiger-striped Dant, a creature constructed of resilient metal, with four terrible arms, and a squat black head which seemed all gaping jaw.

"Look," came the husky voice of Isak Comandore. "There is Keyril." Keyril was rather more humanoid and armed with a cutlass. Dant spied Keyril. The jaws gaped wider, it sprang to the attack.

The battle was a thing of horror; the two demons rolled, twisted, bit, frothed, uttered soundless shrieks, tore each other apart. Suddenly Dant sprang away, circled Keyril with dizzying speed, faster, faster; became a blur, a wild coruscation of colors that seemed to give off a high-pitched wailing sound, rising higher and higher in pitch. Keyril hacked brutally with his cutlass, then seemed to grow feeble and wan. The light that once had been Dant blazed white, exploded in a mental shriek; Keyril was gone and Isak Comandore lay moaning.

Hein Huss drew a deep breath, wiped his face, looked about him with a complacent grin. The entire company sat rigid as stones, staring, all except the apprentice Sam Salazar, who met Hein Huss's glance with a cheerful smile.

"So," growled Huss, panting from his exertion, "you consider yourself superior to the illusion; you sit and smirk at one of Hein Huss's best efforts."

"No, no," cried Sam Salazar, "I mean no disrespect! I want to learn, so I watched you rather than the demons. What could they teach me? Nothing!"

"Ah," said Huss, mollified. "And what did you learn?"

"Likewise, nothing," said Sam Salazar, "but at least I do not sit like a fish."

Comandore's voice came soft but crackling with wrath. "You see in me the resemblance to a fish?"

"I except you, Jinxman Comandore, naturally," Sam Salazar explained.

"Please go to my cabinet, Apprentice Salazar, and fetch me the doll that is your likeness. The steward will bring a basin of water, and we shall have some sport. With your knowledge of fish you perhaps can breathe under water. If not—you may suffocate."

"I prefer not, Jinxman Comandore," said Sam Salazar. "In fact, with your permission, I now resign your service."

Comandore motioned to one of his cabalmen. "Fetch me

the Salazar doll. Since he is no longer my apprentice, it is likely indeed that he will suffocate."

"Come now, Comandore," said Hein Huss gruffly. "Do not torment the lad. He is innocent and a trifle addled. Let this be an occasion of placidity and ease."

"Certainly, Hein Huss," said Comandore. "Why not? There is ample time in which to discipline this upstart."

"Jinxman Huss," said Sam Salazar, "since I am now relieved of my duties to Jinxman Comandore, perhaps you will accept me into your service."

Hein Huss made a noise of vast distaste. "You are not my responsibility."

"There are many futures, Hein Huss," said Sam Salazar. "You have said as much yourself."

Hein Huss looked at Sam Salazar with his water-clear eyes. "Yes, there are many futures. And I think that tonight sees the full amplitude of jinxmanship. . . . I think that never again will such power and skill gather at the same table. We shall die one by one and there shall be none to fill our shoes. . . . Yes, Sam Salazar. I will take you as apprentice. Isak Comandore, do you hear? This youth is now of my company."

"I must be compensated," growled Comandore.

"You have coveted my doll of Tharon Faide, the only one in existence. It is yours."

"Ah, ha!" cried Isak Comandore leaping to his feet. "Hein Huss, I salute you! You are generous indeed! I thank you and accept!"

Hein Huss motioned to Sam Salazar. "Move your effects to my wagon. Do not show your face again tonight."

Sam Salazar bowed with dignity and departed the hall.

The banquet continued, but now something of melancholy filled the room. Presently a messenger from Lord Faide came to warn all to bed, for the party returned to Faide Keep at dawn.

VII

The victorious Faide troops gathered on the heath before Ballant Keep. As a parting gesture Lord Faide ordered the great gate torn off the hinges, so that ingress could never again be denied him. But even after sixteen hundred years the hinges were proof to all the force the horses could muster, and the gates remained in place.

Lord Faide accepted the fact with good grace and bade farewell to his cousin Renfroy, whom he had appointed bailiff. He climbed into his car, settled himself, snapped the switch. The car groaned and moved forward. Behind came the knights and the foot soldiers, then the baggage train, laden with booty, and finally the wagons of the jinxmen.

Three hours the column marched across the mossy downs. Ballant Keep dwindled behind; ahead appeared North and South Wildwood, darkening all the sweep of the western horizon. Where once the break had existed, the First Folk's new planting showed a smudge lower and less intense than the old woodlands.

Two miles from the woodlands Lord Faide called a halt and signaled up his knights. Hein Huss laboriously dismounted from his wagon, came forward.

"In the event of resistance," Lord Faide told the knights, "do not be tempted into the forest. Stay with the column and at all times be on your guard against traps."

Hein Huss spoke. "You wish me to parley with the First Folk once more?"

"No," said Lord Faide. "It is ridiculous that I must ask permission of savages to ride over my own land. We return as we came; if they interfere, so much the worse for them."

"You are rash," said Huss with simple candor.

Lord Faide glanced down at him with black eyebrows raised. "What damage can they do if we avoid their traps? Blow foam at us?"

"It is not my place to advise or to warn," said Hein Huss. "However, I point out that they exhibit a confidence which does not come from conscious weakness; also, that they carried tubes, apparently hollow grasswood shoots, which imply missiles."

Lord Faide nodded. "No doubt. However, the knights wear armor, the soldiers carry bucklers. It is not fit that I, Lord Faide of Faide Keep, choose my path to suit the whims of the First Folk. This must be made clear, even if the exercise involves a dozen or so First Folk corpses."

"Since I am not a fighting man," remarked Hein Huss, "I will keep well to the rear, and pass only when the way is secure."

"As you wish." Lord Faide pulled down the visor of his helmet. "Forward."

The column moved toward the forest, along the previous track, which showed plain across the moss. Lord Faide rode in the lead, flanked by his brother, Gethwin Faide, and his cousin, Mauve Dermont-Faide.

A half-mile passed, and another. The forest was only a mile distant. Overhead the great sun rode at zenith; brightness and heat poured down; the air carried the oily scent of thorn and tarbush. The column moved on, more slowly; the only sounds the clanking of armor, the muffled thud of hooves in the moss, the squeal of wagon wheels.

Lord Faide rose up in his car, watching for any sign of hostile preparation. A half-mile from the planting the forms of the First Folk, waiting in the shade along the forest's verge, became visible. Lord Faide ignored them, held a steady pace along the track they had traveled before.

The half-mile became a quarter-mile. Lord Faide turned to order the troops into single file and was just in time to see a hole suddenly open into the moss and his brother, Gethwin Faide, drop from sight. There was a rattle, a thud, the howling of the impaled horse; Gethwin's wild calls as the horse kicked and crushed him into the stakes. Mauve Dermont-

Faide, riding beside Gethwin, could not control his own horse, which leaped aside from the pit and blundered upon a trigger. Up from the moss burst a tree trunk studded with foot-long thorns. It snapped, quick as a scorpion's tail; the thorns punctured Mauve Dermont-Faide's armor, his chest, and whisked him from his horse to carry him suspended, writhing and screaming. The tip of the scythe pounded into Lord Faide's car, splintered against the hull. The car swung groaning through the air. Lord Faide clutched at the windscreen to prevent himself from falling.

The column halted; several men ran to the pit, but Gethwin Faide lay twenty feet below, crushed under his horse. Others took Mauve Dermont-Faide down from the swaying scythe, but he, too, was dead.

Lord Faide's skin tingled with a gooseflesh of hate and rage. He looked toward the forest. The First Folk stood motionless. He beckoned to Bernard, sergeant of the foot soldiers. "Two men with lances to try out the ground ahead. All others ready with darts. At my signal spit the devils."

Two men came forward, and marching before Lord Faide's car, probed at the ground. Lord Faide settled in his seat. "Forward."

The column moved slowly toward the forest, every man tense and ready. The lances of the two men in the vanguard presently broke through the moss, to disclose a nettle trap— a pit lined with nettles, each frond ripe with globes of acid. Carefully they probed out a path to the side, and the column filed around, each man walking in the other's tracks.

At Lord Faide's side now rode his two nephews, Scolford and Edwin. "Notice," said Lord Faide in a voice harsh and tight. "These traps were laid since our last passage; an act of malice."

"But why did they guide us through before?"

Lord Faide smiled bitterly. "They were willing that we should die at Ballant Keep. But we have disappointed them."

"Notice, they carry tubes," said Scolford.

"Blowguns possibly," suggested Edwin.

Scolford disagreed. "They cannot blow through their foam-vents."

"No doubt we shall soon learn," said Lord Faide. He rose in his seat, called to the rear. "Ready with the darts!"

The soldiers raised their crossbows. The column advanced slowly, now only a hundred yards from the planting. The white shapes of the First Folk moved uneasily at the forest's edges. Several of them raised their tubes, seemed to sight along the length. They twitched their great hands.

One of the tubes was pointed toward Lord Faide. He saw a small black object leave the opening, flit forward, gathering speed. He heard a hum, waxing to a rasping, clicking flutter. He ducked behind the windscreen; the projectile swooped in pursuit, struck the windscreen like a thrown stone. It fell crippled upon the forward deck of the car—a heavy black insect like a wasp, its broken proboscis oozing ocher liquid, horny wings beating feebly, eyes like dumbbells fixed on Lord Faide. With his mailed fist, he crushed the creature.

Behind him other wasps struck knights and men; Corex Faide-Battaro took the prong through his visor into the eye, but the armor of the other knights defeated the wasps. The foot soldiers, however, lacked protection; the wasps half buried themselves in flesh. The soldiers called out in pain, clawed away the wasps, squeezed the wounds. Corex Faide-Battaro toppled from his horse, ran blindly out over the heath, and after fifty feet fell into a trap. The stricken soldiers began to twitch, then fell on the moss, thrashed, leaped up to run with flapping arms, threw themselves in wild somersaults, foaming and thrashing.

In the forest, the First Folk raised their tubes again. Lord Faide bellowed, "Spit the creatures! Bowmen, launch your darts!"

There came the twang of crossbows, darts snapped at the quiet white shapes. A few staggered and wandered aimlessly away; most, however, plucked out the darts or ignored them. They took capsules from small sacks, put them to the end of their tubes.

"Beware the wasps!" cried Lord Faide. "Strike with your bucklers! Kill the cursed things in flight!"

The rasp of horny wings came again; certain of the soldiers found courage enough to follow Lord Faide's orders, and battered down the wasps. Others struck home as before; behind came another flight. The column became a tangle of struggling, crouching men.

"Footmen, retreat!" called Lord Faide furiously. "Footmen back! Knights to me!"

The soldiers fled back along the track, taking refuge behind the baggage wagons. Thirty of their number lay dying, or dead, on the moss.

Lord Faide cried out to his knights in a voice like a bugle. "Dismount, follow slow after me! Turn your helmets, keep the wasps from your eyes! One step at a time, behind the car! Edwin, into the car beside me, test the footing with your lance. Once in the forest there are no traps! Then attack!"

The knights formed themselves into a line behind the car. Lord Faide drove slowly forward, his kinsman Edwin prodding the ground ahead. The First Folk sent out a dozen more wasps, which dashed themselves vainly against the armor. Then there was silence . . . cessation of sound, activity. The First Folk watched impassively as the knights approached, step by step.

Edwin's lance found a trap, the column moved to the side. Another trap—and the column was diverted from the planting toward the forest. Step by step, yard by yard—another trap, another detour, and now the column was only a hundred feet from the forest. A trap to the left, a trap to the right: the safe path led directly toward an enormous heavy-branched tree. Seventy feet, fifty feet, then Lord Faide drew his sword.

"Prepare to charge, kill till your arms tire!"

From the forest came a crackling sound. The branches of the great tree trembled and swayed. The knights stared, for a moment frozen into place. The tree toppled forward, the knights madly tried to flee—to the rear, to the sides. Traps opened; the knights dropped upon sharp stakes. The tree fell; boughs cracked armored bodies like nuts; there was the hoarse yelling of pinned men, screams from the traps, the crackling subsidence of breaking branches. Lord Faide had been battered down into the car, and the car had been pressed groaning into the moss. His first instinctive act was to press the switch to rest position; then he staggered erect, clambered up through the boughs. A pale unhuman face peered at him; he swung his fist, crushed the faceted eyebulge, and roaring with rage scrambled through the branches. Others of his knights were working themselves free, although almost a third were either crushed or impaled.

The First Folk came scrambling forward, armed with enormous thorns, long as swords. But now Lord Faide could reach them at close quarters. Hissing with vindictive joy he sprang into their midst, swinging his sword with both hands, as if demon-possessed. The surviving knights joined him and the ground became littered with dismembered First Folk. They drew back slowly, without excitement. Lord Faide reluctantly called back his knights. "We must succor those still pinned, as many as still are alive."

As well as possible branches were cut away, injured knights drawn forth. In some cases the soft moss had cushioned the impact of the tree. Six knights were dead, another four crushed beyond hope of recovery. To these Lord Faide himself gave the *coup de grace*. Ten minutes further hacking and chopping freed Lord Faide's car, while the First Folk watched incuriously from the forest. The knights wished to charge once more, but Lord Faide ordered retreat. Without interference they returned the way they had come, back to the baggage train.

Lord Faide ordered a muster. Of the original war party, less than two-thirds remained. Lord Faide shook his head bitterly. Galling to think how easily he had been led into a trap! He swung on his heel, strode to the rear of the column, to the wagons of the magicians. The jinxmen sat around a small fire, drinking tea. "Which of you will hoodoo these white forest vermin? I want them dead—stricken with sickness, cramps, blindness, the most painful afflictions you can contrive!"

There was general silence. The jinxmen sipped their tea.

"Well?" demanded Lord Faide. "Have you no answer? Do I not make myself plain?"

Hein Huss cleared his throat, spat into the blaze. "Your wishes are plain. Unfortunately we cannot hoodoo the First Folk."

"And why?"

"There are technical reasons."

Lord Faide knew the futility of argument. "Must we slink home around the forest? If you cannot hoodoo the First Folk, then bring out your demons! I will march on the forest and chop out a path with my sword!"

"It is not for me to suggest tactics," grumbled Hein Huss.

"Go on, speak! I will listen."

"A suggestion has been put to me, which I will pass to you. Neither I nor the other jinxmen associate ourselves with it, since it recommends the crudest of physical principles."

"I await the suggestion," said Lord Faide.

"It is merely this. One of my apprentices tampered with your car, as you may remember."

"Yes, and I will see he gets the hiding he deserves."

"By some freak he caused the car to rise high into the air. The suggestion is this: that we load the car with as much oil as the baggage train affords, that we send the car aloft and let it drift over the planting. At a suitable moment, the occupant of the car will pour the oil over the trees, then hurl

down a torch. The forest will burn. The First Folk will be at
least discomfited; at best a large number will be destroyed."

Lord Faide slapped his hands together. "Excellent! Quickly, to work!" He called a dozen soldiers, gave them orders;
four kegs of cooking oil, three buckets of pitch, six demijohns
of spirit were brought and lifted into the car. The engines
grated and protested, and the car sagged almost to the moss.

Lord Faide shook his head sadly. "A rude use of the relic,
but all in good purpose. Now, where is that apprentice? He
must indicate which switches and which buttons he turned."

"I suggest," said Hein Huss, "that Sam Salazar be sent up
with the car."

Lord Faide looked sidewise at Sam Salazar's round, bland
countenance. "An efficient hand is needed, a seasoned judgment. I wonder if he can be trusted?"

"I would think so," said Hein Huss, "inasmuch as it was
Sam Salazar who evolved the scheme in the first place."

"Very well. In with you, Apprentice! Treat my car with
reverence! The wind blows away from us; fire this edge of the
forest, in as long a strip as you can manage. The torch, where
is the torch?"

The torch was brought and secured to the side of the car.

"One more matter," said Sam Salazar. "I would like to
borrow the armor of some obliging knight, to protect myself
from the wasps. Otherwise—"

"Armor!" bawled Lord Faide. "Bring armor!"

At last, fully accoutered and with visor down, Sam Salazar
climbed into the car. He seated himself, peered intently at
the buttons and switches. In truth he was not precisely certain as to which he had manipulated before. . . . He considered, reached forward, pushed, turned. The motors roared
and screamed; the car shuddered, sluggishly rose into the air.
Higher, higher, twenty feet, forty feet, sixty feet—a hundred,
two hundred. The wind eased the car toward the forest; in
the shade the First Folk watched. Several of them raised
tubes, opened the shutters. The onlookers saw wasps dart

through the air to dash against Sam Salazar's armor.

The car drifted over the trees; Sam Salazar began ladling out the oil. Below, the First Folk stirred uneasily. The wind carried the car too far over the forest; Sam Salazar worked the controls, succeeded in guiding himself back. One keg was empty, and another; he tossed them out, presently emptied the remaining two, and the buckets of pitch. He soaked a rag in spirit, ignited it, threw it over the side, poured the spirit after.

The flaming rag fell into leaves. A crackle; fire blazed and sprang. The car now floated at a height of five hundred feet. Salazar poured over the remaining spirits, dropped the demi-johns, guided the car back over the heath, and fumbling nervously with the controls dropped the car in a series of swoops back to the moss.

Lord Faide sprang forward, clapped him on the shoulder. "Excellently done! The forest blazes like tinder!"

The men of Faide Keep stood back, rejoicing to see the flames soar and lick. The First Folk scurried back from the heat, waving their arms; foam of a peculiar purple color issued from their vents as they ran, small useless puffs discharged as if by accident or through excitement. The flames ate through first the forest, then spread into the new planting, leaping through the leaves.

"Prepare to march!" called Lord Faide. "We pass directly behind the flames, before the First Folk return."

Off in the forest the First Folk perched in the trees, blowing out foam in great puffs and billows, building a wall of insulation. The flames had eaten half across the new planting, leaving behind smoldering saplings.

"Forward! Briskly!"

The column moved ahead. Coughing in the smoke, eyes smarting, they passed under still blazing trees and came out on the western downs.

Slowly the column moved forward, led by a pair of soldiers prodding the moss with lances. Behind followed Lord

Faide with the knights, then came the foot soldiers, then the rumbling baggage train, and finally the six wagons of the jinxmen.

A thump, a creak, a snap. A scythe had broken up from the moss; the soldiers in the lead dropped flat; the scythe whipped past, a foot from Lord Faide's face. At the same time a plaintive cry came from the rear guard. "They pursue! The First Folk come!"

Lord Faide turned to inspect the new threat. A clot of First Folk, two hundred or more, came across the moss, moving without haste or urgency. Some carried wasp tubes, others thorn-rapiers.

Lord Faide looked ahead. Another hundred yards should bring the army out upon safe ground; then he could deploy and maneuver. "Forward!"

The column proceeded, the baggage train and the jinxmen's wagons pressing close up against the soldiers. Behind and to one side came the First Folk, moving casually and easily.

At last Lord Faide judged they had reached secure ground. "Forward, now! Bring the wagons out, hurry now!"

The troops needed no urging; they trotted out over the heath, the wagons trundling after. Lord Faide ordered the wagons into a close double line, stationed the soldiers between, with the horses behind them protected from the wasps. The knights, now dismounted, waited in front.

The First Folk came listlessly, formlessly forward. Blank white faces stared; huge hands grasped tubes and thorns; traces of the purplish foam showed at the lips of their underarm orifices.

Lord Faide walked along the line of knights. "Swords ready. Allow them as close as they care to come. Then a quick charge." He motioned to the foot soldiers. "Choose a target. . .!" A volley of darts whistled overhead, to plunge into white bodies. With chisel-bladed fingers the First Folk plucked them out, discarded them with no evidence of vexation. One or two staggered, wandered confusedly across the line of approach. Others raised their tubes, withdrew the shutter. Out flew the insects, horny wings rasping, prongs thrust forward. Across the moss they flickered, to crush themselves against the armor of the knights, to drop to the ground, to be stamped upon. The soldiers cranked their crossbows back into tension, discharged another flight of darts, caused several more First Folk casualties.

The First Folk spread into a long line, surrounding the Faide troops. Lord Faide shifted half his knights to the other side of the wagons.

The First Folk wandered closer. Lord Faide called for a charge. The knights stepped smartly forward, swords swinging. The First Folk advanced a few more steps, then stopped short. The flaps of skin at their backs swelled, pulsed; white foam gushed through their vents; clouds and billows rose up around them. The knights halted uncertainly, prodding and slashing into the foam but finding nothing. The foam piled higher, rolling in and forward, pushing the knights back toward the wagons. They looked questioningly toward Lord Faide.

Lord Faide waved his sword. "Cut through to the other side! Forward!" Slashing two-handed with his sword, he sprang into the foam. He struck something solid, hacked blindly at it, pushed forward. Then his legs were seized; he was upended and fell with a spine-rattling jar. Now he felt the grate of a thorn searching his armor. It found a crevice under his corselet and pierced him. Cursing he raised on his hands and knees, and plunged blindly forward. Enormous hard hands grasped him, heavy forms fell on his shoulders. He tried to breathe, but the foam clogged his visor; he began to smother. Staggering to his feet he half ran, half fell out into the open air, carrying two of the First Folk with him. He had lost his sword, but managed to draw his dagger. The First Folk released him and stepped back into the foam. Lord Faide sprang to his feet. Inside the foam came the sounds of

combat; some of his knights burst into the open; others called
for help. Lord Faide motioned to the knights. "Back within;
the devils slaughter our kinsmen! In and on to the center!"

He took a deep breath. Seizing his dagger he thrust himself back into the foam. A flurry of shapes came at him: he
pounded with his fists, cut with his dagger, stumbled over a
mass of living tissue. He kicked the softness, and stepped on
metal. Bending, he grasped a leg but found it limp and dead.
First Folk were on his back, another thorn found its mark; he
groaned and thrust himself forward, and once again fell out
into the open air.

A scant fifty of his knights had won back into the central
clearing. Lord Faide cried out, "To the center; mount your
horses!" Abandoning his car, he himself vaulted into a saddle.
The foam boiled and billowed closer. Lord Faide waved his
arm. "Forward, all; at a gallop! After us the wagons—out into
the open!"

They charged, thrusting the frightened horses into the
foam. There was white blindness, the feel of forms underneath, then the open air once again. Behind came the wagons,
and the foot soldiers, running along the channel cut by the
wagons. All won free—all but the knights who had fallen
under the foam.

Two hundred yards from the great white clot of foam,
Lord Faide halted, turned, looked back. He raised his fist,
shook it in a passion. "My knights, my car, my honor! I'll
burn your forests, I'll drive you into the sea, there'll be no
peace till all are dead!" He swung around. "Come," he called
bitterly to the remnants of his war party. "We have been
defeated. We retreat to Faide Keep."

VIII

Faide Keep, like Ballant Keep, was constructed of a black,
glossy substance, half metal, half stone, impervious to heat,

force, and radiation. A parasol roof, designed to ward off hostile energy, rested on five squat outer towers, connected by walls almost as high as the lip of the overhanging roof.

The homecoming banquet was quiet and morose. The soldiers and knights ate lightly and drank much, but instead of becoming merry, lapsed into gloom. Lord Faide, overcome by emotion, jumped to his feet. "Everyone sits silent, aching with rage. I feel no differently. We shall take revenge. We shall put the forests to the torch. The cursed white savages will smother and burn. Drink now with good cheer; not a moment will be wasted. But we must be ready. It is no more than idiocy to attack as before. Tonight I take council with the jinxmen, and we will start a program of affliction."

The soldiers and knights rose to their feet, raised their cups and drank a somber toast. Lord Faide bowed and left the hall.

He went to his private trophy room. On the walls hung escutcheons, memorials, deathmasks, clusters of swords like many-petaled flowers; a rack of side arms, energy pistols, electric stilettos; a portrait of the original Faide, in ancient spacefarer's uniform, and a treasured, almost unique, photograph of the great ship that had brought the first Faide to Pangborn.

Lord Faide studied the ancient face for several moments, then summoned a servant. "Ask the Head Jinxman to attend me."

Hein Huss presently stumped into the room. Lord Faide turned away from the portrait, seated himself, motioned to Hein Huss to do likewise. "What of the keep-lords?" he asked. "How do they regard the setback at the hands of the First Folk?"

"There are various reactions," said Hein Huss. "At Boghoten, Candelwade, and Havve there is distress and anger."

Lord Faide nodded. "These are my kinsmen."

"At Gisborne, Graymar, Castle Cloud, and Alder there is satisfaction, veiled calculation."

"To be expected," muttered Lord Faide. "These lords must be humbled; in spite of oaths and undertakings, they still think rebellion."

"At Star Home, Julian-Douray, and Oak Hall I read surprise at the abilities of the First Folk, but in the main disinterest."

Lord Faide nodded sourly. "Well enough. There is no actual rebellion in prospect; we are free to concentrate on the First Folk. I will tell you what is in my mind. You report that new plantings are in progress between Wildwood, Old Forest, Sarrow Copse, and elsewhere—possibly with the intent of surrounding Faide Keep." He looked inquiringly at Hein Huss, but no comment was forthcoming. Lord Faide continued. "Possibly we have underestimated the cunning of the savages. They seem capable of forming plans and acting with almost human persistence. Or, I should say, more than human persistence, for it appears that after sixteen hundred years they still consider us invaders and hope to exterminate us."

"That is my own conclusion," said Hein Huss.

"We must take steps to strike first. I consider this a matter for the jinxmen. We gain no honor dodging wasps, falling into traps, or groping through foam. It is a needless waste of lives. Therefore, I want you to assemble your jinxmen, cabalmen, and spellbinders; I want you to formulate your most potent hoodoos—"

"Impossible!"

Lord Faide's black eyebrows rose high. "'Impossible'?"

Hein Huss seemed vaguely uncomfortable. "I read the wonder in your mind. You suspect me of disinterest, irresponsibility. Not true. If the First Folk defeat you, we suffer likewise."

"Exactly," said Lord Faide drily, "You will starve."

"Nevertheless, the jinxmen cannot help you." He hoisted himself to his feet, started for the door.

"Sit," said Lord Faide. "It is necessary to pursue this matter."

Hein Huss looked around with his bland, water-clear eyes. Lord Faide met his gaze. Hein Huss sighed deeply. "I see I must ignore the precepts of my trade, break the habits of a lifetime. I must explain." He took his bulk to the wall, fingered the side arms in the rack, studied the portrait of the ancestral Faide. "These miracle workers of the old times—unfortunately we cannot use their magic! Notice the bulk of the spaceship! As heavy as Faide Keep." He turned his gaze on the table, teleported a candelabra two or three inches. "With considerably less effort they gave that spaceship enormous velocity, using ideas and forces they knew to be imaginary and irrational. We have advanced since then, of course. We no longer employ mysteries, arcane constructions, wild nonhuman forces. We are rational and practical—but we cannot achieve the effects of the ancient magicians."

Lord Faide watched Hein Huss with saturnine eyes. Hein Huss gave his deep rumbling laugh. "You think that I wish to distract you with talk? No, this is not the case. I am preparing to enlighten you." He returned to his seat, lowered his bulk with a groan. "Now I must talk at length, to which I am not accustomed. But you must be given to understand what we jinxmen can do and what we cannot do.

"First, unlike the ancient magicians, we are practical men. Naturally there is difference in our abilities. The best jinxman combines great telepathic facility, implacable personal force, and intimate knowledge of his fellow humans. He knows their acts, motives, desires, and fears; he understands the symbols that most vigorously represent these qualities. Jinxmanship in the main is drudgery—dangerous, difficult, and unromantic—with no mystery except that which we employ to confuse our enemies." Hein Huss glanced at Lord Faide to encounter the same saturnine gaze. "Ha! I still have told you nothing; I still have spent many words talking around my inability to confound the First Folk. Patience."

"Speak on," said Lord Faide.

"Listen then. What happens when I hoodoo a man? First I must enter into his mind telepathically. There are three operational levels: the conscious, the unconscious, the cellular. The most effective jinxing is done if all three levels are influenced. I feel into my victim, I learn as much as possible, supplementing my previous knowledge of him, which is part of my stock in trade. I take up his doll, which carries his traces. The doll is highly useful but not indispensable. It serves as a focus for my attention; it acts as a pattern, or a guide, as I fix upon the mind of the victim, and he is bound by his own telepathic capacity to the doll which bears his traces.

"So! Now! Man and doll are identified in my mind, and at one or more levels in the victim's mind. Whatever happens to the doll the victim feels to be happening to himself. There is no more to simple hoodooing than that, from the standpoint of the jinxmen. But naturally the victims differ greatly. Susceptibility is the key idea here. Some men are more susceptible than others. Fear and conviction breed susceptibility. As a jinxman succeeds he becomes ever more feared, and consequently the more efficacious he becomes. The process is self-generative.

"Demon-possession is a similar technique. Susceptibility is again essential; again conviction creates susceptibility. It is easiest and most dramatic when the characteristics of the demon are well known, as in the case of Comandore's Keyril. For this reason, demons can be exchanged or traded among jinxmen. The commodity actually traded is public acceptance and familiarity with the demon."

"Demons then do not actually exist?" inquired Lord Faide half-incredulously.

Hein Huss grinned vastly, showing enormous yellow teeth. "Telepathy works through a superstratum. Who knows what is created in this superstratum? Maybe the demons live on after they have been conceived; maybe they now are real.

This of course is speculation, which we jinxmen shun.

"So much for demons, so much for the lesser techniques of jinxmanship. I have explained sufficient to serve as background to the present situation."

"Excellent," said Lord Faide. "Continue."

"The question, then, is: How does one cast a hoodoo into a creature of an alien race?" He looked inquiringly at Lord Faide. "Can you tell me?"

"I?" asked Lord Faide, surprised. "No."

"The method is basically the same as in the hoodooing of men. It is necessary to make the creature believe, in every cell of his being, that he suffers or dies. This is where the problems begin to arise. Does the creature think—that is to say, does he arrange the processes of his life in the same manner as men? This is a very important distinction. Certain creatures of the universe use methods other than the human nerve-node system to control their environments. We call the human system 'intelligence'—a word which properly should be restricted to human activity. Other creatures use different agencies, different systems, arriving sometimes at similar ends. To bring home these generalities, I cannot hope to merge my mind with the corresponding capacity in the First Folk. The key will not fit the lock. At least, not altogether. Once or twice when I watched the First Folk trading with men at Forest Market, I felt occasional weak significances. This implies that the First Folk mentality creates something similar to human telepathic impulses. Nevertheless, there is no real sympathy between the two races.

"This is the first and the least difficulty. If I were able to make complete telepathic contact—what then? The creatures are different from us. They have no words for 'fear,' 'hate,' 'rage,' 'pain,' 'bravery,' 'cowardice.' One may deduce that they do not feel these emotions. Undoubtedly they know other sensations, possibly as meaningful. Whatever these may be, they are unknown to me, and therefore I cannot either form or project symbols for these sensations."

Lord Faide stirred impatiently. "In short, you tell me that you cannot efficiently enter these creatures' minds; and that if you could, you do not know what influences you could plant there to do them harm."

"Succinct," agreed Hein Huss. "Substantially accurate."

Lord Faide rose to his feet. "In that case you must repair these deficiencies. You must learn to telepathize with the First Folk; you must find what influences will harm them. As quickly as possible."

Hein Huss stared reproachfully at Lord Faide. "But I have gone to great lengths to explain the difficulties involved! To hoodoo the First Folk is a monumental task! It would be necessary to enter Wildwood, to live with the First Folk, to become one of them, as my apprentice thought to become a tree. Even then an effective hoodoo is improbable! The First Folk must be susceptible to conviction! Otherwise there would be no bite to the hoodoo! I could guarantee no success. I would predict failure. No other jinxman would dare tell you this, no other would risk his *mana*. I dare because I am Hein Huss, with life behind me."

"Nevertheless we must attempt every weapon at hand," said Lord Faide in a dry voice. "I cannot risk my knights, my kinsmen, my soldiers against these pallid half-creatures. What a waste of good flesh and blood to be stuck by a poison insect! You must go to Wildwood; you must learn how to hoodoo the First Folk."

Hein Huss heaved himself erect. His great round face was stony; his eyes were like bits of water-worn glass. "It is likewise a waste to go on a fool's errand. I am no fool and I will not undertake a hoodoo which is futile from the beginning."

"In that case," said Lord Faide, "I will find someone else." He went to the door, summoned a servant. "Bring Isak Commandore here."

Hein Huss lowered his bulk into the chair. "I will remain during the interview, with your permission."

"As you wish."

Isak Commandore appeared in the doorway, tall, loosely articulated, head hanging forward. He darted a glance of swift appraisal at Lord Faide, at Hein Huss, then stepped into the room.

Lord Faide crisply explained his desires. "Hein Huss refuses to undertake the mission. Therefore I call on you."

Isak Commandore calculated. The pattern of his thinking was clear: he possibly could gain much *mana*; there was small risk of diminution, for had not Hein Huss already dodged away from the project? Comandore nodded. "Hein Huss has made clear the difficulties; only a very clever and very lucky jinxman can hope to succeed. But I accept the challenge. I will go."

"Good," said Hein Huss. "I will go, too." Isak Comandore darted him a sudden hot glance. "I wish only to observe. To Isak Comandore goes the responsibility and whatever credit may ensue."

"Very well," said Comandore presently. "I welcome your company. Tomorrow morning we leave. I go to order our wagon."

Late in the evening Apprentice Sam Salazar came to Hein Huss where he sat brooding in his workroom. "What do you wish?" growled Huss.

"I have a request to make of you, Head Jinxman Huss."

"Head Jinxman in name only," grumbled Hein Huss. "Isak Comandore is about to assume my position."

Sam Salazar blinked, laughed uncertainly. Hein Huss fixed wintry-pale eyes on him. "What do you wish?"

"I have heard that you go on an expedition to Wildwood, to study the First Folk."

"True, true. What then?"

"Surely they will now attack all men?"

"Hein Huss shrugged. "At Forest Market they trade with men. At Forest Market men have always entered the forest. Perhaps there will be change, perhaps not."

"I would go with you, if I may," said Sam Salazar.

"This is no mission for apprentices."

"An apprentice must take every opportunity to learn," said Sam Salazar. "Also you will need extra hands to set up tents, to load and unload cabinets, to cook, to fetch water, and other such matters."

"Your argument is convincing," said Hein Huss. "We depart at dawn; be on hand."

IX

As the sun lifted over the heath the jinxmen departed Faide Keep. The high-wheeled wagon creaked north over the moss, Hein Huss and Isak Comandore riding the front seat, Sam Salazar with his legs hanging over the tail. The wagon rose and fell with the dips and mounds of the moss, wheels wobbling, and presently passed out of sight behind Skywatcher's Hill.

Five days later, an hour before sunset, the wagon reappeared. As before, Hein Huss and Isak Comandore rode the front seat, with Sam Salazar perched behind. They approached the keep, and without giving so much as a sign or a nod, drove through the gate into the courtyard.

Isak Comandore unfolded his long legs, stepped to the ground like a spider; Hein Huss lowered himself with a grunt. Both went to their quarters, while Sam Salazar led the wagon to the jinxmen's warehouse.

Somewhat later Isak Comandore presented himself to Lord Faide, who had been waiting in his trophy room, forced to a show of indifference through considerations of position, dignity, and protocol. Isak Comandore stood in the doorway, grinning like a fox. Lord Faide eyed him with sour dislike, waiting for Comandore to speak. Hein Huss might have stationed himself an entire day, eyes placidly fixed on Lord Faide, awaiting the first word; Isak Comandore lacked the absolute serenity. He came a step forward. "I have returned from Wildwood."

"With what results?"

"I believe that it is possible to hoodoo the First Folk."

Hein Huss spoke from behind Comandore. "I believe that such an undertaking, if feasible, would be useless, irresponsible, and possibly dangerous." He lumbered forward.

Isak Comandore's eyes glowed hot red-brown; he turned back to Lord Faide. "You ordered me forth on a mission; I will render a report."

"Seat yourselves. I will listen."

Isak Comandore, nominal head of the expedition, spoke. "We rode along the river bank to Forest Market. Here was no sign of disorder or of hostility. A hundred First Folk traded timber, planks, posts, and poles for knife blades, iron wire, and copper pots. When they returned to their barge we followed them aboard, wagon, horses, and all. They showed no surprise—"

"Surprise," said Hein Huss heavily, "is an emotion of which they have no knowledge."

Isak Comandore glared briefly. "We spoke to the barge-tenders, explaining that we wished to visit the interior of Wildwood. We asked if the First Folk would try to kill us to prevent us from entering the forest. They professed indifference as to either our well-being or our destruction. This was by no means a guarantee of safe conduct; however, we accepted it as such, and remained aboard the barge." He spoke on with occasional emendations from Hein Huss.

They had proceeded up the river, into the forest, the First Folk poling against the slow current. Presently they put away the poles; nevertheless the barge moved as before. The mystified jinxmen discussed the possibility of teleportation, or symbological force, and wondered if the First Folk had developed jinxing techniques unknown to men. Sam Salazar, however, noticed that four enormous water beetles, each twelve feet long with oil-black carapaces and blunt heads, had risen from the river bed and pushed the barge from behind—apparently without direction or command. The First Folk stood at the bow, turning the nose of the barge this way or

that to follow the winding of the river. They ignored the jinxmen and Sam Salazar as if they did not exist.

The beetles swam tirelessly; the barge moved for four
hours as fast as a man could walk. Occasionally, First Folk
peered from the forest shadows, but none showed interest or
concern in the barge's unusual cargo. By midafternoon the
river widened, broke into many channels and became a marsh;
a few minutes later the barge floated out into the open water
of a small lake. Along the shore, behind the first line of trees,
appeared a large settlement. The jinxmen were interested and
surprised. It had always been assumed that the First Folk
wandered at random through the forest, as they had originally lived in the moss of the downs.

The barge grounded; the First Folk walked ashore, the
men followed with the horses and wagon. Their immediate
impressions were of swarming numbers, of slow but incessant
activity, and they were attacked by an overpoweringly evil
smell.

Ignoring the stench, the men brought the wagon in from
the shore, paused to take stock of what they saw. The settlement appeared to be a center of many diverse activities.
The trees had been stripped of lower branches, and supported
blocks of hardened foam three hundred feet long, fifty feet
high, twenty feet thick, with a space of a man's height intervening between the underside of the foam and the ground.
There were a dozen of these blocks, apparently of cellular
construction. Certain of the cells had broken open and seethed
with small white fishlike creatures—the First Folk young.

Below the blocks masses of First Folk engaged in various
occupations, in the main unfamiliar to the jinxmen. Leaving
the wagon in the care of Sam Salazar, Hein Huss and Isak
Comandore moved forward among the First Folk, repelled by
the stench and the pressure of alien flesh, but drawn by curiosity. They were neither heeded nor halted; they wandered
everywhere about the settlement. One area seemed to be an
enormous zoo, divided into a number of sections. The purpose

of one of these sections—a kind of range two hundred feet long—was all too clear. At one end a human corpse hung on a rope—a Faide casualty from the battle at the new planting. Certain of the wasps flew straight at the corpse; just before contact they were netted and removed. Others flew up and away or veered toward the First Folk who stood along the side of the range. These latter also were netted and killed at once.

The purpose of the business was clear enough. Examining some of the other activity in this new light, the jinxmen were able to interpret much that had hitherto puzzled them.

They saw beetles tall as dogs with heavy saw-toothed pincers attacking objects resembling horses; pens of insects even larger, long, narrow, segmented, with dozens of heavy legs and nightmare heads. All these creatures—wasps, beetles, centipedes—in smaller and less formidable form were indigenous to the forest; it was plain that the First Folk had been practicing selective breeding for many years, perhaps centuries.

Not all the activity was warlike. Moths were trained to gather nuts, worms to gnaw straight holes through timber; in another section caterpillars chewed a yellow mash, molded it into identical spheres. Much of the evil odor emanated from the zoo; the jinxmen departed without reluctance, and returned to the wagon. Sam Salazar pitched the tent and built a fire, while Hein Huss and Isak Comandore discussed the settlement.

Night came; the blocks of foam glowed with imprisoned light; the activity underneath proceeded without cessation. The jinxmen retired to the tent and slept, while Sam Salazar stood guard.

The following day Hein Huss was able to engage one of the First Folk in conversation; it was the first attention of any sort given to them.

The conversation was long; Hein Huss reported only the gist of it to Lord Faide. (Isak Comandore turned away, ostentatiously disassociating himself from the matter.)

Hein Huss first of all had inquired as to the purpose of the sinister preparations: the wasps, beetles, centipedes, and the like.

"We intend to kill men," the creature had reported ingenuously. "We intend to return to the moss. This has been our purpose ever since men appeared on the planet."

Huss had stated that such an ambition was shortsighted, that there was ample room for both men and First Folk on Pangborn. "The First Folk," said Hein Huss, "should remove their traps and cease their efforts to surround the keeps with forest."

"No," came the response. "men are intruders. They mar the beautiful moss. All will be killed."

Isak Comandore returned to the conversation. "I noticed here a significant fact. All the First Folk within sight had ceased their work; all looked toward us, as if they, too, participated in the discussion. I reached the highly important conclusion that the First Folk are not complete individuals but components of a larger unity, joined to a greater or less extent by a telepathic phase not unlike our own."

Hein Huss continued placidly, "I remarked that if we were attacked, many of the First Folk would perish. The creature showed no concern, and in fact implied much of what Jinxman Comandore had already induced: 'There are always more in the cells to replace the elements which die. But if the community becomes sick, all suffer. We have been forced into the forests, into a strange existence. We must arm ourselves and drive away the men, and to this end we have developed the methods of men to our own purposes!'"

Isak Comandore spoke. "Needless to say, the creature referred to the ancient men, not ourselves."

"In any event," said Lord Faide, "they leave no doubt as to their intentions. We should be fools not to attack them at once, with every weapon at our disposal."

Hein Huss continued imperturbably. "The creature went

on at some length. 'We have learned the value of irrationality.' 'Irrationality' of course was not his word or even his meaning. He said something like 'a series of vaguely motivated trials'—as close as I can translate. He said, 'We have learned to change our environment. We use insects and trees and plants and waterslugs. It is an enormous effort for us who would prefer a placid life in the moss. But you men have forced this life on us, and now you must suffer the consequences.' I pointed out once more that men were not helpless, that many First Folk would die. The creature seemed unworried. 'The community persists.' I asked a delicate question, 'If your purpose is to kill men, why do you allow us here?' He said, 'The entire community of men will be destroyed.' Apparently they believe the human society to be similar to their own, and therefore regard the killing of three wayfaring individuals as pointless effort."

Lord Faide laughed grimly. "To destroy us they must first win past Hellmouth, then penetrate Faide Keep. This they are unable to do."

Isak Comandore resumed his report. "At this time I was already convinced that the problem was one of hoodooing not an individual but an entire race. In theory this should be no more difficult than hoodooing one. It requires no more effort to speak to twenty than to one. With this end in view I ordered the apprentice to collect substances associated with the creatures. Skinflakes, foam, droppings, all other exudations obtainable. While he did so, I tried to put myself in rapport with the creatures. It is difficult, for their telepathy works across a different stratum from ours. Nevertheless, to a certain extent I have succeeded."

"Then you can hoodoo the First Folk?" asked Lord Faide.

"I vouchsafe nothing until I try. Certain preparations must be made."

"Go then; make your preparations."

Comandore rose to his feet and with a sly side glance for Hein Huss left the room. Huss waited, pinching his chin with heavy fingers. Lord Faide looked at him coldly. "You have something to add?"

Huss grunted, hoisted himself to his feet. "I wish that I did. But my thoughts are confused. Of the many futures, all seem troubled and angry. Perhaps our best is not good enough."

Lord Faide looked at Hein Huss with surprise; the massive Head Jinxman had never before spoken in terms so pessimistic and melancholy. "Speak then; I will listen."

Hein Huss said gruffly, "If I knew any certainties I would speak gladly. But I am merely beset by doubts. I fear that we can no longer depend on logic and careful jinxmanship. Our ancestors were miracle workers, magicians. They drove the First Folk into the forest. To put us to flight in our turn the First Folk have adopted the ancient methods: random trial and purposeless empiricism. I am dubious. Perhaps we must turn our backs on sanity and likewise return to the mysticism of our ancestors."

Lord Faide shrugged. "If Isak Comandore can hoodoo the First Folk, such a retreat may be unnecessary."

"The world changes," said Hein Huss. "Of so much I feel sure: the old days of craft and careful knowledge are gone. The future is for men of cleverness, and imagination untroubled by discipline; the unorthodox Sam Salazar may become more effective than I. The world changes."

Lord Faide smiled his sour dyspeptic smile. "When that day comes I will appoint Sam Salazar Head Jinxman and also name him Lord Faide, and you and I will retire together to a hut on the downs."

Hein Huss made a heavy fateful gesture and departed.

X

Two days later Lord Faide, coming upon Isak Comandore, inquired as to his progress. Comandore took refuge in generalities. After another two days Lord Faide inquired again and this time insisted on particulars. Comandore grudgingly led the way to his workroom, where a dozen cabalmen, spell-binders, and apprentices worked around a large table, building a model of the First Folk settlement in Wildwood.

"Along the lakeshore," said Comandore, "I will range a great number of dolls, daubed with First Folk essences. When this is complete I will work up a hoodoo and blight the creatures."

"Good. Perform well." Lord Faide departed the workroom, mounted to the topmost pinnacle of the keep, to the cupola where the ancestral weapon Hellmouth was housed. "Jambart! Where are you?"

Weapon-tender Jambart, short, blue-jowled, red-nosed and big-bellied, appeared. "My lord?"

"I come to inspect Hellmouth. It is prepared for instant use?"

"Prepared, my lord, and ready. Oiled, greased, polished, scraped, burnished, tended—every part smooth as an egg."

Lord Faide made a scowling examination of Hellmouth—a heavy cylinder six feet in diameter, twelve feet long, studded with half-domes interconnected with tubes of polished copper. Jambart undoubtedly had been diligent. No trace of dirt or rust or corrosion showed; all was gleaming metal. The snout was covered with a heavy plate of metal and tarred canvas; the ring upon which the weapon swiveled was well greased.

Lord Faide surveyed the four horizons. To the south was fertile Faide Valley; to the west open downs; to north and east the menacing loom of Wildwood.

He turned back to Hellmouth and pretended to find a smear of grease. Jambart boiled with expostulations and protestations; Lord Faide uttered a grim warning, enjoining less laxity, then descended to the workroom of Hein Huss. He found the Head Jinxman reclining on a couch, staring at the ceiling. At a bench stood Sam Salazar surrounded by bottles, flasks, and dishes.

Lord Faide stared balefully at the confusion. "What are you doing?" he asked the apprentice.

Sam Salazar looked up guiltily. "Nothing in particular, my lord."

"If you are idle, go then and assist Isak Comandore."

"I am not idle, Lord Faide."

"Then what do you do?"

Sam Salazar gazed sulkily at the bench. "I don't know."

"Then you are idle!"

"No, I am occupied. I pour various liquids on this foam. It is First Folk foam. I wonder what will happen. Water does not dissolve it, nor spirits. Heat chars and slowly burns it, emitting a foul smoke."

Lord Faide turned away with a sneer. "You amuse yourself as a child might. Go to Isak Comandore; he can find use for you. How do you expect to become a jinxman, dabbling and prattling like a baby among pretty rocks?"

Hein Huss gave a deep sound: a mingling of sigh, snort, grunt, and clearing of the throat. "He does no harm, and Isak Comandore has hands enough. Salazar will never become a jinxman; that has been clear a long time."

Lord Faide shrugged. "He is your apprentice, and your responsibility. Well, then. What news from the keeps?"

Hein Huss, groaning and wheezing, swung his legs over the edge of the couch. "The lords share your concern, to greater or lesser extent. Your close allies will readily place troops at your disposal; the others likewise if pressure is brought to bear."

Lord Faide nodded in dour satisfaction. "For the moment there is no urgency. The First Folk hold to their forests. Faide Keep of course is impregnable, although they might ravage the valley. . . ." he paused thoughtfully. "Let Isak Comandore cast his hoodoo. Then we will see."

From the direction of the bench came a hiss, a small explosion, a whiff of acrid gas. Sam Salazar turned guiltily to look at them, his eyebrows singed. Lord Faide gave a snort of disgust and strode from the room.

"What did you do?" Hein Huss inquired in a colorless voice.

"I don't know."

Now Hein Huss likewise snorted in disgust. "Ridiculous. If you wish to work miracles, you must remember your procedures. Miracle working is not jinxmanship, with established rules and guides. In matters so complex it is well that you take notes, so that the miracles may be repeated."

Sam Salazar nodded in agreement and turned back to the bench.

XI

Late during the day, news of new First Folk truculence reached Faide Keep. On Honeymoss Hill, not far west of Forest Market, a camp of shepherds had been visited by a wandering group of First Folk, who began to kill the sheep with thorn-swords. When the shepherds protested they, too, were attacked, and many were killed. The remainder of the sheep were massacred.

The following day came other news: four children swimming in Brastock River at Gilbert Ferry had been seized by enormous water-beetles and cut into pieces. On the other side of Wildwood, in the foothills immediately below Castle Cloud, peasants had cleared several hillsides and planted them to vines. Early in the morning they had discovered a horde of black disklike flukes devouring the vines—leaves, branches, trunks, and roots. They set about killing the flukes with spades and at once were stung to death by wasps.

Adam McAdam reported the incidents to Lord Faide, who went to Isak Comandore in a fury. "How soon before you are prepared?"

"I am prepared now. But I must rest and fortify myself. Tomorrow morning I work the hoodoo."

"The sooner the better! The creatures have left their forest; they are out killing men!"

Isak Comandore pulled his long chin. "That was to be expected; they told us as much."

Lord Faide ignored the remark. "Show me your tableau."

Isak Comandore took him into his workroom. The model was now complete, with the masses of simulated First Folk properly daubed and sensitized, each tied with a small wad of foam. Isak Comandore pointed to a pot of dark liquid. "I will explain the basis of the hoodoo. When I visited the camp I watched everywhere for powerful symbols. Undoubtedly there were many at hand, but I could not discern them. However, I remembered a circumstance from the battle at the planting; when the creatures were attacked, threatened with fire and about to die, they spewed foam of dull purple color. Evidently this purple foam is associated with death. My hoodoo will be based upon this symbol."

"Rest well, then, so that you may hoodoo to your best capacity."

The following morning Isak Comandore dressed in long robes of black, and set a mask of the demon Nard on his head to fortify himself. He entered his workroom, closed the door.

An hour passed, two hours. Lord Faide sat at breakfast with his kin, stubbornly maintaining a pose of cynical unconcern. At last he could contain himself no longer and went out into the courtyard where Comandore's underlings stood fidgeting and uneasy. "Where is Hein Huss?" demanded Lord Faide. "Summon him here."

Hein Huss came stumping out of his quarters. Lord Faide motioned to Comandore's workshop. "What is happening? Is he succeeding?"

Hein Huss looked toward the workshop. "He is casting a powerful hoodoo. I feel confusion, anger—"

"In Comandore, or in the First Folk?"

"I am not in rapport. I think he has conveyed a message to their minds. A very difficult task, as I explained to you. In this preliminary aspect he has succeeded."

" 'Preliminary'? What else remains?"

"The two most important elements of the hoodoo: the susceptibility of the victim and the appropriateness of the symbol."

Lord Faide frowned. "You do not seem optimistic."

"I am uncertain. Isak Comandore may be right in his assumption. If so, and if the First Folk are highly susceptible, today marks a great victory, and Comandore will achieve tremendous *mana*!"

Lord Faide stared at the door to the workshop. "What now?"

Hein Huss's eyes went blank with concentration. "Isak Comandore is near death. He can hoodoo no more today."

Lord Faide turned, waved his arm to the cabalmen. "Enter the workroom! Assist your master!"

The cabalmen raced to the door, flung it open. Presently they emerged supporting the limp form of Isak Comandore, his black robe spattered with purple foam. Lord Faide pressed close. "What did you achieve? Speak!"

Isak Comandore's eyes were half closed, his mouth hung loose and wet. "I spoke to the First Folk, to the whole race. I sent the symbol into their minds—" His head fell limply sidewise.

Lord Faide moved back. "Take him to his quarters. Put him on his couch." He turned away, stood indecisively, chewing at his drooping lower lip. "Still we do not know the measure of his success."

"Ah," said Hein Huss, "but we do!"

Lord Faide jerked around. "What is this? What do you say?"

"I saw into Comandore's mind. He used the symbol of purple foam; with tremendous effort he drove it into their minds. Then he learned that purple foam means not death—

purple foam means fear for the safety of the community, purple foam means desperate rage."

"In any event," said Lord Faide after a moment, "there is no harm done. The First Folk can hardly become more hostile."

Three hours later a scout rode furiously into the courtyard, threw himself off his horse, ran to Lord Faide. "The First Folk have left the forest! A tremendous number! Thousands! They are advancing on Faide Keep!"

"Let them advance!" said Lord Faide. "The more the better! Jambart, where are you?"

"Here, sir."

"Prepare Hellmouth! Hold all in readiness!"

"Hellmouth is always ready, sir!"

Lord Faide struck him across the shoulders. "Off with you! Bernard!"

The sergeant of the Faide troops came forward. "Ready, Lord Faide."

"The First Folk attack. Armor your men against wasps, feed them well. We will need all our strength."

Lord Faide turned to Hein Huss. "Send to the keeps, to the manor houses, order our kinsmen to join us, with all their troops and all their armor. Send to Bellgard Hall, to Boghoten, Camber, and Candelwade. Haste, haste, it is only hours from Wildwood."

Huss held up his hand. "I have already done so. The keeps are warned. They know your need."

"And the First Folk—can you feel their minds?"

"No."

Lord Faide walked away. Hein Huss lumbered out the main gate, walked around the keep, casting appraising glances up the black walls of the squat towers, windowless and proof even against the ancient miracle-weapons. High on top the great parasol roof Jambart the weapon-tender worked in the cupola, polishing that which already glistened, greasing surfaces already heavy with grease.

Hein Huss returned within. Lord Faide approached him, mouth hard, eyes bright. "What have you seen?"

"Only the keep, the walls, the towers, the roof, and Hellmouth."

"And what do you think?"

"I think many things."

"You are noncommital; you know more than you say. It is best that you speak, because if Faide Keep falls to the savages you die with the rest of us."

Hein Huss's water-clear eyes met the brilliant black gaze of Lord Faide. "I know only what you know. The First Folk attack. They have proved they are not stupid. They intend to kill us. They are not jinxmen; they cannot afflict us or force us out. They cannot break in the walls. To burrow under, they must dig through solid rock. What are their plans? I do not know. Will they succeed? Again, I do not know. But the day of the jinxman and his orderly array of knowledge is past. I think that we must grope for miracles, blindly and foolishly, like Salazar pouring liquids on foam."

A troop of armored horsemen rode in through the gates: warriors from nearby Bellgard Hall. And as the hours passed contingents from other keeps came to Faide Keep, until the courtyard was dense with troops and horses.

Two hours before sunset the First Folk were sighted across the downs. They seemed a very large company, moving in an undisciplined clot with a number of stragglers, forerunners and wanderers out on the flanks.

The hotbloods from outside keeps came clamoring to Lord Faide, urging a charge to cut down the First Folk; they found no seconding voices among the veterans of the battle at the planting. Lord Faide, however, was pleased to see the dense mass of First Folk. "Let them approach only a mile more—and Hellmouth will take them! Jambart!"

"At your call, Lord Faide."

"Come, Hellmouth speaks!" He strode away with Jambart after. Up to the cupola they climbed.

"Roll forth Hellmouth, direct it against the savages!"

Jambart leaped to the glistening array of wheels and levers. He hesitated in perplexity, then tentatively twisted a wheel. Hellmouth responded by twisting slowly around on its radial track, to the groan and chatter of long-frozen bearings. Lord Faide's brows lowered into a menacing line. "I hear evidence of neglect."

"Neglect, my lord never! Find one spot of rust, a shadow of grime, you may have me whipped!"

"What is that sound?"

"That is internal and invisible—none of my responsibility."

Lord Faide said nothing. Hellmouth now pointed toward the great pale tide from Wildwood. Jambart twisted a second wheel and Hellmouth thrust forth its heavy snout. Lord Faide, in a voice harsh with anger, cried, "The cover, fool!"

"An oversight, my lord, easily repaired." Jambart crawled out along the top of Hellmouth, clinging to the protuberances for dear life, with below only the long smooth sweep of roof. With considerable difficulty he tore the covering loose, then grunting and cursing, inched himself back, jerking with his knees, rearing his buttocks.

The First Folk had slowed their pace a trifle, the main body only a half-mile distant.

"Now," said Lord Faide in high excitement, "before they disperse, we exterminate them!" He sighted through a telescopic tube, squinting through the dimness of internal films and incrustations, signaled to Jambart for the final adjustments. "Now! Fire!"

Jambart pulled the firing lever. Within the great metal barrel came a sputter of clicking sounds. Hellmouth whined, roared. Its snout glowed red, orange, white, and out poured a sudden gout of blazing purple radiation—which almost instantly died. Hellmouth's barrel quivered with heat, fumed, seethed, hissed. From within came a faint pop. Then there was silence.

A hundred yards in front of the First Folk a patch of

moss burnt black where the bolt had struck. The aiming device was inaccurate. Hellmouth's bolt had killed perhaps twenty of the First Folk vanguard.

Lord Faide made feverish signals. "Quick! Raise the barrel. Now! Fire again!"

Jambart pulled the firing arm, to no avail. He tried again, with the same lack of success. "Hellmouth evidently is tired."

"Hellmouth is dead," cried Lord Faide. "You have failed me. Hellmouth is extinct."

"No, no," protested Jambart. "Hellmouth rests! I nurse it as my own child! It is polished like glass! Whenever a section wears off or breaks loose, I neatly remove the fracture, and every trace of cracked glass."

Lord Faide threw up his arms, shouted in vast, inarticulate grief, ran below. "Huss! Hein Huss!"

Hein Huss presented himself. "What is your will?"

"Hellmouth has given up its fire. Conjure me more fire for Hellmouth, and quickly!"

"Impossible."

"Impossible!" cried Lord Faide. "That is all I hear from you! Impossible, useless, impractical! You have lost your ability. I will consult Isak Comandore."

"Isak Comandore can put no more fire into Hellmouth than can I."

"What sophistry is this? He puts demons into men, surely he can put fire into Hellmouth!"

"Come, Lord Faide, you are overwrought. You know the difference between jinxmanship and miracle working."

Lord Faide motioned to a servant. "Bring Isak Comandore here to me!"

Isak Comandore, face haggard, skin waxy, limped into the courtyard. Lord Faide waved preemptorily. "I need your skill. You must restore fire to Hellmouth."

Comandore darted a quick glance at Hein Huss, who stood solid and cold. Comandore decided against dramatic promises that could not be fulfilled. "I cannot do this, my lord."

"What! You tell me this, too?"

"Remark the difference, Lord Faide, between man and
metal. A man's normal state is something near madness; he is
at all times balanced on a knife-edge between hysteria and
apathy. His senses tell him far less of the world than he
thinks they do. It is a simple trick to deceive a man, to possess
him with a demon, to drive him out of his mind, to kill him.
But metal is insensible; metal reacts only as its shape and condition dictates, or by the working of miracles."

"Then you must work miracles!"

"Impossible."

Lord Faide drew a deep breath, collected himself. He
walked swiftly across the court. "My armor, my horse. We
attack."

The column formed, Lord Faide at the head. He led the
knights through the portals, with armored footmen behind.

"Beware the foam!" called Lord Faide. "Attack, strike,
cut, draw back. Keep your visors drawn against the wasps!
Each man must kill a hundred! Attack!"

The troop rode forth against the horde of First Folk,
knights in the lead. The hooves of the horses pounded softly
over the thick moss; in the west the large pale sun hung close
to the horizon.

Two hundred yards from the First Folk the knights
touched the club-headed horses into a lope. They raised their
swords, and shouting, plunged forward, each man seeking to
be first. The clotted mass of First Folk separated: black
beetles darted forth and after them long segmented centipede
creatures. They dashed among the horses, mandibles clicking,
snouts slashing. Horses screamed, reared, fell over backwards;
beetles cut open armored knights as a dog cracks a bone.
Lord Faide's horse threw him and ran away; he picked himself up, hacked at a nearby beetle, lopped off its front leg. It
darted forward, he lopped off the leg opposite; the heavy
head dipped, tore up the moss. Lord Faide cut off the
remaining legs, and it lay helpless.

"Retreat," he bellowed. "Retreat!"

The knights moved back, slashing and hacking at beetles and centipedes, killing or disabling all which attacked.

"Form into a double line, knights and men. Advance slowly, supporting each other!"

The men advanced. The First Folk dispersed to meet them, armed with their thorn-swords and carrying pouches. Ten yards from the men they reached into the pouches, brought forth dark balls which they threw at the men. The balls broke and spattered on the armor.

"Charge!" bawled Lord Faide. The men sprang forward into the mass of First Folk, cutting, slashing, killing. "Kill!" called Lord Faide in exultation. "Leave not one alive!"

A pang struck him, a sting inside his armor, followed by another and another. Small things crawled inside the metal, stinging, biting, crawling. He looked about: on all sides were harrassed expressions, faces working in anguish. Sword arms fell limp as hands beat on the metal, futilely trying to scratch, rub. Two men suddenly began to tear off their armor.

"Retreat," cried Lord Faide. "Back to the keep!"

The retreat was a rout, the soldiers shedding articles of armor as they ran. After them came a flight of wasps—a dozen or more, and half as many men cried out as the poison prongs struck into their backs.

Inside the keep stormed the disorganized company, casting aside the last of their armor, slapping their skin, scratching, rubbing, crushing the ferocious red mites that infested them.

"Close the gates," roared Lord Faide.

The gates slid shut. Faide Keep was besieged.

XII

During the night the First Folk surrounded the keep, forming a ring fifty yards from the walls. All night there was motion, ghostly shapes coming and going in the starlight.

Lord Faide watched from a parapet until midnight, with Hein Huss at his side. Repeatedly, he asked, "What of the other keeps? Do they send further reinforcements?" to which Hein Huss each time gave the same reply: "There is confusion and doubt. The keep-lords are anxious to help but do not care to throw themselves away. At this moment they consider and take stock of the situation."

Lord Faide at last left the parapet, signaling Hein Huss to follow. He went to his trophy room, threw himself into a chair, motioned Hein Huss to be seated. For a moment he fixed the jinxman with a cool, calculating stare. Hein Huss bore the appraisal without discomfort.

"You are Head Jinxman," said Lord Faide finally. "For twenty years you have worked spells, cast hoodoos, performed auguries—more effectively than any other jinxman of Pangborn. But now I find you inept and listless. Why is this?"

"I am neither inept nor listless. I am unable to achieve beyond my abilities. I do not know how to work miracles. For this you must consult my apprentice Sam Salazar, who does not know either, but who earnestly tries every possibility and many impossibilities."

"You believe in this nonsense yourself! Before my very eyes you become a mystic!"

Hein Huss shrugged. "There are limitations to my knowledge. Miracles occur—that we know. The relics of our ancestors lie everywhere. Their methods were supernatural, repellent to our own mental processes—but think! Using these same methods the First Folk threaten to destroy us. In the place of metal they use living flesh—but the result is similar. The men of Pangborn, if they assemble and accept casualties, can drive the First Folk back to Wildwood—but for how long? A year? Ten years? The First Folk plant new trees, dig more traps—and presently come forth again, with more terrible weapons: flying beetles, large as a horse; wasps strong enough to pierce armor, lizards to scale the walls of Faide Keep."

Lord Faide pulled at his chin. "And the jinxmen are helpless?"

"You saw for yourself. Isak Comandore intruded enough into their consciousness to anger them, no more."

"So then—what must we do?"

Hein Huss held out his hands. "I do not know. I am Hein Huss, jinxman. I watch Sam Salazar with fascination. He learns nothing, but he is either too stupid or too intelligent to be discouraged. If this is the way to work miracles, he will work them."

Lord Faide rose to his feet. "I am deathly tired. I cannot think, I must sleep. Tomorrow we will know more."

Hein Huss left the trophy room, returned to the parapet. The ring of First Folk seemed closer to the walls, almost within dart-range. Behind them and across the moors stretched a long pale column of marching First Folk. A little back from the keep a pile of white material began to grow, larger and larger as the night proceeded.

Hours passed, the sky lightened; the sun rose in the east. The First Folk tramped the downs like ants, bringing long bars of hardened foam down from the north, dropping them into piles around the keep, returning into the north once more.

Lord Faide came up on the parapet, haggard and unshaven. "What is this? What do they do?"

Bernard the sergeant responded. "They puzzle us all, my lord."

"Hein Huss! What of the other keeps?"

"They have armed and mounted; they approach cautiously."

"Can you communicate our urgency?"

"I can, and I have done so. I have only accentuated their caution."

"Bah!" cried Lord Faide in disgust. "Warriors they call themselves! Loyal and faithful allies!"

"They know of your bitter experience," said Hein Huss.
"They ask themselves, reasonably enough, what they can ac-
complish which you who are already here cannot do first."

Lord Faide laughed sourly. "I have no answer for them.
In the meantime we must protect ourselves against the wasps.
Armor is useless; they drive us mad with mites. . . . Bernard!"

"Yes, Lord Faide."

"Have each of your men construct a frame two-feet
square, fixed with a short handle. To these frames should be
sewed a net of heavy mesh. When these frames are built we
will sally forth, two soldiers to guard one half-armored knight
on foot."

"In the meantime," said Hein Huss, "the First Folk proceed with their plans."

Lord Faide turned to watch. The First Folk came close
up under the walls carrying rods of hardened foam. "Bernard!
Put your archers to work! Aim for the heads!"

Along the walls bowmen cocked their weapons. Darts
spun down into the First Folk. A few were affected, turned
and staggered away; others plucked away the bolts without
concern. Another flight of bolts, a few more First Folk were
disabled. The others planted the rods in the moss, exuded
foam in great gushes, their back-flaps vigorously pumping air.
Other First Folk brought more rods, pushed them into the
foam. Entirely around the keep, close under the walls, extended the mound of foam. The ring of First Folk now came
close and all gushed foam; it bulked up swiftly. More rods
were brought, thrust into the foam, reinforcing and stiffening
the mass.

"More darts!" barked Lord Faide. "Aim for the heads!
Bernard—your men, have they prepared the wasp nets?"

"Not yet, Lord Faide. The project requires some little
time."

Lord Faide became silent. The foam, now ten feet high,
rapidly piled higher. Lord Faide turned to Hein Huss. "What
do they hope to achieve?"

Hein Huss shook his head. "For the moment I am uncertain."

The first layer of foam had hardened; on top of this the First Folk spewed another layer, reinforcing again with the rods, crisscrossing, horizontal and vertical. Fifteen minutes later, when the second layer was hard the First Folk emplaced and mounted rude ladders to raise a third layer. Surrounding the keep now was a ring of foam thirty feet high and forty feet thick at the base.

"Look," said Hein Huss. He pointed up. The parasol roof overhanging the walls ended only thirty feet above the foam. "A few more layers and they will reach the roof."

"So then?" asked Lord Faide. "The roof is as strong as the walls."

"And we will be sealed within."

Lord Faide studied the foam in the light of this new thought. Already the First Folk, climbing laboriously up ladders along the outside face of their wall of foam, were preparing to lay on a fourth layer. First—rods, stiff and dry, then great gushes of white. Only twenty feet remained between roof and foam.

Lord Faide turned to the sergeant. "Prepare the men to sally forth."

"What of the wasp nets, sir?"

"Are they almost finished?"

"Another ten minutes, sir."

"Another ten minutes will see us smothering. We must force a passage through the foam."

Ten minutes passed, and fifteen. The First Folk created ramps behind their wall: first, dozens of the rods, then foam, and on top, to distribute the weight, reed mats.

Bernard the sergeant reported to Lord Faide. "We are ready."

"Good." Lord Faide descended into the courtyard. He faced the men, gave then their orders. "Move quickly, but stay together; we must not lose ourselves in the foam. As we proceed, slash ahead and to the sides. The First Folk see through the foam; they have the advantage of us. When we break through, we use the wasp nets. Two foot soldiers must guard each knight. Remember, quickly through the foam, that we do not smother. Open the gates."

The gates slid back, the troops marched forth. They faced an unbroken blank wall of foam. No enemy could be seen.

Lord Faide waved his sword. "Into the foam." He strode forward, pushed into the white mass, now crisp and brittle and harder than he had bargained for. It resisted him; he cut and hacked. His troops joined him, carving a way into the foam. First Folk appeared above them, crawling carefully on the mats. Their back flaps puffed, pumped; foam issued from their vents, falling in a cascade over the troops.

Hein Huss sighed. He spoke to Apprentice Sam Salazar. "Now they must retreat, otherwise they smother. If they fail to win through, we all smother."

Even as he spoke the foam, piling up swiftly, in places reached the roof. Below, bellowing and cursing, Lord Faide backed out from under, wiped his face clear. Once again, in desperation, he charged forward, trying at a new spot.

The foam was friable and cut easily, but the chunks detached still blocked the opening. And again down tumbled a cascade of foam, covering the soldiers.

Lord Faide retreated, waved his men back into the keep. At the same moment First Folk crawling on mats on the same level as the parapet over the gate laid rods up from the foam to rest against the projecting edge of the roof. They gushed foam; the view of the sky was slowly blocked from the view of Hein Huss and Sam Salazar.

"In an hour, perhaps two, we will die," said Hein Huss. "They have now sealed us in. There are many men here in the keep, and all will now breathe deeply."

Sam Salazar said nervously, "There is a possibility we might be able to survive—or at least not smother."

"Ah?" inquired Hein Huss with heavy sarcasm. "You plan to work a miracle?"

"If a miracle, the most trivial sort. I observed that water has no effect on the foam, nor a number of other liquids: milk, spirits, wine, or caustic. Vinegar, however, instantly dissolves the foam."

"Aha," said Hein Huss. "We must inform Lord Faide."

"Better that you do so," said Sam Salazar. "He will pay me no heed."

XIII

Half an hour passed. Light filtered into Faide Keep only as a dim gray gloom. Air tasted flat, damp, and heavy. Out from the gates sallied the troops. Each carried a crock, a jug, a skin, or a pan containing strong vinegar.

"Quickly now," called Lord Faide, "but careful! Spare the vinegar, don't throw it wildly. In close formation now—forward."

The soldiers approached the wall, threw ladles of vinegar ahead. The foam crackled, melted.

"Waste no vinegar," shouted Lord Faide, "Forward, quickly now; bring forward the vinegar!"

Minutes later they burst out upon the downs. The First Folk stared at them, blinking.

"Charge," croaked Lord Faide, his throat thick with fumes, "Mind now, wasp nets! Two soldiers to each knight! Charge, double-quick. Kill the white beasts."

The men dashed ahead. Wasp tubes were leveled. "Halt!" yelled Lord Faide. "Wasps!"

The wasps came, wings rasping. Nets rose up; wasps struck with a thud. Down went the nets; hard feet crushed the insects. The beetles and the lizard-centipedes appeared, not so many as of the last evening, for a great number had been killed. They darted forward, and a score of men died,

but the insects were soon hacked into chunks of reeking
brown flesh. Wasps flew, and some struck home; the agonies
of the dying men were unnerving. Presently the wasps likewise decreased in number, and soon there were no more.

The men faced the First Folk, armored only with thorn-
swords and their foam, which now came purple with rage.

Lord Faide waved his sword: the men advanced and began to kill the First Folk, by dozens, by hundreds.

Hein Huss came forth and approached Lord Faide. "Call
a halt."

"A halt? Why? Now we kill these bestial things."

"Far better not. Neither need kill the other. Now is the
time to show great wisdom."

"They have besieged us, caught us in their traps, stung us
with their wasps! And you say halt?"

"They nourish a grudge sixteen hundred years old. Best
not to add another one."

Lord Faide stared at Hein Huss. "What do you propose?"

"Peace between the two races, peace and cooperation."

"Very well. No more traps, no more plantings, no more
breeding of deadly insects."

"Call back your men. I will try."

Lord Faide cried out, "Men, fall back. Disengage."

Reluctantly the troops drew back. Hein Huss approached
the huddled mass of purple-foaming First Folk. He waited a
moment. They watched him intently. He spoke in their
language.

"You have attacked Faide Keep; you have been defeated.
You planned well, but we have proved stronger. At this moment we can kill you. Then we can go on to fire the forest,
starting a hundred blazes. Some of the fires you can control.
Others not. We can destroy Wildwood. Some First Folk may
survive, to hide in the thickets and breed new plans to kill
men. This we do not want. Lord Faide has agreed to peace, if
you likewise agree. This means no more death traps. Men will
freely approach and pass through the forests. In your turn

you may freely come out on the moss. Neither race shall molest the other. Which do you choose? Extinction—or peace?"

The purple foam no longer dribbled from the vents of the First Folk. "We choose peace."

"There must be no more wasps, beetles. The death traps must be disarmed and never replaced."

"We agree. In our turn we must be allowed freedom of the moss."

"Agreed. Remove your dead and wounded, haul away the foam rods."

Hein Huss returned to Lord Faide. "They have chosen peace."

Lord Faide nodded. "Very well. It is for the best." He called to his men. "Sheathe your weapons. We have won a great victory." He ruefully surveyed Faide Keep, swathed in foam and invisible except for the parasol roof. "A hundred barrels of vinegar will not be enough."

Hein Huss looked off into the sky. "Your allies approach quickly. Their jinxmen have told them of your victory."

Lord Faide laughed his sour laugh. "To my allies will fall the task of removing the foam from Faide Keep."

XIV

In the hall of Faide Keep, during the victory banquet, Lord Faide called jovially across to Hein Huss. "Now, Head Jinxman, we must deal with your apprentice, the idler and the waster Sam Salazar."

"He is here, Lord Faide. Rise, Sam Salazar, take cognizance of the honor being done you."

Sam Salazar rose to his feet, bowed.

Lord Faide proffered him a cup. "Drink, Sam Salazar, enjoy yourself. I freely admit that your idiotic tinkerings saved the lives of us all. Sam Salazar, we salute you, and thank you. Now, I trust that you will put frivolity aside, apply yourself to your work, and learn honest jinxmanship. When the time comes, I promise that you shall find a lifetime of employment at Faide Keep."

"Thank you," said Sam Salazar modestly. "However, I doubt if I will become a jinxman."

"No? You have other plans?"

Sam Salazar stuttered, grew faintly pink in the face, then straightened himself, and spoke as clearly and distinctly as he could. "I prefer to continue what you call my frivolity. I hope I can persuade others to join me."

"Frivolity is always attractive," said Lord Faide. "No doubt you can find other idlers and wasters, runaway farm boys and the like."

Sam Salazar said staunchly, "This frivolity might become serious. Undoubtedly the ancients were barbarians. They used symbols to control entities they were unable to understand. We are methodical and rational; why can't we systematize and comprehend the ancient miracles?"

"Well, why can't we?" asked Lord Faide. "Does anyone have an answer?"

No one responded, although Isak Comandore hissed between his teeth and shook his head.

"I personally may never be able to work miracles; I suspect it is more complicated than it seems," said Sam Salazar. "However, I hope that you will arrange for a workshop where I and others who might share my views can make a beginning. In this matter I have the encouragement and the support of Head Jinxman Hein Huss."

Lord Faide lifted his goblet. "Very well, Apprentice Sam Salazar. Tonight I can refuse you nothing. You shall have exactly what you wish, and good luck to you. Perhaps you will produce a miracle during my lifetime."

Isak Comandore said huskily to Hein Huss, "This is a sad event! It signalizes intellectual anarchy, the degradation of jinxmanship, the prostitution of logic. Novelty has a way of attracting youth; already I see apprentices and spellbinders whispering in excitement. The jinxmen of the future will be sorry affairs. How will they go about demon-possession? With a cog, a gear, and a push-button. How will they cast a hoodoo? They will find it easier to strike their victim with an axe."

"Times change," said Hein Huss. "There is now the one rule of Faide on Pangborn, and the keeps no longer need to employ us. Perhaps I will join Sam Salazar in his workshop."

"You depict a depressing future," said Isak Comandore with a sniff of disgust.

"There are many futures, some of which are undoubtedly depressing."

Lord Faide raised his glass. "To the best of your many futures, Hein Huss. Who knows? Sam Salazar may conjure a spaceship to lead us back to home planet."

"Who knows?" said Hein Huss. He raised his goblet. "To the best of the futures!"

The Moon Moth

THE HOUSEBOAT had been built to the most exacting standards of Sirenese craftmanship, which is to say, as close to the absolute as human eye could detect. The planking of waxy dark wood showed no joints, the fastenings were platinum rivets countersunk and polished flat. In style, the boat was massive, broadbeamed, steady as the shore itself, without ponderosity or slackness of line. The bow bulged like a swan's breast, the stem rising high, then crooking forward to support an iron lantern. The doors were carved from slats of a mottled blackgreen wood; the windows were many-sectioned, paned with squares of mica, stained rose, blue, pale green and violet. The bow was given to service facilities and quarters for the slaves; amidships were a pair of sleeping cabins, a dining saloon, and a parlor saloon, opening upon an observation deck at the stern.

Such was Edwer Thissell's housebout, but ownership brought him neither pleasure nor pride. The houseboat had become shabby. The carpeting had lost its pile; the carved screens were chipped; the iron lantern at the bow sagged with rust. Seventy years ago the first owner, on accepting the boat, had honored the builder and had been likewise honored; the transaction (for the process represented a great deal more than simple giving and taking) had augmented the prestige of

both. That time was far gone; the houseboat now commanded no prestige whatever. Edwer Thissell, resident on Sirene
only three months, recognized the lack but could do nothing
about it; this particular houseboat was the best he could get.
He sat on the rear deck practising the *ganga*, a zither-like
instrument not much larger than his hand. A hundred yards
inshore, surf defined a strip of white beach; beyond rose
jungle, with the silhouette of craggy black hills against the
sky. Mireille shone hazy and white overhead, as if through a
tangle of spider web; the face of the ocean had become as
familiar, though not as boring, as the *ganga*, at which he had
worked two hours, twanging out the Sirenese scales, forming
chords, traversing simple progressions. Now he put down the
ganga for the *zachinko*, this a small sound-box studded with
keys, played with the right hand. Pressure on the keys forced
air through reeds in the keys themselves, producing a concer-
tina-like tone. Thissell ran off a dozen quick scales, making
very few mistakes. Of the six instruments he had set himself
to learn, the *zachinko* had proved the least refractory (with
the exception, of course, of the *hymerkin*, that clacking,
slapping, clattering device of wood and stone used exclusively
with the slaves).

Thissell practised another ten minutes, then put aside the
zachinko. He flexed his arms, wrung his aching fingers. Every
waking moment since his arrival had been given to the instruments: the *hymerkin*, the *ganga*, the *zachinko*, the *kiv*, the
strapan, the *gomapard*. He had practised scales in nineteen
keys and four modes, chords without number, intervals never
imagined on the Home Planets. Trills, arpeggios, slurs; click-
stops and nasalization; damping and augmentation of overtones; vibratos and wolf-tones; concavities and convexities.
He practiced with a dogged, deadly diligence, in which his
original concept of music as a source of pleasure had long
become lost. Looking over the instruments, Thissell resisted
an urge to fling all six into the Titanic.

He rose to his feet, went forward through the parlor

saloon, the dining-saloon, along a corridor past the galley and came out on the fore-deck. He bent over the rail, peered down into the underwater pens where Toby and Rex, the slaves, were harnessing the dray-fish for the weekly trip to Fan, eight miles north. The youngest fish, either playful or captious, ducked and plunged. Its streaming black muzzle broke water, and Thissell, looking into its face felt a peculiar qualm: the fish wore no mask!

Thissell laughed uneasily, fingering his own mask, the Moon Moth. No question about it, he was becoming acclimated to Sirene! A significant stage had been reached when the naked face of a fish caused him shock!

The fish were finally harnessed; Toby and Rex climbed aboard, red bodies glistening, black cloth masks clinging to their faces. Ignoring Thissell they stowed the pen, hoisted anchor. The dray-fish strained, the harness tautened, the houseboat moved north.

Returning to the after-deck, Thissell took up the *strapan* —this a circular sound-box eight inches in diameter. Forty-six wires radiated from a central hub to the circumference where they connected to either a bell or a tinkle-bar. When plucked, the bells rang, the bars chimed; when strummed, the instrument gave off a twanging, jingling sound. When played with competence, the pleasantly acid dissonances produced an expressive effect; in an unskilled hand, the results were less felicitous, and might even approach random noise. The *strapan* was Thissell's weakest instrument and he practised with concentration during the entire trip north.

In due course the houseboat approached the floating city. The dray-fish were curbed, the houseboat warped to a mooring. Along the dock a line of idlers weighed and gauged every aspect of the houseboat, the slaves and Thissell himself, according to Sirenese habit. Thissell, not yet accustomed to such penetrating inspection, found the scrutiny unsettling, all the more so for the immobility of the masks. Self-consciously adjusting his own Moon Moth, he climbed the ladder to the dock.

A slave rose from where he had been squatting, touched knuckles to the black cloth at his forehead, and sang on a three-tone phrase of interrogation: "The Moon Moth before me possibly expresses the identity of Ser Edwer Thissell?"

Thissell tapped the *hymerkin* which hung at his belt and sang: "I am Ser Thissell."

"I have been honored by a trust," sang the slave. "Three days from dawn to dusk I have waited on the dock; three nights from dusk to dawn I have crouched on a raft below this same dock listening to the feet of the Night-men. At last I behold the mask of Ser Thissell."

Thissell evoked an impatient clatter from the *hymerkin*. "What is the nature of this trust?"

"I carry a message, Ser Thissell. It is intended for you."

Thissell held out his left hand, playing the *hymerkin* with his right. "Give me the message."

"Instantly, Ser Thissell."

The message bore a heavy superscription:

EMERGENCY COMMUNICATION! RUSH!

Thissell ripped open the envelope. The message was signed by Castel Cromartin, Chief Executive of the Interworld Policies Board, and after the formal salutation read:

> ABSOLUTELY URGENT the following orders be executed! Aboard *Carina Cruzeiro*, destination Fan, date of arrival January 10 U.T., is notorious assassin, Haxo Angmark. Meet landing with adequate authority, effect detention and incarceration of this man. These instructions must be successfully implemented. Failure is unacceptable.
>
> ATTENTION! Haxo Angmark is superlatively dangerous. Kill him without hesitation at any show of resistance.

Thissel considered the message with dismay. In coming to Fan as Consular Representative he had expected nothing like this; he felt neither inclination nor competence in the matter of dealing with dangerous assassins. Thoughtfully he rubbed the fuzzy gray cheek of his mask. The situation was not completely dark; Esteban Rolver, Director of the Space-Port, would doubtless cooperate, and perhaps furnish a platoon of slaves.

More thoughtfully, Thissell reread the message. January 10, Universal Time. He consulted a conversion calendar. Today, 40th in the Season of Bitter Nectar—Thissell ran his finger down the column, stopped. January 10. Today.

A distant rumble caught his attention. Dropping from the mist came a dull shape: the lighter returning from contact with the *Carina Cruzeiro*.

Thissell once more re-read the note, raised his head, studied the descending lighter. Aboard would be Haxo Angmark. In five minutes he would emerge upon the soil of Sirene. Landing formalities would detain him possibly twenty minutes. The landing field lay a mile and a half distant, joined to Fan by a winding path through the hills.

Thissell turned to the slave. "When did this message arrive?"

The slave leaned forward uncomprehendingly. Thissell reiterated his question, singing to the clack of the *hymerkin*: "This message: you have enjoyed the honor of its custody how long?"

The slave sang: "Long days have I waited on the wharf, retreating only to the raft at the onset of dusk. Now my vigil is rewarded; I behold Ser Thissell."

Thissell turned away, walked furiously up the dock. Ineffective, inefficient Sirenese! Why had they not delivered the message to his houseboat? Twenty-five minutes—twenty-two now . . .

At the esplanade Thissell stopped, looked right then left, hoping for a miracle: some sort of air-transport to whisk him to the space-port, where with Rolver's aid, Haxo Angmark might still be detained. Or better yet, a second message cancelling the first. Something, anything . . . But air-cars were not to be found on Sirene, and no second message appeared.

Across the esplanade rose a meager row of permanent structures, built of stone and iron and so proof against the efforts of the Night-men. A hostler occupied one of these structures, and as Thissell watched a man in a splendid pearl and silver mask emerged riding one of the lizard-like mounts of Sirene.

Thissell sprang forward. There was still time; with luck he might yet intercept Haxo Angmark. He hurried across the esplanade.

Before the line of stalls stood the hostler, inspecting his stock with solicitude, occasionally burnishing a scale or whisking away an insect. There were five of the beasts in prime condition, each as tall as a man's shoulder, with massive legs, thick bodies, heavy wedge-shaped heads. From their forefangs, which had been artificially lengthened and curved into near-circles, gold rings depended; the scales of each had been stained in diaper-pattern: purple and green, orange and black, red and blue, brown and pink, yellow and silver.

Thissell came to a breathless halt in front of the hostler. He reached for his *kiv**, then hesitated. Could this be considered a casual personal encounter? The *zachinko* perhaps? But the statement of his needs hardly seemed to demand the formal approach. Better the *kiv* after all. He struck a chord, but by error found himself stroking the *ganga*. Beneath his mask Thissell grinned apologetically; his relationship with this hostler was by no means on an intimate basis. He hoped that the hostler was of sanguine disposition, and in any event the urgency of the occasion allowed no time to select an exactly appropriate instrument. He struck a second chord, and, playing as well as agitation, breathlessness and lack of skill

---

*Kiv: five banks of resilient metal strips, fourteen to the bank, played by touching, twisting, twanging.

allowed, sang out a request: "Ser Hostler, I have immediate need of a swift mount. Allow me to select from your herd."

The hostler wore a mask of considerable complexity which Thissell could not identify: a construction of varnished brown cloth, pleated gray leather and high on the forehead two large green and scarlet globes, minutely segmented like insect eyes. He inspected Thissell a long moment, then, rather ostentatiously selecting his *stimic**, executed a brilliant progression of trills and rounds, of an import Thissell failed to grasp. The hostler sang, "Ser Moon Moth, I fear that my steeds are unsuitable to a person of your distinction."

Thissell earnestly twanged at the *ganga*. "By no means; they all seem adequate. I am in great haste and will gladly accept any of the group."

The hostler played a brittle cascading crescendo. "Ser Moon-Moth," he sang, "the steeds are ill and dirty. I am flattered that you consider them adequate to your use. I cannot accept the merit you offer me. And"—here, switching instruments, he struck a cool tinkle from his *krodatch***—"somehow I fail to recognize the boon-companion and co-craftsman who accosts me so familiarly with his *ganga*."

The implication was clear. Thissell would receive no mount. He turned, set off at a run for the landing field.

------

*stimic: three flute-like tubes equipped with plungers. Thumb and forefinger squeeze a bag to force air across the mouth-pieces; the second, third and fourth little fingers manipulate the slide. The *stimic* is an instrument well-adapted to the sentiments of cool withdrawal, or even disapproval.

**krodatch: a small square sound-box strung with resined gut. The musician scratches the strings with his fingernail, or strokes them with his fingertips, to produce a variety of quietly formal sounds. The *krodatch* is also used as an instrument of insult.

Behind him sounded a clatter of the hostler's *hymerkin*—whether directed toward the hostler's slaves, or toward himself Thissell did not pause to learn.

The previous Consular Representative of the Home Planets on Sirene had been killed at Zundar. Masked as a Tavern Bravo he had accosted a girl beribboned for the Equinoctial Attitudes, a solecism for which he had been instantly beheaded by a Red Demiurge, a Sun Sprite and a Magic Hornet. Edwer Thissell, recently graduated from the Institute, had been named his successor, and allowed three days to prepare himself. Normally of a contemplative, even cautious, disposition, Thissell had regarded the appointment as a challenge. He learned the Sirenese language by sub-cerebral techniques, and found it uncomplicated. Then, in the Journal of Universal Anthropology, he read:

"The population of the Titanic littoral is highly individualistic, possibly in response to a bountiful environment which puts no premium upon group activity. The language, reflecting this trait, expresses the individual's mood, his emotional attitude toward a given situation. Factual information is regarded as a secondary concomitant. Moreover, the language is sung, characteristically to the accompaniment of a small instrument. As a result, there is great difficulty in ascertaining fact from a native of Fan, or the forbidden city Zundar. One will be regaled with elegant arias and demonstrations of astonishing virtuosity upon one or another of the numerous musical instruments. The visitor to this fascinating world, unless he cares to be treated with the most consummate contempt, must therefore learn to express himself after the approved local fashion."

Thissell made a note in his memorandum book: *Procure*

small musical instrument, together with directions as to use.
He read on.

"There is everywhere and at all times a plenitude,
not to say, superfluity of food, and the climate is benign. With a fund of racial energy and a great deal of
leisure time, the population occupies itself with intricacy. Intricacy in all things: intricate craftsmanship,
such as the carved panels which adorn the houseboat;
intricate symbolism, as exemplified in the masks worn
by everyone; the intricate half-musical language which
admirably expresses subtle moods and emotions; and
above all the fantastic intricacy of inter-personal rela-
tionships. Prestige, face, *mana*, repute, glory: the Sirenese word is *strakh*. Every man has his characteristic
strakh, which determines whether, when he needs a
houseboat, he will be urged to avail himself of a floating palace, rich with gems, alabaster lanterns, peacock
faience and carved wood, or grudgingly permitted an
abandoned shack on a raft. There is no medium of exchange on Sirene; the single and sole currency is
strakh . . .

Thissell rubbed his chin and read further.

"Masks are worn at all times, in accordance with the
philosophy that a man should not be compelled to use
a similitude foisted upon him by factors beyond his
control; that he should be at liberty to choose that
semblance most consonant with his *strakh*. In the civilized areas of Sirene—which is to say the Titanic littoral
—a man literally never shows his face; it is his basic
secret.

"Gambling, by this token, is unknown on Sirene; it
would be catastrophic to Sirenese self-respect to gain

advantage by means other than the exercise of *strakh*. The word 'luck' has no counterpart in the Sirenese language."

Thissell made another note: *Get mask. Museum? Drama guild?*

He finished the article, hastened forth to complete his preparations, and the next day embarked aboard the *Robert Astroguard* for the first leg of the passage to Sirene.

The lighter settled upon the Sirenese space-port, a topaz disk isolated among the black, green and purple hills. The lighter grounded, and Edwer Thissell stepped forth. He was met by Esteban Rolver, the local agent for Spaceways. Rolver threw up his hands, stepped back. "Your mask," he cried huskily. "Where is your mask?"

Thissell held it up rather self-consciously. "I wasn't sure—"

"Put it on," said Rolver, turning away. He himself wore a fabrication of dull green scales, blue-lacquered wood. Black quills protruded at the cheeks, and under his chin hung a black and white checked pom-pom, the total effect creating a sense of sardonic supple personality.

Thissell adjusted the mask to his face, undecided whether to make a joke about the situation or to maintain a reserve suitable to the dignity of his post.

"Are you masked?" Rolver inquired over his shoulder.

Thissell replied in the affirmative and Rolver turned. The mask hid the expression of his face, but his hand unconsciously flicked a set of keys strapped to his thigh. The instrument sounded a trill of shock and polite consternation. "You can't wear that mask!" sang Rolver. "In fact—how, where, did you get it?"

"It's copied from a mask owned by the Polypolis museum," declared Thissell stiffly. "I'm sure it's authentic."

Rolver nodded, his own mask more sardonic-seeming than ever. "It's authentic enough. It's a variant of the type known as the Sea-Dragon Conqueror, and is worn on cere-monial occasions by persons of enormous prestige: princes, heroes, master craftsmen, great musicians."

"I wasn't aware—"

Rolver made a gesture of languid understanding. "It's something you'll learn in due course. Notice my mask. Today I'm wearing a Tarn-Bird. Persons of minimal prestige—such as you, I, any other out-worlder—wear this sort of thing."

"Odd," said Thissell as they started across the field toward a low concrete blockhouse. "I assumed that a person wore whatever mask he liked."

"Certainly," said Rolver. "Wear any mask you like—if you can make it stick. This Tarn-Bird for instance. I wear it to indicate that I presume nothing. I make no claims to wis-dom, ferocity, versatility, musicianship, truculence, or any of a dozen other Sirenese virtues."

"For the sake of argument," said Thissell, "what would happen if I walked through the streets of Zundar in this mask?"

Rolver laughed, a muffled sound behind his mask. "If you walked along the docks of Zundar—there are no streets—in any mask, you'd be killed within the hour. That's what happened to Benko, your predecessor. He didn't know how to act. None of us out-worlders know how to act. In Fan we're tolerated—so long as we keep our place. But you couldn't even walk around Fan in that regalia you're sport-ing now. Somebody wearing a Fire-snake or a Thunder Gob-lin—masks, you understand—would step up to you. He'd play his *krodatch*, and if you failed to challenge his audacity with a passage on the *skaranyi**, a devilish instrument, he'd play his *hymerkin*—the instrument we use with the slaves. That's

---

skaranyi: a miniature bag-pipe, the sac squeezed be-tween thumb and palm, the four fingers controlling the stops along four tubes.

the ultimate expression of contempt. Or he might ring his duelling-gong and attack you then and there."

"I had no idea that people here were quite so irascible," said Thissell in a subdued voice.

Rolver shrugged and swung open the massive steel door into his office. "Certain acts may not be committed on the Concourse at Polypolis without incurring criticism."

"Yes, that's quite true," said Thissell. He looked around the office. "Why the security? The concrete, the steel?"

"Protection against the savages," said Rolver. "They come down from the mountains at night, steal what's available, kill anyone they find ashore." He went to a closet, brought forth a mask. "Here. Use this Moon-Moth; it won't get you in trouble."

Thissell unenthusiastically inspected the mask. It was constructed of mouse-colored fur; there was a tuft of hair at each side of the mouth-hole, a pair of feather-like antennae at the forehead. White lace flaps dangled beside the temples and under the eyes hung a series of red folds, creating an effect at once lugubrious and comic.

Thissell asked, "Does this mask signify any degree of prestige?"

"Not a great deal."

"After all, I'm Consular Representative," said Thissell. "I represent the Home Planets, a hundred billion people—"

"If the Home Planets want their representative to wear a Sea-Dragon Conqueror mask, they'd better send out a Sea-Dragon Conqueror type of man."

"I see," said Thissell in a subdued voice. "Well, if I must . . ."

Rolver politely averted his gaze while Thissell doffed the Sea-Dragon Conqueror and slipped the more modest Moon Moth over his head. "I suppose I can find something just a bit more suitable in one of the shops," Thissell said. "I'm told a person simply goes in and takes what he needs, correct?"

Rolver surveyed Thissell critically. "That mask—temporarily, at least—is perfectly suitable. And it's rather important not to take anything from the shops until you know the *strakh* value of the article you want. The owner loses prestige if a person of low *strakh* makes free with his best work."

Thissell shook his head in exasperation. "Nothing of this was explained to me! I knew of the masks, of course, and the painstaking integrity of the craftsmen, but this insistence on prestige—*strakh*, whatever the word is . . ."

"No matter," said Rolver. "After a year or two you'll begin to learn your way around. I suppose you speak the language?"

"Oh, indeed. Certainly."

"And what instruments do you play?"

"Well—I was given to understand that any small instrument was adequate, or that I could merely sing."

"Very inaccurate. Only slaves sing without accompaniment. I suggest that you learn the following instruments as quickly as possible: the *hymerkin* for your slaves, the *ganga* for conversation between intimates or one a trifle lower than yourself in *strakh*. The *kiv* for casual polite intercourse. The *zachinko* for more formal dealing. The *strapan* or the *krodatch* for your social inferiors—in your case, should you wish to insult someone. The *gomapard**** or the double-*kamanthil******* for ceremonials." He considered a moment. "The *crebarin*, the water-flute and the *slobo* are highly useful also—but perhaps you'd better learn the other instruments first. They should provide at least a rudimentary means of communication."

---

*gomapard: one of the few electric instruments used on Sirene. An oscillator produces an oboe-like tone which is modulated, choked, vibrated, raised and lowered in pitch by four keys.

***double-*kamanthil*: an instrument similar to the *ganga*, except the tones are produced by twisting and inclining a disk of resined leather against one or more of the forty-six strings.

"Aren't you exaggerating?" suggested Thissell. "Or joking?"

Rolver laughed his saturnine laugh. "Not at all. First of all, you'll need a houseboat. And then you'll want slaves."

Rolver took Thissell from the landing field to the docks of Fan, a walk of an hour and a half along a pleasant path under enormous trees loaded with fruit, cereal pods, sacs of sugary sap.

"At the moment," said Rolver, "there are only four out-worlders in Fan, counting yourself. I'll take you to Welibus, our Commercial Factor. I think he's got an old houseboat he might let you use."

Cornely Welibus had resided fifteen years in Fan, acquiring sufficient *strakh* to wear his South Wind mask with authority. This consisted of a blue disk inlaid with cabochons of lapis-lazuli, surrounded by an aureole of shimmering snake-skin. Heartier and more cordial than Rolver, he not only provided Thissell with a houseboat, but also a score of various musical instruments and a pair of slaves.

Embarrassed by the largesse, Thissell stammered something about payment, but Welibus cut him off with an expansive gesture. "My dear fellow, this is Sirene. Such trifles cost nothing."

"But a houseboat—"

Welibus played a courtly little flourish on his *kiv*. "I'll be frank, Ser Thissell. The boat is old and a trifle shabby. I can't afford to use it; my status would suffer." A graceful melody accompanied his words. "Status as yet need not concern you. You require merely shelter, comfort and safety from the Night-men."

"Night-men?"

"The cannibals who roam the shore after dark."

"Oh yes. Ser Rolver mentioned them."

"Horrible things. We won't discuss them." A shuddering little trill issued from his *kiv*. "Now, as to slaves." He tapped the blue disk of his mask with a thoughtful forefinger. "Rex and Toby should serve you well." He raised his voice, played a swift clatter on the *hymerkin*. "*Avan esx trobu!*"

A female slave appeared wearing a dozen tight bands of pink cloth, and a dainty black mask sparkling with mother-of-pearl sequins.

"*Fascu etz Rex ae Toby.*"

Rex and Toby appeared, wearing loose masks of black cloth, russet jerkins. Welibus addesssed them with a resonant clatter of *hymerkin*, enjoining them to the service of their new master, on pain of return to their native islands. They prostrated themselves, sang pledges of servitude to Thissell in soft husky voices. Thissell laughed nervously and essayed a sentence in the Sirenese language. "Go to the houseboat, clean it well, bring aboard food."

Toby and Rex stared blankly through the holes in their masks. Welibus repeated the orders with *hymerkin* accompaniment. The slaves bowed and departed.

Thissell surveyed the musical instruments with dismay. "I haven't the slightest idea how to go about learning these things."

Welibus turned to Rolver. "What about Kershaul? Could he be persuaded to give Ser Thissell some basic instruction?"

Rolver nodded judicially. "Kershaul might undertake the job."

Thissell asked, "Who is Kershaul?"

"The third of our little group of expatriates," replied Welibus, "an anthropologist. You've read *Zundar the Splendid? Rituals of Sirene? The Faceless Folk?* No? A pity. All excellent works. Kershaul is high in prestige, and I believe visits Zundar from time to time. Wears a Cave Owl, sometimes a Star-wanderer or even a Wise Arbiter."

"He's taken to an Equatorial Serpent," said Rolver. "The variant with the gilt tusks."

"Indeed!" marvelled Welibus. "Well, I must say he's earned it. A fine fellow, good chap indeed." And he strummed his *zachinko* thoughtfully.

Three months passed. Under the tutelage of Mathew Kershaul Thissell practised the *hymerkin*, the *ganga*, the *strapan*,
the *kiv*, the *gomapard*, and the *zachinko*. The double-*kamanthil*, the *krodatch*, the *slobo*, the water-flute and a number of
others could wait, said Kershaul, until Thissell had mastered
the six basic instruments. He lent Thissell recordings of note-
worthy Sirenese conversing in various moods and to various
accompaniments, so that Thissell might learn the melodic
conventions currently in vogue, and perfect himself in the
niceties of intonation, the various rhythms, cross-rhythms,
compound rhythms, implied rhythms and suppressed rhythms.
Kershaul professed to find Sirenese music a fascinating study,
and Thissell admitted that it was a subject not readily exhausted. The quarter-tone tuning of the instruments admitted the
use of twenty-four tonalities which, multiplied by the five
modes in general use, resulted in one hundred and twenty
separate scales. Kershaul, however, advised that Thissell
primarily concentrate on learning each instrument in its fundamental tonality, using only two of the modes.

With no immediate business at Fan except the weekly
visits to Mathew Kershaul, Thissell took his houseboat eight
miles south and moored it in the lee of a rocky promontory.
Here, if it had not been for the incessant practising, Thissell
lived an idyllic life. The sea was calm and crystal-clear; the
beach, ringed by the gray, green and purple foliage of the
forest, lay close at hand if he wanted to stretch his legs.

Toby and Rex occupied a pair of cubicles forward. Thissell had the after-cabins to himself. From time to time he
toyed with the idea of a third slave, possibly a young female,
to contribute an element of charm and gayety to the menage,
but Kershaul advised against the step, fearing that the intensity of Thissell's concentration might somehow be diminished.
Thissell acquiesced and devoted himself to the study of the
six instruments.

The days passed quickly. Thissell never became bored
with the pageantry of dawn and sunset; the white clouds and

blue sea of noon; the night sky blazing with the twenty-nine stars of Cluster SI 1-715. The weekly trip to Fan broke the tedium. Toby and Rex foraged for food; Thissell visited the luxurious houseboat of Mathew Kershaul for instruction and advice. Then, three months after Thissell's arrival, came the message completely disorganizing the routine: Haxo Angmark, assassin, *agent provocateur*, ruthless and crafty criminal, had come to Sirene. *Effective detention and incarceration of this man!* read the orders. *Attention! Haxo Angmark superlatively dangerous. Kill without hesitation!*

Thissell was not in the best of condition. He trotted fifty yards until his breath came in gasps, then walked: through low hills crowned with white bamboo and black tree-ferns; across meadows yellow with grass-nuts, through orchards and wild vineyards. Twenty minutes passed, twenty-five minutes; with a heavy sensation in his stomach Thissell knew that he was too late. Haxo Angmark had landed, and might be traversing this very road toward Fan. But along the way Thissell met only four persons: a boy-child in a mock-fierce Alk-Islander mask; two young women wearing the Red-bird and the Green-bird; a man masked as a Forest Goblin. Coming upon the man, Thissell stopped short. Could this be Angmark?

Thissell assayed a strategem. He went boldly to the man, stared into the hideous mask. "Angmark," he called in the language of the Home Planets, "you are under arrest!"

The Forest Goblin stared uncomprehendingly, then started forward along the track.

Thissell put himself in the way. He reached for his *ganga*, then recalling the hostler's reaction, instead struck a chord on the *zachinko*. "You travel the road from the space-port," he sang. "What have you seen there?"

The Forest Goblin grasped his hand-bugle, an instrument used to deride opponents on the field of battle, to summon animals, or occasionally to evince a rough and ready truculence. "Where I travel and what I see are the concern solely of myself. Stand back or I walk upon your face." He marched forward, and had not Thissell leapt aside the Forest Goblin might well have made good his threat.

Thissell stood gazing after the retreating back. Angmark? Not likely, with so sure a touch on the hand-bugle. Thissell hesitated, then turned and continued on his way.

Arriving at the space-port, he went directly to the office. The heavy door stood ajar; as Thissell approached, a man appeared in the doorway. He wore a mask of dull green scales, mica plates, blue-lacquered wood and black quills—the Tarn-Bird.

"Ser Rolver," Thissell called out anxiously, "who came down from the *Carina Cruzeiro?*"

Rolver studied Thissell a long moment. "Why do you ask?"

"Why do I ask?" demanded Thissell. "You must have seen the space-gram I received from Castel Cromartin!"

"Oh yes," said Rolver. "Of course. Naturally."

"It was delivered only half an hour ago," said Thissell bitterly. "I rushed out as fast as I could. Where is Angmark?"

"In Fan, I assume," said Rolver.

Thissell cursed softly. "Why didn't you hold him up, delay him in some way?"

Rolver shrugged. "I had neither authority, inclination nor the capability to stop him."

Thissell fought back his annoyance. In a voice of studied calm he said, "On the way I passed a man in rather a ghastly mask—saucer eyes, red wattles."

"A Forest Goblin," said Rolver. "Angmark brought the mask with him."

"But he played the hand-bugle," Thissell protested. "How could Angmark—"

"He's well-acquainted with Sirene; he spent five years here in Fan."

Thissell grunted in annoyance. "Cromartin made no mention of this."

"It's common knowledge," said Rolver with a shrug. "He was Commercial Representative before Welibus took over."

"Were he and Welibus acquainted?"

Rolver laughed shortly. "Naturally. But don't suspect poor Welibus of anything more venal than juggling his accounts; I assure you he's no consort of assassins."

"Speaking of assassins," said Thissell, "do you have a weapon I might borrow?"

Rolver inspected him in wonder. "You came out here to take Angmark bare-handed?"

"I had no choice," said Thissell. "When Cromartin gives orders he expects results. In any event you were here with your slaves."

"Don't count on me for help," Rolver said testily. "I wear the Tarn-Bird and make no pretensions of valor. But I can lend you a power pistol. I haven't used it recently; I won't guarantee its charge."

"Anything is better than nothing," said Thissell.

Rolver went into the office and a moment later returned with his gun. "What will you do now?"

Thissell shook his head wearily. "I'll try to find Angmark in Fan. Or might he head for Zundar?"

Rolver considered. "Angmark might be able to survive in Zundar. But he'd want to brush up on his musicianship. I imagine he'll stay in Fan a few days."

"But how can I find him? Where should I look?"

That I can't say," replied Rolver. "You might be safer not finding him. Angmark is a dangerous man."

Thissell returned to Fan the way he had come.

Where the path swung down from the hills into the esplanade a thick-walled *pisé-de-terre* building had been constructed. The door was carved from a solid black plank; the windows were guarded by enfoliated bands of iron. This was the office of Cornely Welibus, Commercial Factor, Importer and Exporter. Thissell found Welibus sitting at his ease on the tiled verandah, wearing a modest adaptation of the Waldemar mask. He seemed lost in thought, and might or might not have recognized Thissell's Moon Moth; in any event he gave no signal of greeting.

Thissell approached the porch. "Good morning, Ser Welibus."

Welibus nodded abstractedly and said in a flat voice, plucking at his *krodatch*. "Good morning."

Thissell was rather taken aback. This was hardly the instrument to use toward a friend and fellow out-worlder, even if he did wear the Moon-Moth.

Thissell said coldly, "May I ask how long you have been sitting here?"

Welibus considered half a minute, and now when he spoke he accompanied himself on the more cordial *crebarin*. But the recollection of the *krodatch* chord still rankled in Thissell's mind.

"I've been here fifteen or twenty minutes. Why do you ask?"

"I wonder if you noticed a Forest Goblin pass?"

Welibus nodded. "He went on down the esplanade—turned into that first mask shop, I believe."

Thissell hissed between his teeth. This would naturally be Angmark's first move. "I'll never find him once he changes masks," he muttered.

"Who is this Forest Goblin?" asked Welibus, with no more than casual interest.

Thissell could see no reason to conceal the name. "A notorious criminal; Haxo Angmark."

"Haxo Angmark!" croaked Welibus, leaning back in his chair. "You're sure he's here?"

"Reasonably sure."

Welibus rubbed his shaking hands together. "This is bad news—bad news indeed! He's an unscrupulous scoundrel."

"You know him well?"

"As well as anyone." Welibus was now accompanying himself with the *kiv*. "He held the post I now occupy. I came out as an inspector and found that he was embezzling four thousand UMI's a month. I'm sure he feels no great gratitude toward me." Welibus glanced nervously up the esplanade. "I hope you catch him."

"I'm doing my best. He went into the mask shop, you say?"

"I'm sure of it."

Thissell turned away. As he went down the path he heard the black plank door thud shut behind him.

He walked down the esplanade to the mask-maker's shop, paused outside as if admiring the display; a hundred miniature masks, carved from rare woods and minerals, dressed with emerald flakes, spider-web silk, wasp wings, petrified fish scales and the like. The shop was empty except for the mask-maker, a gnarled knotty man in a yellow robe, wearing a deceptively simple Universal Expert mask, fabricated from over two thousand bits of articulated wood.

Thissell considered what he would say, how he would accompany himself, then entered. The mask-maker, noting the Moon Moth and Thissell's diffident manner, continued with his work.

Thissell, selecting the easiest of his instruments, stroked his *strapan*—possibly not the most felicitous choice, for it conveyed a certain degree of condescension. Thissell tried to counteract this flavor by singing in warm, almost effusive, tones, shaking the *strapan* whimsically when he struck a wrong note: "A stranger is an interesting person to deal with: his habits are unfamiliar, he excites curiosity. Not twenty minutes ago a stranger entered this fascinating shop, to exchange his drab Forest Goblin for one of the remarkable and adventurous creations assembled on the premises."

The mask-maker turned Thissell a side glance, and without words played a progression of chords on an instrument

Thissell had never seen before: a flexible sac gripped in the palm with three short tubes leading between the fingers. When the tubes were squeezed almost shut and air forced through the slit, an oboe-like tone ensued. To Thissell's developing ear the instrument seemed difficult, the mask-maker expert, and the music conveyed a profound sense of disinterest.

Thissell tried again, laboriously manipulating the *strapan*. He sang, "To an out-worlder on a foreign planet, the voice of one from his home is like water to a wilting plant. A person who could unite two such persons might find satisfaction in such an act of mercy."

The mask-maker casually fingered his own *strapan*, and drew forth a set of rippling scales, his fingers moving faster than the eyes could follow. He sang in the formal style: "An artist values his moments of concentration; he does not care to spend time exchanging banalities with persons of at best average prestige." Thissell attempted to insert a counter melody, but the mask-maker struck a new set of complex chords whose portent evaded Thissell's understanding, and continued: "Into the shop comes a person who evidently has picked up for the first time an instrument of unparalleled complication, for the execution of his music is open to criticism. He sings of home-sickness and longing for the sight of others like himself. He dissembles his enormous *strakh* behind a Moon Moth, for he plays the *strapan* to a Master Craftsman, and sings in a voice of contemptuous raillery. The refined and creative artist ignores the provocation. He plays a polite instrument, remains noncommittal, and trusts that the stranger will tire of his sport and depart."

Thissell took up his *kiv*. "The noble mask-maker completely misunderstands me—"

He was interrupted by staccato rasping of the mask-maker's *strapan*. "The stranger now sees fit to ridicule the artist's comprehension."

Thissell scratched furiously at his *strapan*: "To protect myself from the heat, I wander into a small and unpretentious mask-shop. The artisan, though still distracted by the novelty of his tools, gives promise of development. He works zealously to perfect his skill, so much so that he refuses to converse with strangers, no matter what their need."

The mask-maker carefully laid down his carving tool. He rose to his feet, went behind a screen, and shortly returned wearing a mask of gold and iron, with simulated flames licking up from the scalp. In one hand he carried a *skaranyi*, in the other a scimitar. He struck off a brilliant series of wild tones, and sang: "Even the most accomplished artist can augment his *strakh* by killing sea-monsters, Night-men and importunate idlers. Such an occasion is at hand. The artist delays his attack exactly ten seconds, because the offender wears a Moon Moth." He twirled his scimitar, spun it in the air.

Thissell desperately pounded the *strapan*. "Did a Forest Goblin enter the shop? Did he depart with a new mask?"

"Five seconds have elapsed," sang the mask-maker in steady ominous rhythm.

Thissell departed in frustrated rage. He crossed the square, stood looking up and down the esplanade. Hundreds of men and women sauntered along the docks, or stood on the decks of their houseboats, each wearing a mask chosen to express his mood, prestige and special attributes, and everywhere sounded the twitter of musical instruments.

Thissell stood at a loss. The Forest Goblin had disappeared. Haxo Angmark walked at liberty in Fan, and Thissell had failed the urgent instructions of Castel Cromartin.

Behind him sounded the casual notes of a *kiv*. "Ser Moon Moth Thissell, you stand engrossed in thought."

Thissell turned, to find beside him a Cave Owl, in a somber cloak of black and gray. Thissell recognized the mask, which symbolized erudition and patient exploration of abstract ideas; Mathew Kershaul had worn it on the occasion of their meeting a week before.

"Good morning, Ser Kershaul," muttered Thissell.

"And how are the studies coming? Have you mastered the C-Sharp Plus scale on the *gomapard*? As I recall, you were finding those inverse intervals puzzling."

"I've worked on them," said Thissell in a gloomy voice. "However, since I'll probably be recalled to Polypolis, it may be all time wasted."

"Eh? What's this?"

Thissell explained the situation in regard to Haxo Angmark. Kershaul nodded gravely. "I recall Angmark. Not a gracious personality, but an excellent musician, with quick fingers and a real talent for new instruments." Thoughtfully he twisted the goatee of his Cave-Owl mask. "What are your plans?"

"They're non-existent," said Thissell, playing a doleful phrase on the *kiv*. "I haven't any idea what masks he'll be wearing and if I don't know what he looks like, how can I find him?"

Kershaul tugged at his goatee. "In the old days he favored the Exo Cambian Cycle, and I believe he used an entire set of Nether Denizens. Now of course his tastes may have changed."

"Exactly," Thissell complained. "He might be twenty feet away and I'd never know it." He glanced bitterly across the esplanade toward the mask-maker's shop. "No one will tell me anything; I doubt if they care that a murderer is walking their docks."

"Quite correct," Kershaul agreed. "Sirenese standards are different from ours."

"They have no sense of responsibility," declared Thissell. "I doubt if they'd throw a rope to a drowning man."

"It's true that they dislike interference," Kershaul agreed. "They emphasize individual responsibility and self-sufficiency."

"Interesting," said Thissell, "but I'm still in the dark about Angmark."

Kershaul surveyed him gravely. "And should you locate Angmark, what will you do then?"

"I'll carry out the orders of my superior," said Thissell doggedly.

"Angmark is a dangerous man," mused Kershaul. "He's got a number of advantages over you."

"I can't take that into account. It's my duty to send him back to Polypolis. He's probably safe, since I haven't the remotest idea how to find him."

Kershaul reflected. "An out-worlder can't hide behind a mask, not from the Sirenese, at least. There are four of us here at Fan—Rolver, Welibus, you and me. If another out-worlder tries to set up housekeeping the news will get around in short order."

"What if he heads for Zundar?"

Kershaul shrugged. "I doubt if he'd dare. On the other hand—" Kershaul paused, then noting Thissell's sudden inattention, turned to follow Thissell's gaze.

A man in a Forest Goblin mask came swaggering toward them along the esplanade. Kershaul laid a restraining hand on Thissell's arm, but Thissell stepped out into the path of the Forest Goblin, his borrowed gun ready. "Haxo Angmark," he cried, "don't make a move, or I'll kill you. You're under arrest."

"Are you sure this is Angmark?" asked Kershaul in a worried voice.

"I'll find out," said Thissell. "Angmark, turn around, hold up your hands."

The Forest Goblin stood rigid with surprise and puzzlement. He reached to his *zachinko*, played an interrogatory arpeggio, and sang, "Why do you molest me, Moon-Moth?"

Kershaul stepped forward and played a placatory phrase on his *slobo*. "I fear that a case of confused identity exists, Ser Forest Goblin. Ser Moon-Moth seeks an out-worlder in a Forest Goblin mask."

The Forest Goblin's music became irritated, and he suddenly switched to his *stimic*. "He asserts that I am an outworlder? Let him prove his case, or he has my retaliation to face."

Kershaul glanced in embarrassment around the crowd which had gathered and once more struck up an ingratiating melody. "I am sure that Ser Moon Moth—"

The Forest Goblin interrupted with a fanfare of *skaranyi* tones. "Let him demonstrate his case or prepare for the flow of blood."

Thissell said, "Very well, I'll prove my case." He stepped forward, grasped the Forest Goblin's mask. "Let's see your face, that'll demonstrate your identity!"

The Forest Goblin sprang back in amazement. The crowd gasped, then set up an ominous strumming and toning of various instruments.

The Forest Goblin reached to the nape of his neck, jerked the cord to his duel-gong, and with his other hand snatched forth his scimitar.

Kershaul stepped forward, playing the *slobo* with great agitation. Thissell, now abashed, moved aside, conscious of the ugly sound of the crowd.

Kershaul sang explanations and apologies, the Forest Goblin answered; Kershaul spoke over his shoulder to Thissell: "Run for it, or you'll be killed! Hurry!"

Thissell hesitated; the Forest Goblin put up his hand to thrust Kershaul aside. "Run!" screamed Kershaul. "To Welibus' office, lock yourself in!"

Thissell took to his heels. The Forest Goblin pursued him a few yards, then stamped his feet, sent after him a set of raucous and derisive blasts of the hand-bugle, while the crowd produced a contemptuous counterpoint of clacking *hymerkins*.

There was no further pursuit. Instead of taking refuge in the Import-Export office, Thissell turned aside and after cautious reconnaissance proceeded to the dock where his houseboat was moored.

The hour was not far short of dusk when he finally returned aboard. Toby and Rex squatted on the forward deck, surrounded by the provisions they had brought back: reed baskets of fruit and cereal, blue-glass jugs containing wine, oil and pungent sap, three young pigs in a wicker pen. They were cracking nuts between their teeth, spitting the shells over the side. They looked up at Thissell, and it seemed that they rose to their feet with a new casualness. Toby muttered something under his breath; Rex smothered a chuckle.

Thissell clacked his *hymerkin* angrily. He sang, "Take the boat off-shore; tonight we remain at Fan."

In the privacy of his cabin he removed the Moon Moth, stared into a mirror at his almost unfamiliar features. He picked up the Moon Moth, examined the detested lineaments: the furry gray skin, the blue spines, the ridiculous lace flaps. Hardly a dignified presence for the Consular Representative of the Home Planets. If, in fact, h₂ still held the position when Cromartin learned of Angmark's winning free!

Thissell flung himself into a chair, stared moodily into space. Today he'd suffered a series of setbacks, but he wasn't defeated yet, not by any means. Tomorrow he'd visit Mathew Kershaul; they'd discuss how best to locate Angmark. As Kershaul had pointed out, another out-world establishment could not be camouflaged; Haxo Angmark's identity would soon become evident. Also tomorrow he must procure another mask. Nothing extreme or vainglorious, but a mask which expressed a modicum of dignity and self-respect.

At this moment one of the slaves tapped on the door-panel, and Thissell hastily pulled the hated Moon Moth back over his head.

Early next morning, before the dawn-light had left the sky, the slaves sculled the houseboat back to that section of

the dock set aside for the use of out-worlders. Neither Rolver nor Welibus nor Kershaul had yet arrived and Thissell
waited impatiently. An hour passed, and Welibus brought
his boat to the dock. Not wishing to speak to Welibus, Thissell remained inside his cabin.

A few moments later Rolver's boat likewise pulled in
alongside the dock. Through the window Thissell saw Rolver,
wearing his usual Tarn-bird, climb to the dock. Here he was
met by a man in a yellow-tufted Sand Tiger mask, who
played a formal accompaniment on the *gomapard* to whatever message he brought Rolver.

Rolver seemed surprised and disturbed. After a moment's
thought he manipulated his own *gomapard*, and as he sang,
he indicated Thissell's houseboat. Then, bowing, he went on
his way.

The man in the Sand Tiger mask climbed with rather
heavy dignity to the float and rapped on the bulwark of
Thissell's houseboat.

Thissell presented himself. Sirenese etiquette did not demand that he invite a casual visitor aboard, so he merely
struck an interrogation on his *zachinko*.

The Sand Tiger played his *gomapard* and sang. "Dawn
over the bay of Fan is customarily a splendid occasion; the
sky is white with yellow and green colors; when Mireille rises,
the mists burn and writhe like flames. He who sings derives a
greater enjoyment from the hour when the floating corpse of
an out-worlder does not appear to mar the serenity of the
view."

Thissell's *zachinko* gave off a startled interrogation almost
of its own accord; the Sand Tiger bowed with dignity. "The
singer acknowledges no peer in steadfastness of disposition;
however, he does not care to be plagued by the antics of a
dissatisfied ghost. He therefore has ordered his slaves to
attach a thong to the ankle of the corpse, and while we have
conversed they have linked the corpse to the stern of your

houseboat. You will wish to administer whatever rites are prescribed in the Out-world. He who sings wishes you a good morning and now departs."

Thissell rushed to the stern of his houseboat. There, near-naked and mask-less, floated the body of a mature man, supported by air trapped in his pantaloons.

Thissell studied the dead face, which seemed character-less and vapid—perhaps in direct consequence of the mask-wearing habit. The body appeared of medium stature and weight, and Thissell estimated the age as between forty-five and fifty. The hair was nondescript brown, the features bloated by the water. There was nothing to indicate how the man had died.

This must be Haxo Angmark, thought Thissell. Who else could it be? Mathew Kershaul? Why not? Thissell asked himself uneasily. Rolver and Welibus had already disembarked and gone about their business. He searched across the bay to locate Kershaul's houseboat, and discovered it already tying up to the dock. Even as he watched, Kershaul jumped ashore, wearing his Cave-Owl mask.

He seemed in an abstracted mood, for he passed Thissell's houseboat without lifting his eyes from the dock.

Thissell turned back to the corpse. Angmark, then, be-yond a doubt. Had not three men disembarked from the houseboats of Rolver, Welibus and Kershaul, wearing masks characteristic of these men? Obviously, the corpse of Ang-mark . . . The easy solution refused to sit quiet in Thissell's mind. Kershaul had pointed out that another out-worlder would be quickly identified. How else could Angmark main-tain himself unless he . . . Thissell brushed the thought aside. The corpse was obviously Angmark.

And yet . . .

Thissell summoned his slaves, gave orders that a suitable container be brought to the dock, that the corpse be trans-ferred therein, and conveyed to a suitable place of repose.

The slaves showed no enthusiasm for the task and Thissell was forced to thunder forcefully, if not skillfully, on the *hymerkin* to emphasize his orders.

He walked along the dock, turned up the esplanade, passed the office of Cristofer Welibus and set out along the pleasant little lane to the landing field.

When he arrived, he found that Rolver had not yet made an appearance. An over-slave, given status by a yellow rosette on his black cloth mask, asked how he might be of service. Thissell stated that he wished to dispatch a message to Polypolis.

There was no difficulty here, declared the slave. If Thissell would set forth his message in clear block-print it would be dispatched immediately.

Thissell wrote:

OUT-WORLDER FOUND DEAD, POSSIBLY ANGMARK.
AGE 48, MEDIUM PHYSIQUE, BROWN HAIR, OTHER
MEANS OF IDENTIFICATION LACKING. AWAIT
ACKNOWLEDGEMENT AND/OR INSTRUCTIONS.

He addressed the message to Castel Cromartin at Polypolis and handed it to the over-slave. A moment later he heard the characteristic sputter of the trans-space discharge.

An hour passed. Rolver made no appearance. Thissell paced restlessly back and forth in front of the office. There was no telling how long he would have to wait: trans-space transmission time varied unpredictably. Sometimes the message snapped through unknowable regions for hours; and there were several authenticated examples of messages being received before they had been transmitted.

Another half-hour passed, and Rolver finally arrived, wearing his customary Tarn-Bird. Coincidentally Thissell heard the hiss of the incoming message.

Rolver seemed surprised to see Thissell. "What brings you out so early?"

Thissell explained. "It concerns the body which you referred to me this morning. I'm communicating with my superiors about it."

Rolver raised his head and listened to the sound of the incoming message. "You seem to be getting an answer. I'd better attend to it."

"Why bother?" asked Thissell. "Your slave seems efficient."

"It's my job," declared Rolver. "I'm responsible for the accurate transmission and receipt of all space-grams."

"I'll come with you," said Thissell. "I've always wanted to watch the operation of the equipment."

"I'm afraid that's irregular," said Rolver. He went to the door which led into the inner compartment. "I'll have your message in a moment."

Thissell protested, but Rolver ignored him and went into the inner office.

Five minutes later he reappeared, carrying a small yellow envelope. "Not too good news," he announced with unconvincing commiseration.

Thissell glumly opened the envelope. The message read:

BODY NOT ANGMARK. ANGMARK HAS BLACK
HAIR. WHY DID YOU NOT MEET LANDING. SERIOUS
INFRACTION, HIGHLY DISSATISFIED. RETURN TO
POLYPOLIS NEXT OPPORTUNITY.
                              CASTEL CROMARTIN

Thissell put the message in his pocket. "Incidentally, may I inquire the color of your hair?"

Rolver played a surprised little trill on his *kiv*. "I'm quite blond. Why do you ask?"

"Mere curiosity."

Rolver played another run on the *kiv*. "Now I understand. My dear fellow, what a suspicious nature you have! Look!" He turned and parted the folds of his mask at the nape of his neck. Thissell saw that Rolver was blond indeed.

"Are you reassured?" asked Rolver jocularly.

"Oh, indeed," said Thissell. "Incidentally, have you another mask you could lend me? I'm sick of this Moon Moth."

"I'm afraid not," said Rolver. "But you need merely go into a mask-maker's shop and make a selection."

"Yes, of course," said Thissell. He took his leave of Rolver and returned along the trail to Fan. Passing Welibus' office he hesitated, then turned in. Today Welibus wore a dazzling confection of green glass prisms and silver beads, a mask Thissell had never seen before.

Welibus greeted him cautiously to the accompaniment of a *kiv*. "Good morning, Ser Moon Moth."

"I won't take too much of your time," said Thissell, "but I have a rather personal question to put to you. What color is your hair?"

Welibus hesitated a fraction of a second, then turned his back, lifted the flap of his mask. Thissell saw heavy black ringlets. "Does that answer your question?" inquired Welibus.

"Completely," said Thissell. He crossed the esplanade, went out on the dock to Kershaul's houseboat. Kershaul greeted him without enthusiasm, and invited him aboard with a resigned wave of the hand.

"A question I'd like to ask," said Thissell. "What color is your hair?"

Kershaul laughed woefully. "What little remains is black. Why do you ask?"

"Curiosity."

"Come, come," said Kershaul with an unaccustomed bluffness. "There's more to it than that."

Thissell, feeling the need of counsel, admitted as much. "Here's the situation. A dead out-worlder was found in the harbor this morning. His hair was brown. I'm not entirely certain, but the chances are—let me see, yes, two out of three that Angmark's hair is black."

Kershaul pulled at the Cave-Owl's goatee. "How do you arrive at that probability?"

"The information came to me through Rolver's hands. He has blond hair. If Angmark has assumed Rolver's identity, he would naturally alter the information which came to me this morning. Both you and Welibus admit to black hair."

"Hm," said Kershaul. "Let me see if I follow your line of reasoning. You feel that Haxo Angmark has killed either Rolver, Welibus or myself and assumed the dead man's identity. Right?"

Thissell looked at him in surprise. "You yourself emphasized that Angmark could not set up another out-world establishment without revealing himself! Don't you remember?"

"Oh, certainly. To continue. Rolver delivered a message to you stating that Angmark was dark, and announced himself to be blond."

"Yes. Can you verify this? I mean for the old Rolver?"

"No," said Kershaul sadly. "I've seen neither Rolver nor Welibus without their masks."

"If Rolver is not Angmark," Thissell mused, "if Angmark indeed has black hair, then both you and Welibus come under suspicion."

"Very interesting," said Kershaul. He examined Thissell warily. "For that matter, you yourself might be Angmark. What color is your hair?"

"Brown," said Thissell curtly. He lifted the gray fur of the Moon Moth mask at the back of his head.

"But you might be deceiving me as to the text of the message," Kershaul put forward.

"I'm not," said Thissell wearily. "You can check with Rolver if you care to."

Kershaul shook his head. "Unnecessary. I believe you. But another matter: what of voices? You've heard all of us before and after Angmark arrived. Isn't there some indication there?"

"No. I'm so alert for any evidence of change that you all sound rather different. And the masks muffle your voices."

Kershaul tugged the goatee. "I don't see any immediate

solution to the problem." He chuckled. "In any event, need there be? Before Angmark's advent, there were Rolver, Welibus, Kershaul and Thissell. Now—for all practical purposes— there are still Rolver, Welibus, Kershaul and Thissell. Who is to say that the new member may not be an improvement upon the old?"

"An interesting thought," agreed Thissell, "but it so happens that I have a personal interest in identifying Angmark. My career is at stake."

"I see," mumured Kershaul. "The situation then becomes an issue between yourself and Angmark."

"You won't help me?"

"Not actively. I've become pervaded with Sirenese individualism. I think you'll find that Rolver and Welibus will respond similarly." He sighed. "All of us have been here too long."

Thissell stood deep in thought. Kershaul waited patiently a moment, then said, "Do you have any further questions?"

"No," said Thissell. "I have merely a favor to ask you."

"I'll oblige if I possibly can," Kershaul replied courteously.

"Give me, or lend me, one of your slaves, for a week or two."

Kershaul played an exclamation of amusement on the *ganga*. "I hardly like to part with my slaves; they know me and my ways—"

"As soon as I catch Angmark you'll have him back."

"Very well," said Kershaul. He rattled a summons on his *hymerkin*, and a slave appeared. "Anthony," sang Kershaul, "you are to go with Ser Thissell and serve him for a short period."

The slave bowed, without pleasure.

Thissell took Anthony to his houseboat, and questioned him at length, noting certain of the responses upon a chart. He then enjoined Anthony to say nothing of what had passed, and consigned him to the care of Toby and Rex. He gave further instructions to move the houseboat away from the dock and allow no one aboard until his return.

He set forth once more along the way to the landing field, and found Rolver at a lunch of spiced fish, shredded bark of the salad tree, and a bowl of native currants. Rolver clapped an order on the *hymerkin*, and a slave set a place for Thissell. "And how are the investigations proceeding?"

"I'd hardly like to claim any progress," said Thissell. "I assume that I can count on your help?"

Rolver laughed briefly. "You have my good wishes."

"More concretely," said Thissell, "I'd like to borrow a slave from you. Temporarily."

Rolver paused in his eating. "Whatever for?"

"I'd rather not explain," siad Thissell. "But you can be sure that I make no idle request."

Without graciousness Rolver summoned a slave and consigned him to Thissell's service.

On the way back to his houseboat, Thissell stopped at Welibus' office.

Welibus looked up from his work. "Good afternoon, Ser Thissell."

Thissell came directly to the point. "Ser Welibus, will you lend me a slave for a few days?"

Welibus hesitated, then shrugged. "Why not?" He clacked his *hymerkin*; a slave appeared. "Is he satisfactory? Or would you prefer a young female?" He chuckled rather offensively, to Thissell's way of thinking.

"He'll do very well. I'll return him in a few days."

"No hurry." Welibus made an easy gesture and returned to his work.

Thissell continued to his houseboat, where he separately interviewed each of his two new slaves and made notes upon his chart.

Dusk came soft over the Titanic Ocean. Toby and Rex sculled the houseboat away from the dock, out across the silken waters. Thissell sat on the deck listening to the sound of soft voices, the flutter and tinkle of musical instruments. Lights from the floating houseboats glowed yellow and wan watermelon-red. The shore was dark; the Night-men would presently come slinking to paw through refuse and stare jealously across the water.

In nine days the *Buenaventura* came past Sirene on its regular schedule; Thissell had his orders to return to Polypolis. In nine days, could he locate Haxo Angmark?

Nine days weren't too many, Thissell decided, but they might possibly be enough.

Two days passed, and three and four and five. Every day Thissell went ashore and at least once a day visited Rolver, Welibus and Kershaul.

Each reacted differently to his presence. Rolver was sardonic and irritable; Welibus formal and at least superficially affable; Kershaul mild and suave, but ostentatiously impersonal and detached in his conversation.

Thissell remained equally bland to Rolver's dour jibes, Welibus' jocundity, Kershaul's withdrawal. And every day, returning to his houseboat he made marks on his chart.

The sixth, the seventh, the eighth day came and passed. Rolver, with rather brutal directness, inquired if Thissell wished to arrange for passage on the *Buenaventura*. Thissell considered, and said, "Yes, you had better reserve passage for one."

"Back to the world of faces," shuddered Rolver. "Faces! Everywhere pallid, fish-eyed faces. Mouths like pulp, noses knotted and punctured; flat, flabby faces. I don't think I could stand it after living here. Luckily you haven't become a real Sirenese."

"But I won't be going back," said Thissell.

"I thought you wanted me to reserve passage."

"I do. For Haxo Angmark. He'll be returning to Polypolis, in the brig."

"Well, well," said Rolver. "So you've picked him out."

"Of course," said Thissell. "Haven't you?"

Rolver shrugged. "He's either Welibus or Kershaul, that's as close as I can make it. So long as he wears his mask and calls himself either Welibus or Kershaul, it means nothing to me."

"It means a great deal to me," said Thissell. "What time tomorrow does the lighter go up?"

"Eleven twenty-two sharp. If Haxo Angmark's leaving, tell him to be on time."

"He'll be here," said Thissell.

He made his usual call upon Welibus and Kershaul, then returning to his houseboat, put three final marks on his chart.

The evidence was here, plain and convincing. Not absolutely incontrovertible evidence, but enough to warrant a definite move. He checked over his gun. Tomorrow, the day of decision. He could afford no errors.

The day dawned bright white, the sky like the inside of an oyster shell. Mireille rose through iridescent mists. Toby and Rex sculled the houseboat to the dock. The remaining three out-world houseboats floated somnolently on the slow swells.

One boat Thissell watched in particular, that whose owner Haxo Angmark had killed and dropped into the harbor. This boat presently moved toward the shore, and Haxo Angmark himself stood on the front deck, wearing a mask Thissell had never seen before: a construction of scarlet feathers, black glass and spiked green hair.

Thissell was forced to admire his poise. A clever scheme, cleverly planned and executed—but marred by an insurmountable difficulty.

Angmark returned within. The houseboat reached the dock. Slaves flung out mooring lines, lowered the gang-plank. Thissell, his gun ready in the pocket flap of his robes, walked down the dock, went aboard. He pushed open the door to the saloon. The man at the table raised his red, black and green mask in surprise.

Thissell said, "Angmark, please don't argue or make any—"

Something hard and heavy tackled him from behind; he was flung to the floor, his gun wrested expertly away.

Behind him the *hymerkin* clattered; a voice sang, "Bind the fool's arms."

The man sitting at the table rose to his feet, removed the red, black and green mask to reveal the black cloth of a slave. Thissell twisted his head. Over him stood Haxo Angmark, wearing a mask Thissell recognized as a Dragon-Tamer, fabricated from black metal, with a knife-blade nose, socketed-eyelids, and three crests running back over the scalp.

The mask's expression was unreadable, but Angmark's voice was triumphant. "I trapped you very easily."

"So you did," said Thissell. The slave finished knotting his wrists together. A clatter of Angmark's *hymerkin* sent him away. "Get to your feet," said Angmark. "Sit in that chair."

"What are we waiting for?" inquired Thissell.

"Two of our fellows still remain out on the water. We won't need them for what I have in mind."

"Which is?"

"You'll learn in due course," said Angmark. "We have an hour or so on our hands."

Thissell tested his bonds. They were undoubtedly secure.

Angmark seated himself. "How did you fix on me? I admit to being curious . . . Come, come," he chided as Thissell sat silently. "Can't you recognize that I have defeated you? Don't make affairs unpleasant for yourself."

Thissell shrugged. "I operated on a basic principle. A man can mask his face, but he can't mask his personality."

"Aha," said Angmark. "Interesting. Proceed."

"I borrowed a slave from you and the other two out-worlders, and I questioned them carefully. What masks had their masters worn during the month before your arrival? I prepared a chart and plotted their responses. Rolver wore the Tarn-Bird about eighty percent of the time, the remaining

twenty percent divided between the Sophist Abstraction and
the Black Intricate. Welibus had a taste for the heroes of Kan-
Cachan Cycle. He wore the Chalekun, the Prince Intrepid, the
Seavain most of the time: six days out of eight. The other
two days he wore his South-Wind or his Gay Companion.
Kershaul, more conservative, preferred the Cave Owl, the
Star Wanderer, and two or three other masks he wore at odd
intervals.

"As I say, I acquired this information from possibly its
most accurate source, the slaves. My next step was to keep
watch upon the three of you. Every day I noted what masks
you wore and compared it with my chart. Rolver wore his
Tarn Bird six times, his Black Intricate twice. Kershaul wore
his Cave Owl five times, his Star Wanderer once, his Quin-
cunx once and his Ideal of Perfection once. Welibus wore the
Emerald Mountain twice, the Triple Phoenix three times, and
Prince Intrepid once and the Shark-God twice."

Angmark nodded thoughtfully. "I see my error. I selected
from Welibus's masks, but to my own taste—and as you point
out, I revealed myself. But only to you." He rose and went to
the window. "Kershaul and Rolver are now coming ashore;
they'll soon be past and about their business—though I doubt
if they'd interfere in any case; they've both become good
Sirenese."

Thissell waited in silence. The minutes passed. Then Angmark reached to a shelf and picked up a knife. He looked at
Thissell. "Stand up."

Thissell slowly rose to his feet. Angmark approached
from the side, reached out, lifted the Moon Moth from
Thissell's head. Thissell gasped and made a vain attempt to
seize it. Too late; his face was bare and naked.

Angmark turned away, removed his own mask, donned
the Moon Moth. He struck a call on his *hymerkin*. Two slaves
entered, stopped in shock at the sight of Thissell.

Angmark played a brisk tattoo, sang, "Carry this man up
to the dock."

"Angmark," cried Thissell. "I'm maskless!"

The slaves seized him and in spite of Thissell's desperate struggles, conveyed him out on the deck, along the float and up on the dock.

Angmark fixed a rope around Thissell's neck. He said, "You are now Haxo Angmark, and I am Edwer Thissell. Welibus is dead, you shall soon be dead. I can handle your job without difficulty. I'll play musical instruments like a Nightman and sing like a crow. I'll wear the Moon Moth till it rots and then I'll get another. The report will go to Polypolis, Haxo Angmark is dead. Everything will be serene."

Thissell barely heard. "You can't do this," he whispered. "My mask, my face . . ." A large woman in a blue and pink flower mask walked down the dock. She saw Thissell and emitted a piercing shriek, flung herself prone on the dock.

"Come along," said Angmark brightly. He tugged at the rope, and so pulled Thissell down the dock. A man in a Pirate Captain mask coming up from his houseboat stood rigid in amazement.

Angmark played the *zachinko* and sang, "Behold the notorious criminal Haxo Angmark. Through all the outer-worlds his name is reviled; now he is captured and led in shame to his death. Behold Haxo Angmark!"

They turned into the esplanade. A child screamed in fright; a man called hoarsely. Thissell stumbled; tears tumbled from his eyes; he could see only disorganized shapes and colors. Angmark's voice belled out richly: "Everyone behold, the criminal of the out-worlds, Haxo Angmark! Approach and observe his execution!"

Thissell feebly creid out, "I'm not Angmark; I'm Edwer Thissell; he's Angmark." But no one listened to him; there were only cries of dismay, shock, disgust at the sight of his face. He called to Angmark, "Give me my mask, a slave-cloth . . ."

Angmark sang jubilantly, "In shame he lived, in maskless shame he dies."

A Forest Goblin stood before Angmark. "Moon Moth, we meet once more."

Angmark sang, "Stand aside, friend Goblin; I must execute this criminal. In shame he lived, in shame he dies!"

A crowd had formed around the group; masks stared in morbid titillation at Thissell.

The Forest Goblin jerked the rope from Angmark's hand, threw it to the ground. The crowd roared. Voices cried, "No duel no duel! Execute the monster!"

A cloth was thrown over Thissell's head. Thissell awaited the thrust of a blade. But instead his bonds were cut. Hastily he adjusted the cloth, hiding his face, peering between the folds.

Four men clutched Haxo Angmark. The Forest Goblin confronted him, playing the *skaranyi*. "A week ago you reached to divest me of my mask; you have now achieved your perverse aim!"

"But he is a criminal," cried Angmark. "He is notorious, infamous!"

"What are his misdeeds?" sang the Goblin.

"He has murdered, betrayed; he has wrecked ships; he has tortured, blackmailed, robbed, sold children into slavery; he has—"

The Forest Goblin stopped him. "Your religious differences are of no importance. We can vouch however for your present crimes!"

The hostler stepped forward. He sang fiercely, "This insolent Moon Moth nine days ago sought to pre-empt my choicest mount!"

Another man pushed close. He wore a Universal Expert, and sang, "I am a Master Mask-maker; I recognize this Moon Moth outworlder! Only recently he entered my shop and derided my skill. He deserves death!"

"Death to the out-world monster!" cried the crowd. A wave of men surged forward. Steel blades rose and fell, the deed was done.

Thissell watched, unable to move. The Forest Goblin approached, and playing the *stimic* sang sternly, "For you we have pity, but also contempt. A true man would never suffer such indignities!"

Thissell took a deep breath. He reached to his belt and found his *zachinko*. He sang, "My friend, you malign me! Can you not appreciate true courage? Would you prefer to die in combat or walk maskless along the esplanade?"

The Forest Goblin sang, "There is only one answer. First I would die in combat; I could not bear such shame."

Thissell sang, "I had such a choice. I could fight with my hands tied, and so die—or I could suffer shame, and through this shame conquer my enemy. You admit that you lack sufficient *strakh* to achieve this deed. I have proved myself a hero of bravery! I ask, who here has courage to do what I have done?"

"Courage?" demanded the Forest Goblin. "I fear nothing, up to and beyond death at the hands of the Night-men!"

"Then answer."

The Forest Goblin stood back. He played his double-*kamanthil*. "Bravery indeed, if such were your motives."

The hostler struck a series of subdued *gomapard* chords and sang, "Not a man among us would dare what this maskless man has done."

The crowd muttered approval.

The mask-maker approached Thissell, obsequiously stroking his double-*kamanthil*. "Pray Lord Hero, step into my nearby shop, exhange this vile rag for a mask befitting your quality."

Another mask-maker sang, "Before you choose, Lord Hero, examine my magnificent creations!"

A man in a Bright Sky Bird mask approached Thissell reverently. "I have only just completed a sumptuous houseboat; seventeen years of toil have gone into its fabrication. Grant me the good fortune of accepting and using this splendid craft; aboard waiting to serve you are alert slaves and pleasant maidens; there is ample wine in storage and soft silken carpets on the decks."

"Thank you," said Thissell, striking the *zachinko* with vigor and confidence. "I accept with pleasure. But first a mask."

The mask-maker struck an interrogative trill on the *gomapard*. "Would the Lord Hero consider a Sea-Dragon Conqueror beneath his dignity?"

"By no means," said Thissell. "I consider it suitable and satisfactory. We shall go now to examine it."

The Mitr

A ROCKY HEADLAND made a lee for the bay and the wide empty beach.

The water barely rose and fell. A high overcast grayed the sky, stilled the air. The bay shone with a dull luster, like old pewter.

Dunes bordered the beach, breaking into a nearby forest of pitchy black-green cypress. The forest was holding its own, matting down the drifts with whiskery roots.

Among the dunes were ruins—glass walls ground milky by salt breeze and sand. In the center of these walls a human being had brought grass and ribbon-weed for her bed.

Her name was Mitr, or so the beetles called her. For want of any other, she had taken the word for a name.

The name, the grass bed, and a length of brown cloth stolen from the beetles were her only possessions. Possibly her belongings might be said to include a mouldering heap of bones which lay a hundred yards back in the forest. They interested her strongly, and she vaguely remembered a connection with herself. In the old days, when her arms and legs had been short and round, she had not marked the rather grotesque correspondence of form. Now she had lengthened, and the resemblance was plain. Eyeholes like her eyes, a mouth like her own, teeth, jaw, skull, shoulders, ribs, legs, feet. From time to time she would wander back into the forest and stand wondering, though of late she had not been regular in her visits.

Today was dreary and gray. She felt bored, uneasy, and after some thought decided that she was hungry. Wandering out on the dunes she listlessly ate a number of grass-pods. Perhaps she was not hungry after all.

She walked down to the beach, stood looking out across the bay. A damp wind flapped the brown cloth, rumpled her hair. Perhaps it would rain. She looked anxiously at the sky. Rain made her wet and miserable. She could always take shelter among the rocks of the headland but—sometimes it was better to be wet.

She wandered down along the beach, caught and ate a small shellfish. There was little satisfaction in the salty flesh. Apparently she was not hungry. She picked up a sharp stick and drew a straight line in the damp sand—fifty feet—a hundred feet long. She stopped, looked back over her work with pleasure. She walked back, drawing another line parallel to the first, a hand's-breadth distant.

Very interesting effect. Fired by sudden enthusiasm she drew more lines up and down the beach until she had created an extensive grate of parallel lines.

She looked over her work with satisfaction. Making such marks on the smooth sand was pleasant and interesting. Some other time she would do it again, and perhaps use curving lines or cross-hatching.

But enough for now. She dropped the stick. The feeling of hunger that was not hunger came over her again. She caught a sand-locust but threw it away without eating it.

She began to run at full speed along the beach. This was better, the flash of her legs below her, the air clean in her lungs. Panting, she came to a halt, flung herself down in the sand.

Presently she caught her breath, sat up. She wanted to run some more, but felt a trifle languid. She grimaced, jerked uneasily. Maybe she should visit the beetles over the headland; perhaps the old gray creature called Ti-Sri-Ti would speak to her.

Tentatively she rose to her feet and started back along the beach. The plan gave her no real pleasure. Ti-Sri-Ti had little of interest to say. He answered no questions, but recited interminable data concerned with the colony: how many grubs would be allowed to mature, how many pounds of spider-eggs had been taken to storage, the condition of his mandibles, antenna, eyes. . . .

She hesitated, but after a moment went on. Better Ti-Sri-Ti than no one, better the sound of a voice than the monotonous crash of gray surf. And perhaps he might say something interesting; on occasions his conversation went far afield and then Mitr listened with absorption: "The mountains are ruled by wild lizards and beyond are the Mercaloid Mechanvikis, who live under the ground with only fuming chimneys and slag-runs to tell of activity below. The beetles live along the shore and of the Mitr only one remains by old Glass City, the last of the Mitr."

She had not quite understood, since the flux and stream of time, the concepts of before and after, meant nothing to her. The universe was static; day followed day, not in a series, but as a duplication.

Ti-Sri-Ti had droned on: "Beyond the mountains is endless desert, then endless ice, then endless waste, then a land of seething fire, then the great water and once more the land of life, the rule and domain of the beetles, where every solstice a new acre of leaf mulch is chewed and laid. . . ." And then there had been an hour dealing with beetle fungi-culture.

Mitr wandered along the beach. She passed the beautiful grate she had scratched in the damask sand, passed her glass walls, climbed the first shelves of black rock. She stopped, listened. A sound?

She hesitated, then went on. There was a rush of many feet. A long brown and black beetle sprang upon her, pressed

her against the rocks. She fought feebly, but the fore-feet
pinned her shoulders, arched her back. The beetle pressed his
proboscis to her neck, punctured her skin. She stood limp,
staring into his red eyes while he drank.

He finished, released her. The wound closed of itself,
smarted and ached. The beetle climbed up over the rocks.

Mitr sat for an hour regaining her strength. The thought
of listening to Ti-Sri-Ti now gave her no pleasure.

She wandered listlessly back along the beach, and ate a
few bits of sea-weed and a small fish which had been trapped
in a tide-pool.

She walked to the water's edge and stared out past the
headland to the horizon. She wanted to cry out, to yell;
something of the same urge which had driven her to run so
swiftly along the beach.

She raised her voice, called, a long musical note. The
damp mild breeze seemed to muffle the sound. She turned
away discouraged.

She wandered down the shore to the little stream of fresh
water. Here she drank and ate some of the blackberries that
grew in rank thickets.

She jerked upright, raised her head.

A vast high sound filled the sky, seemed part of all the air.
She stood rigid, then craned her neck, seaching the overcast, legs half-bent for flight.

A long black sky-fish dropped into view, snorting puffs of
fire.

Terrified, she backed into the blackberry bushes. The
brambles tore her legs, brought her to awareness. She dodged
into the forest, crouched under a leaning cypress trunk.

The sky-fish dropped with astounding rapidity, lowered
to the beach, settled with a quiet final belch and sigh.

Mitr watched in frozen fascination. Never had she known
of such a thing, never would she walk the beach again without watching the heavens.

The sky-fish opened. She saw the glint of metal, glass. From the interior jumped three creatures. Her head moved forward in wonder. They were something like herself, but large, red, burly. Strange, frightening things. They made a great deal of noise, talking in hoarse rough voices.

One of them saw the glass walls, and for a space they examined the ruins with great interest.

The brown and black beetle which had drunk her blood chose this moment to scuttle down the rocks to the beach. One of the newcomers set up a loud halloo and the beetle, bewildered and resentful, ran back up toward the rocks. The stranger held a shiny thing in his hand. It spat a lance of fire and the beetle burst into a thousand incandescent pieces.

The three cried out in loud voices, laughing, and Mitr shrank back under the tree trunk, making herself as small as possible.

One of the stangers noticed the place on the beach where she had drawn her grating. He called his companions and they looked with every display of attention, studying her footprints with extreme interest. One of them made a comment which caused the others to break into loud laughter. Then they all turned and searched up and down the beach.

They were seeking her, thought Mitr. She crouched so far under the trunk that the bark bruised her flesh.

Presently their interest waned and they went back to the sky-fish. One of them brought forth a long black tube, which he took down to the edge of the surf and threw far out into the leaden water. The tube stiffened, pulsed, made sucking sounds.

The sky-fish was thirsty and was drinking through his probiscis, thought Mitr.

The three strangers now walked along the beach toward the fresh-water stream. Mitr watched their approach with apprehension. Were they following her tracks? Her hands were sweating, her skin tingled.

They stopped at the water's edge, drank, only a few paces away. Mitr could see them plainly. They had bright copper hair and little hair-wisps around their mouths. They wore shining red carapaces around their chests, gray cloth on their legs, metal foot-wrappings. They were much like herself—but somehow different. Bigger, harder, more energetic. They were cruel, too; they had burnt the brown and black beetle. Mitr watched them fascinatedly. Where was their home? Were there others like them, like her, in the sky?

She shifted her position; the foliage crackled. Tingles of excitement and fear ran along her back. Had they heard? She peered out, ready to flee. No, they were walking back down the beach toward the sky-fish.

Mitr jumped up from under the tree-trunk, stood watching from behind the foliage. Plainly they cared little that another like themselves lived nearby. She became angry. Now she wanted to chide them, and order them off her beach.

She held back. It would be foolish to show herself. They might easily throw a lance of flame to burn her as they had the beetle. In any event they were rough and brutal. Strange creatures.

She stole through the forest, flitting from trunk to trunk, falling flat when necessary until she had approached the sky-fish as closely as shelter allowed.

The strangers were standing close around the base of the monster, and showed no further disposition to explore.

The tube into the bay grew limp. They pulled it back into the sky-fish. Did that mean that they were about to leave? Good. They had no right on her beach. They had committed an outrage, landing so arrogantly, and killing one of her beetles. She almost stepped forward to upbraid them; then remembered how rough and hard and cruel they were, and held back with a tingling skin.

Stand quietly. Presently they will go, and you will be left in possession of the beach.

She moved restlessly.

Rough red brutes.

Don't move or they will see you. And then? She shivered.

They were making preparations for leaving. A lump came into her throat. They had seen her tracks and had never bothered to search. They could have found her so easily, she had hid herself almost in plain sight. And now she was closer then ever.

If she moved forward only a step, then they would see her.

Skin tingling, she moved a trifle out from behind the tree-trunk. Just a little bit. Then she jumped back, heart thudding.

Had they seen her? With a sudden fluttering access of fright she hoped not. What would they do?

She looked cautiously around the trunk. One of the strangers was staring in a puzzled manner, as if he might have glimpsed movement. Even now he didn't see her. He looked straight into her eyes.

She heard him call out, then she was fleeing through the forest. He charged after her, and after him came the other two, battering down the undergrowth.

They left her, bruised and bleeding, in a bed of ferns, and marched back through the forest toward the beach, laughing and talking in their rough hoarse voices.

She lay quiet for a while.

Their voices grew faint. She rose to her feet, staggered, limped after them.

A great glare lit the sky.

Through the trees she saw the sky-fish thunder up—higher, higher, higher. It vanished through the overcast.

There was silence along the beach, only the endless mutter of the surf.

She walked down to the water's edge, where the tide was coming in. The overcast was graying with evening.

She looked for many minutes into the sky, listening.

No sound. The damp wind blew in her face, ruffling her hair.

She sighed, turned back toward the ruined glass walls with tears on her cheeks.

The tide was washing up over the grate of straight lines she had drawn so carefully in the sand. Another few minutes and it would be entirely gone.

The Men Return

HE RELICT came furtively down the crag, a shambling gaunt creature with tortured eyes. He moved in a series of quick dashes using panels of dark air for concealment, running behind each passing shadow, at times crawling on all fours, head low to the ground. Arriving at the final low outcrop of rock, he halted, peered across the plain.

Far away rose low hills, blurring into the sky, which was mottled and sallow like poor milk-glass. The intervening plain spread like rotten velvet, black-green and wrinkled, streaked with ocher and rust. A fountain of liquid rock jetted high in the air, branched out into black coral. In the middle distance a family of gray objects evolved with a sense of purposeful destiny: spheres melted into pyramids, became domes, tufts of white spires, sky-piercing poles; then, as a final *tour de force*, tesseracts.

The Relict cared nothing for this; he needed food: out on the plain were plants. They would suffice in lieu of anything better. They grew in the ground, or sometimes on a floating lump of water, or to a core of hard black gas. There were dank black flaps of leaf, clumps of haggard thorn, pale green bulbs, stalks with leaves and contorted flowers. There were no definite growths or species, and the Relict had no means of

knowing if the leaves and tendrils he had eaten yesterday
would poison him today.

He tested the surface of the plain with his foot. The glassy
surface (though it likewise seemed a construction of red and
gray-green pyramids) accepted his weight, then suddenly
sucked at his leg. In a frenzy he tore himself free, jumped
back, squatted on the temporarily solid rock.

Hunger rasped at his stomach. He must eat. He contemplated the plain. Not too far away a pair of Organisms played
—sliding, diving, dancing, striking flamboyant poses. Should
they approach he would try to kill one of them. They resembled men, and so should make a good meal.

He waited. A long time? A short time? It might have been
either; duration had neither quantitative nor qualitative reality. The sun had vanished, there was no standard cycle or
recurrence. Time was a word blank of meaning.

Matters had not always been so. The Relict retained a few
tattered recollections of the old days, before system and logic
had been rendered obsolete. Man had dominated Earth by
virtue of a single assumption: that an effect could be traced
to a cause, itself the effect of a previous cause.

Manipulation of this basic law yielded rich results; there
seemed no need for any other tool or instrumentality. Man
congratulated himself on his generalized structure. He could
live on desert, on plain or ice, in forest or in city; Nature had
not shaped him to a special environment.

He was unaware of his vulnerability. Logic was the special
environment; the brain was the special tool.

Then came the terrible hour when Earth swam into a
pocket of non-causality, and all the ordered tensions of
cause-effect dissolved. The special tool was useless; it had no
purchase on reality. From the two billions of men, only a few
survived—the mad. They were now the Organisms, lords of
the era, their discords so exactly equivalent to the vagaries of
the land as to constitute a peculiar wild wisdom. Or perhaps
the disorganized matter of the world, loose from the old

organization, was peculiarly sensitive to psycho-kinesis.

A handful of others, the Relicts, managed to exist, but only through a delicate set of circumstances. They were the ones most strongly charged with the old causal dynamic. It persisted sufficiently to control the metabolism of their bodies, but could extend no further. They were fast, fast dying, for sanity provided no leverage against the environment. Sometimes their own minds sputtered and jangled, and they would go raving and leaping out across the plain.

The Organisms observed with neither surprise nor curiosity; how could surprise exist? The mad Relict might pause by an Organism, and try to duplicate the creature's existence. The Organism ate a mouthful of plant; so did the Relict. The Organism rubbed his feet with crushed water; so did the Relict. Then presently the Relict would die of poison or rent bowels or skin lesions, while the Organism relaxed in the dank black grass. Or the Organism might seek to eat the Relict; and the Relict would run off in terror, unable to abide any part of the world—running, bounding, breasting the thick air; eyes wide, mouth open, calling and gasping until finally he foundered in a pool of black iron or blundered into a vacuum pocket, to bat around like a fly in a bottle.

The Relicts now numbered very few. Finn, he who crouched on the rock overlooking the plain, lived with four others. Two of these were old men and soon would die. Finn likewise would die unless he found food.

Out on the plain one of the Organisms, Alpha, sat down, caught a handful of air, a globe of blue liquid, a rock, kneaded them together, pulled the mixture like taffy, gave it a great heave. It uncoiled from his hand like rope. The Relict crouched low. No telling what deviltry would occur to the creature. He and all the rest of them—unpredictable! The Relict valued their flesh to eat; but they also would eat him if opportunity offered. In the competition he was at a great disadvantage. Their random acts baffled him. Seeking to escape, he ran, and then the terror began. The direction he set his face was seldom the direction the varying frictions of the ground let him move. Behind was the Organism, as random and uncommitted as the environment. The double set of vagaries sometimes compounded, sometimes canceled each other. In the latter case the Organism might catch him. . . . It was inexplicable. But then, what was not? The word "explanation" had no meaning.

They were moving toward him. Had they seen him? He flattened himself against the sullen yellow rock.

The Organisms paused not far away. He could hear their sounds, and crouched, sick from conflicting pangs of hunger and fear.

Alpha sank to his knees, lay flat on his back, arms and legs flung out at random, addressing the sky in a series of musical cries, sibilants, gutteral groans. It was a personal language he had only now improvised, but Beta understood him well.

"A vision," cried Alpha. "I see past the sky. I see knots, spinning circles. They tighten into hard points; they will never come undone."

Beta perched on a pyramid, glanced over his shoulder at the mottled sky.

"An intuition," chanted Alpha, "A picture out of the other time. It is hard, merciless, inflexible."

Beta poised on the pyramid, dove through the glassy surface, swam under Alpha, emerged, lay flat beside him.

"Observe the Relict on the hillside. In his blood is the whole of the old race—the narrow men with minds like cracks. He has exuded the intuition. Clumsy thing—a blunderer," said Alpha.

"They are all dead, all of them," cried Beta. "Although three or four remain." (When *past, present* and *future* are no more than ideas left over from another era, like boats on a dry lake—then the completion of a process can never be defined.)

Alpha said, "This is the vision. I see the Relicts swarming

the Earth; then whisking off to nowhere, like gnats in the wind. That is behind us."

The Organisms lay quiet, considering the vision.

A rock, or perhaps a meteor, fell from the sky, struck into the surface of the pond. It left a circular hole which slowly closed. From another part of the pool a gout of fluid splashed into the air, floated away.

Alpha spoke: "Again—the intuition comes strong! There will be lights in the sky."

The fever died in him. He hooked a finger into the air, hoisted himself to his feet.

Beta lay quiet. Slugs, ants, flies, beetles were crawling on him, boring, breeding. Alpha knew that Beta could arise, shake off the insects, stride off. But Beta seemed to prefer passivity. That was well enough. He could produce another Beta should he choose, or a dozen of him. Sometimes the world swarmed with Organisms, all sorts, all colors, tall as steeples, short and squat as flower-pots. Sometimes they hid quietly in deep caves, and sometimes the tentative substance of Earth would shift, and perhaps one, or perhaps thirty, would be shut in the subterranean cocoon, and all would sit gravely waiting, until such time as the ground would open and they could peer blinking and pallid out into the light.

"I feel a lack," said Alpha. "I will eat the Relict." He set forth, and sheer chance brought him near to the ledge of yellow rock. Finn the Relict spring to his feet in panic.

Alpha tried to communicate, so that Finn might pause while Alpha ate. But Finn had no grasp for the many-valued overtones of Alpha's voice. He seized a rock, hurled it at Alpha. The rock puffed into a cloud of dust, blew back into the Relict's face.

Alpha moved closer, extended his long arms. The Relict kicked. His feet went out from under him, he slid out on the plain. Alpha ambled complacently behind him. Finn began to crawl away. Alpha moved off to the right—one direction was

as good as another. He collided with Beta, and began to eat
Beta instead of the Relict. The Relict hesitated; then approached, and joining Alpha, pushed chunks of pink flesh
into his mouth.

Alpha said to the Relict, "I was about to communicate an
intuition to him whom we dine upon. I will speak to you."

Finn could not understand Alpha's personal language. He
ate as rapidly as possible.

Alpha spoke on. "There will be lights in the sky. The
great lights."

Finn rose to his feet and, warily watching Alpha, seized
Beta's legs, began to pull him toward the hill. Alpha watched
with quizzical unconcern.

It was hard work for the spindly Relict. Sometimes Beta
floated; sometimes he wafted off on the air; sometimes he
adhered to the terrain. At last he sank into a knob of granite
which froze around him. Finn tried to jerk Beta loose, pry
him up with a stick, without success.

He ran back and forth in an agony of indecision. Beta
began to collapse, wither, like a jellyfish on hot sand. The
Relict abandoned the hulk. Too late, too late! Food going to
waste! The world was a hideous place of frustration!

Temporarily his belly was full. He started back up the
crag, and presently found the camp, where the four other
Relicts waited—two ancient males, two females. The females,
Gisa and Reak, like Finn, had been out foraging. Gisa had
brought in a slab of lichen; Reak a bit of nameless carrion.

The old men, Boad and Tagart, sat quietly waiting either
for food or for death.

The women greeted Finn sullenly. "Where is the food
you went forth to find?"

"I had a whole carcass," said Finn. "I could not carry it."

Boad had slyly stolen the slab of lichen and was cram-
ming it into his mouth. It had come alive; it quivered and
exuded a red ichor which was poison, and the old man died.

"Now there is food," said Finn. "Let us eat."

But the poison created a putrescence; the body seethed with blue foam, flowed away of its own energy.

The women turned to look at the other old man, who said in a quavering voice, "Eat me if you must—but why not choose Reak, who is younger than I?"

Reak, the younger of the women, gnawing on the bit of carrion, made no reply.

Finn said hollowly, "Why do we worry ourselves? Food is ever more difficult, and we are the last of all men."

"No, no," spoke Reak, "not the last. We saw others on the green mound."

"That is long ago," said Gisa. "Now they are surely dead."

"Perhaps they have found a source of food," suggested Reak.

Finn rose to his feet, looked across the plain. "Who knows? Perhaps there is a more pleasant land beyond the horizon."

"There is nothing anywhere but waste and evil creatures," snapped Gisa.

"What could be worse than here?" Finn argued.

No one could find grounds for disagreement.

"Here is what I propose," said Finn. "Notice this tall peak. Notice the layers of hard air. They bump into the peak; they bounce off; they float in and out and disappear past the edge of sight. Let us all climb this peak, and when a sufficiently large bank of air passes, we will throw ourselves on top, and allow it to carry us to the beautiful regions which may exist just out of sight."

There was an argument. The old man Tagart protested his feebleness; the women derided the possibility of the bountiful regions Finn envisioned, but presently, grumbling and arguing, they began to clamber up the pinnacle.

It took a long time; the obsidian was soft as jelly; Tagart several times professed himself at the limit of his endurance. But still they climbed, and at last reached the pinnacle. There was barely room to stand. They could see in all directions, fa out over the landscape, till vision was lost in the watery gray.

The women bickered and pointed in various directions; but there was small sign of happier territory. In one direction blue-green hills shivered like bladders full of oil. In another direction lay a streak of black—a gorge or a lake of clay. In another direction were blue-green hills—the same they had seen in the first direction; somehow there had been a shift. Below was the plain, gleaming like an iridescent beetle, here and there pocked with black velvet spots, overgrown with questionable vegetation.

They saw Organisms, a dozen shapes loitering by ponds, munching vegetable pods or small rocks or insects. There came Alpha. He moved slowly, still awed by his vision, ignoring the other Organisms. Their play went on, but presently they stood quiet, sharing the oppression.

On the obsidian peak, Finn caught hold of a passing filament of air, drew it in. "Now—all on, and we sail away to the Land of Plenty."

"No," protested Gisa, "there is no room, and who knows if it will fly in the right direction?"

"Where is the right direction?" asked Finn. "Does anyone know?"

No one knew, but the women still refused to climb aboard the filament. Finn turned to Tagart. "Here, old one, show these women how it is; climb on!"

"No, no," he cried. "I fear the air; this is not for me."

"Climb on, old man, then we follow."

Wheezing and fearful, clenching his hands deep into the spongy mass, Tagart put himself out on the air, spindly shanks hanging over into nothing. "Now," spoke Finn, "who next?"

The women still refused. "You go then, yourself," cried Gisa.

"And leave you, my last guarantee against hunger? Aboard now!"

"No. The air is too small; let the old one go and we will follow on a larger."

"Very well." Finn released his grip. The air floated off over the plain, Tagart straddling and clutching for dear life.

They watched him curiously. "Observe," said Finn, "how fast and easily moves the air. Above the Organisms, over all the slime and uncertainty."

But the air itself was uncertain, and the old man's raft dissolved. Clutching at the departing wisps, Tagart sought to hold his cushion together. It fled from under him, and he fell.

On the peak the three watched the spindly shape flap and twist on its way to earth far below.

"Now," Reak exclaimed vexatiously, "we even have no more meat."

"None," said Gisa, "except the visionary Finn himself."

They surveyed Finn. Together they would more than out-match him.

"Careful," cried Finn. "I am the last of the Men. You are my women, subject to my orders."

They ignored him, muttering to each other, looking at him from the side of their faces. "Careful!" cried Finn. "I will throw you both from this peak."

"That is what we plan for you," said Gisa.

They advanced with sinister caution.

"Stop! I am the last man!"

"We are better off without you."

"One moment! Look at the Organisms!"

The women looked. The Organisms stood in a knot, staring at the sky.

"Look at the sky!"

The women looked; the frosted glass was cracking, breaking curling aside.

"The blue! The blue sky of old times!"

A terribly bright light burnt down, seared their eyes. The rays warmed their naked backs.

"The sun," they said in awed voices. "The sun has come back to Earth."

The shrouded sky was gone; the sun rode proud and bright

in a sea of blue. The ground below churned, cracked, heaved, solidified. They felt the obsidian harden under their feet; its color shifted to glossy black. The Earth, the sun, the galaxy, had departed the region of freedom; the other time with its restrictions and logic was once more with them.

"This is Old Earth," cried Finn. "We are Men of Old Earth! The land is once again ours!"

"And what of the Organisms?"

"If this is the Earth of old, then let the Organisms beware!"

The Organisms stood on a low rise of ground beside a runnel of water that was rapidly becoming a river flowing out onto the plain.

Alpha cried, "Here is my intuition! It is exactly as I knew. The freedom is gone; the tightness, the constriction are back!"

"How will we defeat it?" asked another Organism.

"Easily," said a third. "Each must fight a part of the battle. I plan to hurl myself at the sun, and blot it from existence." And he crouched, threw himself into the air. He fell on his back and broke his neck.

"The fault," said Alpha, "is in the air; because the air surrounds all things."

Six Organisms ran off in search of air, and stumbling into the river, drowned.

"In any event," said Alpha, "I am hungry." He looked around for suitable food. He seized an insect which stung him. He dropped it. "My hunger remains."

He spied Finn and the two women descending from the crag. "I will eat one of the Relicts," he said. "Come, let us all eat."

Three of them started off—as usual in random directions. By chance Alpha came face to face with Finn. He prepared to eat, but Finn picked up a rock. The rock remained a rock, hard, sharp, heavy. Finn swung it down, taking joy in the inertia. Alpha died with a crushed skull. One of the other

Organisms attempted to step across a crevasse twenty feet wide and so disappeared; the other sat down, swallowed rocks to assuage his hunger, and presently went into convulsions.

Finn pointed here and there around the fresh new land. "In that quarter, the new city, like that of the legends. Over here the farms, the cattle."

"We have none of these," protested Gisa.

"No," said Finn. "Not now. But once more the sun rises and sets; once more rock has weight and air has none. Once more water falls as rain and flows to the sea." He stepped forward over the fallen Organism. "Let us make plans."

The Narrow Land

PAIR OF NERVES joined across the top of Ern's brain; he became conscious, aware of darkness and constriction. The sensation was uncomfortable. He tensed his members, thrust at the shell, meeting resistance in all directions except one. He kicked, butted and presently created a rupture. The constriction eased somewhat. Ern squirmed around, clawed at the membrane, tore it back and was met by a sudden unpleasant exudation: the juices of a being not himself. It wrenched around, reached forth. Ern recoiled, struck back the probing members, which seemed ominously strong and massive.

There was a period of passivity. Each found the other hateful: they were of the same sort, yet different. Presently the two small creatures fought, with little near-inaudible squeaks and chitters.

Ern eventually strangled his opponent. When he tried to detach himself, he found that an adhesion of tissue had occurred, that the two were now one. Ern expanded himself, surrounded and fused with the defeated individual.

For a further period Ern rested, exploring his consciousness. The constriction once again became oppressive. Ern thrust and kicked, creating a new rupture, and the shell split wide.

Ern struggled forth into soft slime, then up into a glare of light, an acrid dry void. From above came a harsh cry. An enormous shape hurled down. Ern dodged, evaded a pair of clicking black prongs. He flapped, paddled, slid down into cool water, where he submerged himself.

Others inhabited the water; Ern saw their dim shapes to all sides. Some were like himself: pale pop-eyed sprats, narrow-skulled with wisps of film for crests. Others were larger, with the legs and arms definitely articulated, the crests stiffer, the skin tough and silver-gray. Ern bestirred himself, tested his arms and legs. He swam, carefully at first, then with competence. Hunger came; he ate: larvae, nodules on the roots of reeds, trifles of this and that.

So Ern entered his childhood, and gradually became wise in the ways of the waterworld. Duration could not be measured; there was no basis for time: no alteration of light and darkness, no change except for Ern's own growth. The only notable events of the sea-shallows were the tragedies. A water-baby frolicking too far, recklessly, offshore might be caught in a current and swept out under the storm-curtain. The armored birds from time to time carried away a very young baby basking at the surface. Most dreadful of all was the ogre who lived in one of the sea-sloughs: a brutish creature with long arms, a flat face and four bony ridges over the top of its skull. On one occasion Ern almost became its victim. Skulking under the roots of the swamp-reeds, the ogre lunged forth; Ern felt the swirl of water and darted away, the ogre's grasp so near that the claws scraped his leg. The ogre pursued, making idiotic sounds, then jerking aside seized one of Ern's playfellows, and settled to the bottom to munch upon its captive.

After Ern grew large enough to defy the predator birds, he spent much time on the surface, tasting the air and marveling at the largeness of the vistas, though he understood nothing of what he saw. The sky was a dull gray fog, somewhat brighter out over the sea, never changing except for an occasional wind-whipped cloud or a trail of rain. Close at hand was the swamp: sloughs, low-lying islands overgrown with pallid reeds, complicated black shrubs of the utmost fragility, a few spindly dendrons. Beyond hung a wall of black murk. On the seaward side the horizon was obscured by a lightning-shattered wall of cloud and rain. The wall of murk and the wall of storm ran parallel, delineating the borders of the region between.

The larger of the water-children tended to congregate at the surface. There were two sorts. The typical individual was slender and lithe, with a narrow bony skull, a single crest, protuberant eyes. His temperament was mercurial; he tended to undignified wrangling and sudden brisk fights which were over almost as soon as they started. The sex differences were definite: some were male, half as many were female.

In contrast, and much in the minority, were the twin-crested water-children. These were more massive, with broader skulls, less prominent eyes and a more sedate disposition. Their sexual differentiation was not obvious, and they regarded the antics of the single-crested children with disapproval.

Ern identified himself with this latter group though his crest development was not yet definite, and, if anything, he was even broader and more stocky than the others. Sexually he was slow in developing, but he seemed definitely masculine.

The oldest of the children, single- and double-crested alike, knew a few elements of speech, passed down the classes from a time and source unknown. In due course Ern learned the language, and thereafter idled away long periods discussing the events of the sea-shallows. The wall of storm with its incessant dazzle of lightning was continually fascinating, but the children gave most of their attention to the swamp and rising ground beyond, where, by virtue of tradition transmitted along with the language, they knew their destiny lay, among the 'men'.

Occasionally the 'men' would be seen probing the shore mud for flatfish, or moving among the reeds on mysterious errands. At such times the water-children, impelled by some

unknown emotion, would instantly submerge themselves, all
except the most daring of the single-crested who would float
with only their eyes above water, to watch the men at their
fascinating activities.

Each appearance of the men stimulated discussion among
the water-children. The single-crested maintained that all
would become men and walk the dry land, which they declared to be a condition of bliss. The double-crested, more
skeptical, agreed that the children might go ashore—after all,
this was the tradition—but what next? Tradition offered no
information on this score, and the discussions remained
speculative.

At long last Ern saw men close at hand. Searching the
bottom for crustaceans, he heard a strong rhythmic splashing,
and looking up saw three large long figures: magnificent
creatures! They swam with power and grace; even the ogre
might avoid such as these! Ern followed at a discreet distance
wondering if he dared approach and make himself known. It
would be pleasant, he thought, to talk with these men, to
learn about life on the shore . . . The men paused to inspect a
school of playing children, pointing here and there, while the
children halted their play to stare up in wonder. Now occurred
a shocking incident. The largest of the double-crested water-
children was Zim the Name-giver, a creature, by Ern's reckon-
ing, old and wise. It was Zim's prerogative to ordain names
for his fellows: Ern had received his name from Zim. It now
chanced that Zim, unaware of the men, wandered into view.
The men pointed, uttered sharp guttural cries and plunged
below the surface. Zim, startled into immobility, hesitated an
instant, then darted away. The men pursued, harrying him
this way and that, apparently intent on his capture. Zim, wild
with fear, swam far offshore, out over the gulf, where the
current took him and carried him away, out toward the curtain of storm.

The men, exclaiming in anger, plunged landward in foaming strokes of arms and legs.

In fascinated curiosity Ern followed: up a large slough, finally to a beach of packed mud. The men waded ashore, strode off among the reeds. Ern drifted slowly forward, beset by quivering conflict of impulses. How, he wondered, could beings so magnificent hound Zim the Name-giver to his doom? The land was close; the footprints of the men were plain on the mud of the beach; where did they lead? What wonderful new vistas lay beyond the line of reeds? Ern eased forward to the beach. He lowered his feet and tried to walk. His legs felt limp and flexible; only by dint of great concentration was he able to set one foot before the other. Deprived of the support of the water his body felt gross and clumsy. From the reeds came a screech of amazement. Ern's legs, suddenly capable, carried him in wobbling leaps down the beach. He plunged into the water, swam frantically back along the slough. Behind him came men, churning the water. Ern ducked aside, hid behind a clump of rotting reeds. The men continued down the slough, out over the shallows where they spent a fruitless period ranging back and forth.

Ern remained in his cover. The men returned, passing no more than the length of their bodies from Ern's hiding place, so close that he could see their glittering eyes and the dark yellow interior of their oral cavities when they gasped for air. With their spare frames, prow-shaped skulls and single crests they resembled neither Ern nor Zim, but rather the single-crested water-children. These were not his sort! He was not a man! Perplexed, seething with excitement and dissatisfaction, Ern returned to the shallows.

But nothing was as before. The innocence of the easy old life had departed; there was now a portent in the air which soured the pleasant old routines. Ern found it hard to wrench his attention away from the shore and he considered the single-crested children, his erstwhile playmates, with new wariness: they suddenly seemed strange, different from himself, and they in turn watched the double-crested children with distrust, swimming away in startled shoals when Ern or one of the others came by.

Ern became morose and dour. The old satisfactions were gone; there were no compensations. Twice again the men swam out across the shallows, but all the double-crested children, Ern among them, hid under reeds. The men thereupon appeared to lose interest, and for a period life went on more or less as before. But change was in the wind. The shoreline became a preoccupation: what lay behind the reed islands, between the reed islands and the wall of murk? Where did the men live, in what wonderful surroundings? With the most extreme vigilance against the ogre Ern swam up the largest of the sloughs. To either side were islands overgrown with pale reeds, with an occasional black skeleton-tree or a globe of tangle-bush: stuff so fragile as to collapse at a touch. The slough branched, opening into still coves reflecting the gray gloom of the sky, and at last narrowed, dwindling to a channel of black slime.

Ern dared proceed no farther. If someone or something had followed him, he was trapped. And at this moment a strange yellow creature halted overhead to hover on a thousand tinkling scales. Spying Ern it set up a wild ululation. Off in the distance Ern thought to hear a call of harsh voices: men. He swung around and swam back the way he had come, with the tinkle-bird careening above. Ern ducked under the surface, swam down the slough at full speed. Presently he went to the side, cautiously surfaced. The yellow bird swung in erratic circles over the point where he had submerged, its quavering howl now diminished to a mournful hooting sound.

Ern gratefully returned to the shallows. It was now clear to him that if ever he wished to go ashore he must learn to walk. To the perplexity of his fellows, even those of the double-crests, he began to clamber up through the mud of the near island, exercising his legs among the reeds. All went passably well, and Ern presently found himself walking without effort though as yet he dared not try the land behind the islands. Instead he swam along the coast, the storm-wall on his right hand, the shore on his left. On and on he went, further than he had ever ventured before.

The storm-wall was changeless, a roll of rain and a thick vapor lanced with lightning. The wall of murk was the same: dense black at the horizon, lightening by imperceptible gradations to become the normal gray gloom of the sky overhead. The narrow land extended endlessly onward. Ern saw new swamps, reed islands; shelves of muddy foreshore, a spit of sharp rocks. At length the shore curved away, retreated toward the wall of murk, to form a funnel shaped bay, into which poured a freezingly cold river. Ern swam to the shore, crawled up on the shingle, stood swaying on his still uncertain legs. Far across the bay new swamps and islands continued to the verge of vision and beyond. There was no living creature in sight. Ern stood alone on the gravel bar, a small gray figure, swaying on still limber legs, peering earnestly this way and that. The river curved away and out of sight into the darkness. The water of the estuary was bitterly cold, the current ran swift; Ern decided to go no farther. He slipped into the sea and returned the way he had come.

Back in the familiar shallows he took up his old routine: searching the bottom for crustaceans, taunting the ogre, floating on the surface with a wary eye for men, testing his legs on the island. During one of the visits ashore he came upon a most unusual sight: a woman depositing eggs in the mud. From behind a curtain of reeds Ern watched in fascination. The woman was not quite so large as the men and lacked the harsh male facial structure, though her cranial ridge was no less prominent. She wore a shawl of a dark red woven stuff: the first garment Ern had ever seen, and he marveled at the urbanity of the men's way of life.

The woman was busy for some time. When she departed, Ern went to examine the eggs. They had been carefully protected from armored birds by a layer of mud and a neat little

tent of plaited reeds. The nest contained three clutches, each
a row of three eggs, each egg carefully separated from the
next by a wad of mud.

So here, thought Ern, was the origin of the water-babies.
He recalled the circumstances of his own birth; evidently he
had emerged from just such an egg. Rearranging mud and
tent, Ern left the eggs as he had found them and returned to
the water.

Time passed. The men came no more. Ern wondered that
they should abandon an occupation in which they had showed
so vigorous an interest; but then the whole matter exceeded
the limits of his understanding.

He became prey to restlessness once again. In this regard
he seemed unique: none of his fellows had ever wandered
beyond the shallows. Ern set off along the shore, this time
swimming with the storm-wall to his left. He crossed the
slough in which lived the ogre, who glared up as Ern passed
and made a threatening gesture. Ern swam hastily on, though
now he was of a size larger than that which the ogre preferred
to attack.

The shore on this side of the shallows was more interesting and varied than that on the other. He came upon three
high islands crowned with a varied vegetation—black skeleton
trees; stalks with bundles of pink and white foliage clenched
in black fingers; glossy lamellar pillars, the topmost scales
billowing out into gray leaves—then the islands were no more,
and the mainland rose directly from the sea. Ern swam close
to the beach to avoid the currents, and presently came to a
spit of shingle pushing out into the sea. He climbed ashore
and surveyed the landscape. The ground was slanted up under
a cover of umbrella trees, then rose sharply to become a
rocky bluff crested with black and gray vegetation: the most
notable sight of Ern's experience.

Ern slid back into the sea, swam on. The landscape slack-
ened, became flat and swampy. He swam past a bank of black
slime overgrown with squirming yellow-green fibrils, which

he took care to avoid. Some time later he heard a thrashing hissing sound and looking to sea observed an enormous white worm sliding through the water. Ern floated quietly and the worm slid on past and away. Ern continued. On and on he swam until, as before, the shore was broken by an estuary leading away into the murk. Wading up the beach, Ern looked far and wide across a dismal landscape supporting only tatters of brown lichen. The river which flooded the estuary seemed even larger and swifter than the one he had seen previously, and carried an occasional chunk of ice. A bitter wind blew toward the storm-wall, creating a field of retreating white-caps. The opposite shore, barely visible, showed no relief or contrast. There was no apparent termination to the narrow land; it appeared to reach forever between the walls of storm and gloom.

Ern returned to the shallows, not wholly satisfied with what he had learned. He had seen marvels unknown to his fellows, but what had they taught him? Nothing. His questions remained unanswered.

Changes were taking place; they could not be ignored. The whole of Ern's class lived at the surface, breathing air. Infected by some pale dilution of Ern's curiosity, they stared uneasily landward. Sexual differentiation was evident; there were tendencies toward sexual play, from which the double-crested children, with undeveloped organs, stood contemptuously aloof. Social as well as physical distinctions developed; there began to be an interchange of taunts and derogation, occasionally a brief skirmish. Ern ranged himself with the double-crested children, although on exploring his own scalp, he found only indecisive hummocks and hollows, which to some extent embarrassed him.

In spite of the general sense of imminence, the coming of the men took the children by surprise.

In the number of two hundred the men came down the sloughs and swam out to surround the shallows. Ern and a few others instantly clambered up among the reeds of the

island and concealed themselves. The other children milled
and swam in excited circles. The men shouted, slapped the
water with their arms; diving and veering they herded the
water-children up the slough, all the way to the beach of
dried mud. Here they chose and sorted, sending the largest up
the beach, allowing the fingerlings and sprats to return to the
shallows, taking the double-crested children with sharp cries
of exultation.

The selection was complete. The captive children were
marshaled into groups and sent staggering up the trail; those
with legs still soft were carried.

Ern, fascinated by the process, watched from a discreet
distance. When men and children had disappeared, he emerged
from the water, clambered up the beach to look after his
departed friends. What to do now? Return to the shallows?
The old life seemed drab and insipid. He dared not present
himself to the men. They were single-crested; they were
harsh and abrupt. What remained? He looked back and forth,
between water and land, and at last gave his youth a melancholy farewell: henceforth he would live ashore.

He walked a few steps up the path, stopped to listen.

Silence.

He proceeded warily, prepared to duck into the undergrowth at a sound. The soil underfoot became less sodden;
the reeds disappeared and aromatic black cycads lined the
path. Above rose slender supple withes, with gas-filled leaves
half-floating, half-supported. Ern moved ever more cautiously,
pausing to listen ever more frequently. What if he met the
men? Would they kill him? Ern hesitated and even looked
back along the path . . . The decision had been made. He continued forward.

A sound, from somewhere not too far ahead. Ern dodged
off the path, flattened himself behind a hummock.

No one appeared. Ern moved forward through the cycads,
and presently, through the black fronds, he saw the village of
the men: a marvel of ingenuity and complication! Nearby

stood tall bins containing food-stuffs, then, at a little distance, a row of thatched stalls stacked with poles, coils of rope, pots of pigment and grease. Yellow tinkle-birds, perched on the gables, made a constant chuckling clamor. The bins and stalls faced an open space surrounding a large platform, where a ceremony of obvious import was in progress. On the platform stood four men, draped in bands of woven leaves, and four women wearing dark red shawls and tall hats decorated with tinkle-bird scales. Beside the platform, in a miserable gray clot, huddled the single-crested children, the individuals distinguishable only by an occasional gleam of eye or twitch of pointed crest.

One by one the children were lifted up to the four men, who gave each a careful examination. Most of the male children were dismissed and sent down into the crowd. The rejects, about one in every ten, were killed by the blow of a stone mallet and propped up to face the wall of storm. The girl-children were sent to the other end of the platform, where the four women waited. Each of the trembling girl-children was considered in turn. About half were discharged from the platform into the custody of a woman and taken to a booth; about one in every five was daubed along the skull with white paint and sent to a nearby pen where the double-crested children were also confined. The rest suffered a blow of the mallet. The corpses were propped to face the wall of murk . . .

Above Ern's head sounded the mindless howl of a tinkle-bird. Ern darted back into the brush. The bird drifted overhead on clashing scales. Men ran to either side, chased Ern back and forth, and finally captured him. He was dragged to the village, thrust triumphantly up on the platform, amid calls of surprise and excitement. The four priests, or whatever their function, surrounded Ern to make their examination. There was a new set of startled outcries. The priests stood back in perplexity, then after a mumble of discussion signaled to the priest-women. The mallet was brought forward—but

was never raised. A man from the crowd jumped up on the
platform, to argue with the priests. They made a second careful study of Ern's head, muttering to each other. Then one
brought a knife, another clamped Ern's head. The knife was
drawn the length of his cranium, first to the left of the central
ridge, then to the right, to produce a pair of near-parallel
cuts. Orange blood trickled down Ern's face; pain made him
tense and stiff. A woman brought forward a handful of some
vile substance which she rubbed into the wounds. Then all
stood away, murmuring and speculating. Ern glared back,
half-mad with fear and pain.

He was led to a booth, thrust within. Bars were dropped
across the aperture and laced with thongs.

Ern watched the remainder of the ceremony. The corpses
were dismembered, boiled and eaten. The white-daubed girl-
children were marshaled into a group with all those double-
crested children with whom Ern had previously identified
himself. Why, he wondered, had he not been included in this
group? Why had he first been threatened with the mallet, then
wounded with a knife? The situation was incomprehensible.

The girls and the two-crested children were marched
away through the brush. The other girls with no more ado
became members of the community. The male children
underwent a much more formal instruction. Each man took
one of the boys under his sponsorship, and subjected him to
a rigorous discipline. There were lessons in deportment, knot-
tying, weaponry, language, dancing, the various outcries.

Ern received minimal attention. He was fed irregularly, as
occasion seemed to warrant. The period of his confinement
could not be defined, the changeless gray sky providing no
chronometric reference; and indeed, the concept of time as a
succession of definite interims was foreign to Ern's mind. He
escaped apathy only by attending the instruction in adjoining
booths, where single-crested boys were taught language and
deportment. Ern learned the language long before those under
instruction; he and his double-crested fellows had used the

rudiments of this language in the long-gone halcyon past.

The twin wounds along Ern's skull eventually healed, leaving parallel weals of scar-tissue. The black feathery combs of maturity were likewise sprouting, covering his entire scalp with down.

None of his erstwhile comrades paid him any heed. They had become indoctrinated in the habits of the village; the old life of the shallows had receded in their memories. Watching them stride past his prison Ern found them increasingly apart from himself. They were lithe, slender, agile, like tall keen-featured lizards. He was heavier, with blunter features, a broader head; his skin was tougher and thicker, a darker gray. He was now almost as large as the men, though by no means so sinewy and quick: when need arose, they moved with mercurial rapidity.

Once or twice Ern, in a fury, attempted to break the bars of his booth, only to be prodded with a pole for his trouble, and he therefore desisted from this unprofitable exercise. He became fretful and bored. The booths to either side were now used only for copulation, an activity which Ern observed with dispassionate interest.

The booth at last was opened. Ern rushed forth, hoping to surprise his captors and win free, but one man seized him, another looped a rope around his body. Without ceremony he was led from the village.

The men offered no hint of their intentions. Jogging along at a half-trot, they took Ern through the black brush in that direction known as 'sea-left': which was to say, with the sea on the left hand. The trail veered inland, rising over bare hummocks, dropping into dank swales brimming with rank black dendrons.

Ahead loomed a great copse of umbrella trees, impressively tall, each stalk as thick as the body of a man, each billowing leaf large enough to envelop a half-dozen booths like that in which Ern had been imprisoned.

Someone had been at work. A number of the trees had

been cut, the poles trimmed and neatly stacked, the leaves cut
into rectangular sheets and draped over ropes. The racks
supporting the poles had been built with meticulous accuracy,
and Ern wondered who had done such precise work: certainly not the men of the village, whose construction even Ern
found haphazard.

A path led away through the forest: a path straight as a
string, of constant width, delineated by parallel lines of white
stones: a technical achievement far beyond the capacity of
the men, thought Ern.

The men now became furtive and uneasy. Ern tried to
hang back, certain that whatever the men had in mind was
not to his advantage, but willy-nilly he was jerked forward.

The path made an abrupt turn, marched up a swale
between copses of black-brown cycads, turned out upon a
field of soft white moss, at the center of which stood a large
and splendid village. The men, pausing in the shadows, made
contemptuous sounds, performed insulting acts—provoked,
so Ern suspected, by envy, for the village across the meadow
surpassed that of his captors as much as that village excelled
the environment of the shallows. There were eight precisely
spaced rows of huts, built of sawed planks, decorated or
given symbolic import by elaborate designs of blue, maroon
and black. At the sea-right and sea-left ends of the central
avenue stood larger constructions with high-peaked roofs,
shingled, like all the others, with slabs of biotite. Notably
absent were disorder and refuse; this village, unlike the village
of the single-crested men, was fastidiously neat. Behind the
village rose the great bluff Ern had noticed on his exploration
of the coast.

At the edge of the meadow stood a row of six stakes, and
to the first of these the men tied Ern.

"This is the village of the 'Twos'," declared one of the
men. "Folk such as yourself. Do not mention that we cut
your scalp or affairs will go badly."

They moved back, taking cover under a bank of worm

plants. Ern strained at his bonds, convinced that no matter
what the eventuality, it could not be to his benefit.

The villagers had taken note of Ern. Ten persons set forth
across the meadow. In front came four splendid 'Twos', stepping carefully, with an exaggerated strutting gait, followed by
six young One-girls, astoundingly urbane in gowns of wadded
umbrella leaf. The girls had been disciplined; they no longer
used their ordinary sinuous motion but walked in a studied
simulation of the Two attitudes. Ern stared in fascination.
The 'Twos' appeared to be of his own sort, sturdier and heavier than the cleaver-headed 'Ones.'

The pair in the van apparently shared equal authority.
They comported themselves with canonical dignity, and their
garments—fringed shawls of black, brown and purple, boots
of gray membrane with metal clips, metal filigree greaves—
were formalized and elaborate. He on the stormward side
wore a crest of glittering metal barbs; he on the darkward
side a double row of tall black plumes. The Twos at their
back seemed of somewhat lesser prestige. They wore caps of
complicated folds and tucks and carried halberds three times
their own length. At the rear walked the One-girls, carrying
parcels. Ern saw them to be members of his own class, part of
the group which had been led away after the selection ritual.
Their skin had been stained dark red and yellow; they wore
dull yellow caps, yellow shawls, yellow sandals, and walked
with the mincing delicate rigidity in which they had been
schooled.

The foremost Twos, halting at either side of Ern, examined him with portentous gravity. The halberdiers fixed him
with a minatory stare. The girls posed in self-conscious attitudes. The Twos squinted in puzzlement at the double ridges
of scar tissue along his scalp. They arrived at a dubious consensus: "He appears sound, if somewhat gross of body and
oddly ridged."

One of the halberdiers, propping his weapon against a
stake, unbound Ern, who stood tentatively half of a mind to

take to his heels. The Two wearing the crest of metal barbs inquired:

"Do you speak?"

"Yes."

"You must say 'Yes, Preceptor of the Storm Dazzle'; such is the form."

Ern found the admonition puzzling, but no more so than the other attributes of the Twos. His best interests, so he decided, lay in cautious cooperation. The Twos, while arbitrary and capricious, apparently did not intend him harm. The girls arranged the parcels beside the stake: payment, so it seemed, to the One-men.

"Come then," commanded he of the black plumes. "Watch your feet, walk correctly! Do not swing your arms; you are a Two, an important individual; you must act appropriately, according to the Way."

"Yes, Preceptor of the Storm Dazzle."

"You will address me as 'Preceptor of the Dark Chill'!"

Confused and apprehensive, Ern was marched across the meadow of pale moss. The trail, demarcated now by lines of black stones, bestrewn with black gravel, and glistening in the damp, exactly bisected the meadow, which was lined to either side by tall black-brown fan-trees. First walked the preceptors, then Ern, then the halberdiers and finally the six One-girls.

The trail connected with the central avenue of the village, which opened at the center into a square plaza paved with squares of wood. To the darkward side of the plaza stood a tall black tower supporting a set of peculiar black objects; on the stormward side an identical white tower presented lightning symbols. Across and set back in a widening of the avenue was a long two-story hall, to which Ern was conducted and lodged in a cubicle.

A third pair of Twos, a rank higher than the halberdiers but lower than the Preceptors—the 'Pedagogue of the Storm Dazzle' and the 'Pedagogue of the Dark Chill'—took Ern in charge. He was washed, anointed with oil, and again the weals along his scalp received a puzzled inspection. Ern began to suspect that the Ones had used duplicity; that, in order to sell him to the Twos, they had simulated double ridges across his scalp; and that, after all, he was merely a peculiar variety of One. It was indeed a fact that his sexual parts resembled those of the One men rather than the epicene, or perhaps atrophied, organs of the Twos. The suspicion made him more uneasy than ever, and he was relieved when the pedagogues brought him a cap, half of silver scales, half of glossy black bird-fiber, which covered his scalp, and a shawl hanging across his chest and belted at the waist, which concealed his sex organs.

As with every other aspect and activity of the Two-village there were niceties of usage in regard to the cap. "The Way requires that in low-ceremonial activity, you must stand with black toward Night and silver toward Chaos. If a ritual or other urgency impedes, reverse your cap."

This was the simplest and least complicated of the decorums to be observed.

The Pedagogues found much to criticize in Ern's deportment.

"You are somewhat more crude and gross than the usual cadet," remarked the Pedagogue of Storm-Dazzle. "The injury to your head has affected your condition."

"You will be carefully schooled," the Pedagogue of Dark-Chill told him. "As of this moment consider yourself a mental void."

A dozen other young Twos, including four from Ern's class, were undergoing tutelage. As instruction was on an individual basis, Ern saw little of them. He studied diligently and assimilated knowledge with a facility which won him grudging compliments. When he seemed proficient in primary methods, he was introduced to cosmology and religion. "We inhabit the Narrow Land," declared the Pedagogue of Storm-Dazzle. "It extends forever! How can we assert this with such confidence? Because we know that the opposing principles of Storm and Dark Chill, being divine, are infinite. Therefore, the Narrow Land, the region of confrontation, likewise is infinite."

Ern ventured a question. "What exists behind the wall of storm?"

"There is no 'behind.' STORM-CHAOS *is*, and dazzles the dark with his lightnings. This is the masculine principle. DARK-CHILL, the female principle, *is*. She accepts the rage and fire and quells it. We Twos partake of each, we are at equilibrium, and hence excellent."

Ern broached a perplexing topic: "The Two-women do not produce eggs?"

"There are neither Two-women nor Two-men! We are brought into being by dual-divine intervention, when a pair of eggs in a One-woman's clutch are put down in juxtaposition. Through alternation, these are always male and female and so yield a double individual, neutral and dispassionate, symbolized by the paired cranial ridges. One-men and One-women are incomplete, forever driven by the urge to couple; only fusion yields the true Two."

It was evident to Ern that questioning disturbed the Pedagogues, so he desisted from further interrogation, not wishing to call attention to his unusual attributes. During instruction he had sensibly increased in size. The combs of maturity were growing up over his scalp; his sexual organs had developed noticeably. Both, luckily, were concealed, by cap and shawl. In some fashion he was different from other Twos, and the Pedagogues, should they discover this fact, would feel dismay and confusion, at the very least.

Other matters troubled Ern: namely the impulses aroused within himself by the slave One-girls. Such tendencies were defined to be ignoble! This was no way for a Two to act! The Pedagogues would be horrified to learn of his leanings. But if he were not a Two—what was he?

Ern tried to quell his hot blood by extreme diligence. He

began to study the Two technology, which like every other aspect of Two society was rationalized in terms of formal dogma. He learned the methods of collecting bog iron, of smelting, casting, forging, hardening and tempering. Occasionally he wondered how the skills had first been evolved, inasmuch as empiricism, as a mode of thought, was antithetical to the Dual Way.

Ern thoughtlessly touched upon the subject during a recitation. Both Pedagogues were present. The Pedagogue of Storm-Dazzle replied, somewhat tartly, that all knowledge was a dispensation of the two Basic Principles.

"In any event," stated the Pedagogue of Dark-Chill, "the matter is irrelevant. What is, *is*, and by this token is optimum."

"Indeed," remarked the Pedagogue of Storm-Dazzle, "the very fact that you have formed this inquiry betrays a disorganized mind, more typical of a 'Freak' than a Two."

"What is a 'Freak'?" asked Ern.

The Pedagogue of Dark-Chill made a stern gesture. "Once again your mentality tends to random association and discontent with authority!"

"Respectfully, Pedagogue of Dark-Chill, I wish only to learn the nature of 'wrong', so that I may know its distinction from 'right'."

"It suffices that you imbue yourself with 'right', with no reference whatever to 'wrong'!"

With this viewpoint Ern was forced to be content. The Pedagogues, leaving the chamber, glanced back at him. Ern heard a fragment of their muttered conversation. "—surprising perversity—" "—but for the evidence of the cranial ridges—"

In perturbation Ern walked back and forth across his cubicle. He was different from the other cadets: so much was clear.

At the refectory, where the cadets were brought nutriment by One-girls, Ern covertly scrutinized his fellows. While only little less massive than himself, they seemed differently proportioned, almost cylindrical, with features and protrusions less prominent. If he were different, what kind of person was he? A 'Freak'? What was a 'Freak'? A masculine Two? Ern was inclined to credit this theory, for it explained his interest in the One-girls, and he turned to watch them gliding back and forth with trays. In spite of their One-ness, they were undeniably appealing . . .

Thoughtfully Ern returned to his cubicle. In due course a One-girl came past. Ern summoned her into the cubicle and made his wishes known. She showed surprise and uneasiness, though no great disinclination. "You are supposed to be neutral; what will everyone think?"

"Nothing whatever, if they are unaware of the situation."

"True. But is the matter feasible? I am One and you are a Two—"

"The matter may or may not be feasible; how will the truth be known unless it is attempted, orthodoxy not withstanding?"

"Well, then, as you will . . ."

A monitor looked into the cubicle, to stare dumbfounded. "What goes on here?" He looked more closely, then tumbled backward into the compound to shout: "A Freak, a Freak! Here among us, a Freak! To arms, kill the Freak!"

Ern thrust the girl outside. "Mingle with the others, deny everything: I now feel that I must leave." He ran out upon the central avenue, looked up and down. The halberdiers, informed of emergency, were arraying themselves in formally appropriate gear. Ern took advantage of the delay to run from the village. In pursuit came the Twos, calling threats and ritual abuse. The sea-right path toward the pole forest and the swamp was closed to him; Ern fled sea-left, toward the great bluff. Dodging among fan trees and banks of worm-weed, finally hiding under a bank of fungus, he gained a respite while the halberdiers raced past.

Emerging from his covert, Ern stood uncertainly, wondering which way to go. Freak or not, the Twos had exhibited what seemed an irrational antagonism. Why had they attacked him? He had performed no damage, perpetrated no willful deception. The fault lay with the Ones. In order to deceive the Twos they had scarred Ern's head—a situation for which Ern could hardly be held accountable. Bewildered and depressed, Ern started toward the shore, where at least he could find food. Crossing a peat-bog he was sighted by the halberdiers, who instantly set up the outcry: "Freak! Freak! Freak!" And again Ern was forced to run for his life, up through a forest of mingled cycads and pole-trees, toward the great bluff which now loomed ahead.

A massive stone wall barred his way: a construction obviously of great age, overgrown with black and brown lichen. Ern ran staggering and wobbling along the wall, with the halberdiers close upon him, still screaming: "Freak! Freak! Freak!"

A gap appeared in the wall. Ern jumped through to the opposite side, ducked behind a clump of feather-bush. The halberdiers stopped short in front of the gap, their cries stilled, and now they seemed to be engaged in controversy.

Ern waited despondently for discovery and death, since the bush offered scant concealment. One of the halberdiers at last ventured gingerly through the wall, only to give a startled grunt and jump back.

There were receding footsteps, then silence. Ern crawled cautiously from his hiding place, and went to peer through the gap. The Twos had departed. Peculiar, thought Ern. They must have known he was close at hand . . . He turned. Ten paces distant the largest man he had yet seen leaned on a sword, inspecting him with a brooding gaze. The man was almost twice the size of the largest Two. He wore a dull brown smock of soft leather, a pair of shining metal wristbands. His skin was a heavy rugose gray, tough as horn; at the joints of his arms and legs were bony juts, ridges and buttresses, which gave him the semblance of enormous power. His skull was broad, heavy, harshly indented and ridged; his eyes were blazing crystals in deep shrouded sockets. Along his scalp ran three serrated ridges. In addition to his sword, he carried, slung over his shoulder, a peculiar metal device with a long nozzle. He advanced a slow step. Ern swayed back, but for some reason beyond his own knowing was dissuaded from taking to his heels.

The man spoke, in a hoarse voice: "Why do they hunt you?"

Ern took courage from the fact that the man had not killed him out of hand. "They called me 'Freak' and drove me forth."

" 'Freak'?" The Three considered Ern's scalp. "You are a Two."

"The Ones cut my head to make scars, then sold me to the Twos." Ern felt the weals. On either side and at the center, almost as prominent as the scars, were the crests of an adult, three in number. They were growing apace; even had he not compromised himself, the Twos must have found him out on the first occasion he removed his cap. He said humbly: "It appears that I am a 'Freak' like yourself."

The Three made a brusque sound. "Come with me."

They walked back through the grove, to a path which slanted up the bluff, then swung to the side and entered a valley. Beside a pond rose a great stone hall flanked by two towers with steep conical roofs—in spite of age and dilapidation a structure to stagger Ern's imagination.

By a timber portal they entered a courtyard which seemed to Ern a place of unparalleled charm. At the far end boulders and a great overhanging slab created the effect of a grotto. Within were trickling water, growths of feathery black moss, pale cycads, a settle padded with woven reed and sphagnum. The open area was a swamp-garden, exhaling the odors of reed, water-soaked vegetation, resinous wood. Remarkable, thought Ern, as well as enchanting: neither the Ones nor the Twos contrived except for an immediate purpose.

The Three took Ern across the court into a stone chamber, also half-open to the refreshing drizzle, carpeted with packed sphagnum. Under the shelter of the ceiling were the appurtenances of the Three's existence: crocks and bins, a table, a cabinet, tools and implements.

The Three pointed to a bench. "Sit."

Ern gingerly obeyed.

"You are hungry?"

"No."

"How was your imposture discovered?"

Ern related the circumstances which led to his exposure. The Three showed no disapproval, which gave Ern encouragement. "I had long suspected that I was something other than a 'Two'."

"You are obviously a 'Three'," said his host. "Unlike the neuter Twos, Threes are notably masculine, which explains your inclinations for the One-woman. Unluckily there are no Three females." He looked at Ern. "They did not tell how you were born?"

"I am a fusion of One-eggs."

"True. The One-woman lays eggs of alternate sex, in clutches of three. The pattern is male-female-male; such is the nature of her organism. A sheath forms on the interior of her ovipositor; as the eggs emerge, a sphincter closes, to encapsulate the eggs. If she is careless, she will fail to separate the eggs and will put down a clutch with two eggs in contact. The male breaks into the female shell; there is fusion; a Two is hatched. At the rarest of intervals three eggs are so joined. One male fuses with the female, then, so augmented, he breaks into the final egg and assimilates the other male. The result is a male Three."

Ern recalled his first memory. "I was alone. I broke into the male-female shell. We fought at length."

The Three reflected for a lengthy period. Ern wondered if he had committed an annoyance. Finally the Three said, "I am named Mazar the Final. Now that you are here I can be known as 'the Final' no longer. I am accustomed to solitude; I have become old and severe; you may find me poor company.

If such is the case, you are free to pursue existence elsewhere. If you choose to stay, I will teach you what I know, which is perhaps pointless activity, since the Twos will presently come in a great army to kill us both."

"I'll stay," said Ern. "As of now I know only the ceremonies of the Twos, which I may never put to use. Are there no other Threes?"

"The Twos have killed all—all but Mazar the Final."

"And Ern."

"And now Ern."

"What of sea-left and sea-right, beyond the rivers, along other shores? Are there no more men?"

"Who knows? The Wall of Storm confronts the Wall of Dark; the Narrow Land extends—how far? Who knows? If to infinity then all possibilities must be realized; then there are other Ones, Twos and Threes. If the Narrow Land terminates at Chaos, then we may be alone."

"I have traveled sea-right and sea-left until wide rivers stopped me," said Ern. "The Narrow Land continued without any sign of coming to an end. I believe that it must extend to infinity; in fact, it is hard to conceive of a different situation."

"Perhaps, perhaps," said Mazar gruffly. "Come." He conducted Ern about the hall, through workshops and repositories, chambers crowded with mementoes, trophies and nameless paraphernalia.

"Who used these marvelous objects? Were there many Threes?"

"At one time there were many," intoned Mazar, in a voice as hoarse and dreary as the sound of wind. "It was so long ago that I cannot put words to the thought. I am the last."

"Why were there so many then and so few now?"

"It is a melancholy tale. A One-tribe lived along the shore, with customs different from the Ones of the swamp. They were a gentle people, and they were ruled by a Three who had been born by accident. He was Mena the Origin, and he

caused the women to produce clutches with the eggs purpose-
ly joined, so that a large number of Threes came into being.
It was a great era. We were dissatisfied with the harsh life of
the Ones, the rigid life of the Twos; we created a new existence. We learned the use of iron and steel, we built this hall
and many more; the Ones and Twos both learned from us
and profited."

"Why did they war upon you?"

"By our freedom we incurred their fear. We set out to
explore the Narrow Land. We traveled many leagues sea-left
and sea-right. An expedition penetrated the Dark-Chill to a
wilderness of ice, so dark that the explorers walked with
torches. We built a raft and sent it to drift under the Wall of
Storm. There were three Ones aboard. The raft was tethered
with a long cable; when we pulled it back the Ones had been
riven by dazzle and were dead. By these acts we infuriated
the Two preceptors. They declared us impious and marshaled
the Ones of the swamp. They massacred the Ones of the shore,
then they made war on the Threes. Ambush, poison, pitfall:
they showed no mercy. We killed Twos; there were always
more Twos, but never more Threes.

"I could tell long tales of the war, how each of my comrades met death. Of them all, I am the last. I never go beyond
the wall and the Twos are not anxious to attack me, for they
fear my fire gun. But enough for now. Go where you will,
except beyond the wall, where the Twos are dangerous. There
is food in the bins; you may rest in the moss. Reflect upon
what you see; and when you have questions, I will answer."

Mazar went his way. Ern refreshed himself in the falling
water of the grotto, ate from the bins, then walked upon the
gray meadow to consider what he had learned. Here Mazar,
becoming curious, discovered him. "Well then," asked Mazar,
"and what do you think now?"

"I understand many things which have puzzled me," said
Ern. "Also I regret leaving the One-girl, who showed a coop-
erative disposition."

"This varies according to the individual," said Mazar. "In the olden times we employed many such as domestics, though their mental capacity is not great."

"If there were Three-women, would they not produce eggs and eventually Three-children?"

Mazar made a brusque gesture. "There are no Three-women; there have never been Three-women. The process allows none to form."

"What if the process were controlled?"

"Bah. The ovulation of One-women is not susceptible to our control."

"Long ago," said Ern, "I watched a One-woman preparing her nest. She laid in clutches of three. If sufficient eggs were collected, rearranged and joined, in some cases the female principle would dominate."

"This is an unorthodox proposal," said Mazar, "and to my knowledge has never been tried. It cannot be feasible . . . Such women might not be fertile. Or they might be freaks indeed."

"We are a product of the process," Ern argued. "Because there are two male eggs to the clutch, we are masculine. If there were two female and one male, or three female, why should not the result be female? As for fertility, we have no knowledge until the matter is put to test."

"The process is unthinkable!" roared Mazar, drawing himself erect, crests extended. "I will hear no more!"

Dazed by the fury of the old Three's response, Ern stood limp. Slowly he turned and started to walk sea-right, toward the wall.

"Where are you going?" Mazar called after him.

"To the swamps."

"And what will you do there?"

"I will find eggs and try to help a Three-woman into being."

Mazar glared and Ern prepared to flee for his life. Then Mazar said, "If your scheme is sound, all my comrades are dead in vain. Existence becomes a mockery."

"Perhaps nothing will come of the notion," said Ern. "It so, nothing is different."

"The venture is dangerous," grumbled Mazar. "The Twos will be alert."

"I will go down to the shore and swim to the swamp; they will never notice me. In any case, I have no better use to which to put my life."

"Go then," said Mazar in his hoarsest voice. "I am old and without enterprise. Perhaps our race may yet be regenerated. Go then, take care and return safely. You and I are the only Threes alive."

Mazar patrolled the wall. At times he ventured out into the pole-forest, listening, peering down toward the Two village. Ern had been gone a long time, or so it seemed. At last: far-off alarms, the cry of "Freak! Freak! Freak!"

Recklessly, three crests furiously erect, Mazar plunged toward the sound. Ern appeared through the trees, haggard, streaked with mud, carrying a rush-basket. In frantic pursuit came Two halberdiers and somewhat to the side a band of painted One-men. "This way!" roared Mazar. "To the wall!" He brought forth his fire-gun. The halberdiers, in a frenzy, ignored the threat. Ern tottered past him; Mazar pointed the projector, pulled the trigger: flame enveloped four of the halberdiers, who ran thrashing and flailing through the forest. The others halted. Mazar and Ern retreated to the wall, passed through the gap. The halberdiers, excited to rashness, leapt after them. Mazar swung his sword; one of the Twos lost his head. The others retreated in panic, keening in horror at so much death.

Ern slumped upon the ground, cradling the eggs upon his body.

"How many?" demanded Mazar.

"I found two nests. I took three clutches from each."

"Each nest is separate and each clutch as well? Eggs from different nests may not fuse."

"Each is separate."

Mazar carried the corpse to the gap in the wall, flung it forth, then threw the head at the skulking One-men. None came to challenge him.

Once more in the hall Mazar arranged the eggs on a stone settle. He made a sound of satisfaction. "In each clutch are two round eggs and one oval: male and female; and we need not guess at the combinations." He reflected a moment. "Two males and a female produce the masculine Three; two females and a male should exert an equal influence in the opposite direction . . . There will necessarily be an excess of male eggs. They will yield two masculine Threes; possibly more, if three male eggs are able to fuse." He made a thoughtful sound. "It is a temptation to attempt the fusion of four eggs."

"In this case I would urge caution," suggested Ern.

Mazar drew back in surprise and displeasure. "Is your wisdom so much more profound than mine?"

Ern made a polite gesture of self-effacement, one of the graces learned at the Two school. "I was born in the shallows, among the water-babies. Our great enemy was the ogre who lived in a slough. While I searched for eggs, I saw him again. He is larger than you and I together; his limbs are gross; his head is malformed and hung over with red wattles. Upon his head stand four crests."

Mazar was silent. He said at last: "We are Threes. Best that we produce other Threes. Well then, to work."

The eggs lay in the cool mud, three paces from the water of the pond.

"Now to wait," said Mazar. "To wait and wonder."

"I will help them survive," said Ern. "I will bring them food and keep them safe. And—if they are female . . ."

"There will be two females," declared Mazar. "Of this I am certain. I am old—but, well, we shall see."

The Pilgrims

I: At the Inn

FOR THE BETTER PART of a day Cugel had traveled a dreary waste where nothing grew but salt-grass; then, only a few minutes before sunset, he arrived at the bank of a broad slow river, beside which ran a road. A half-mile to his right stood a tall structure of timber and dark brown stucco, evidently an inn. The sight gave Cugel vast satisfaction, for he had eaten nothing the whole of the day, and had spent the previous night in a tree. Ten minutes later he pushed open the heavy iron-bound door, and entered the inn.

He stood in a vestibule. To either side were diamond-paned casements, burnt lavender with age, where the settin' sun scattered a thousand refractions. From the common room came the cheerful hum of voices, the clank of pottery and glass, the smell of ancient wood, waxed tile, leather and simmering cauldrons. Cugel stepped forward to find a score of men gathered about the fire, drinking wine and exchanging the large talk of travelers.

The landlord stood behind a counter: a stocky man hardly as tall as Cugel's shoulder, with a high-domed bald head and a black beard hanging a foot below his chin. His eyes were protuberant and heavy-lidded; his expression was as placid and calm as the flow of the river. At Cugel's request for accommodation he dubiously pulled at his nose. "Already I am over-extended, with pilgrims upon the route to Erze Damath. Those you see upon the benches are not even half of all I must lodge this night. I will put down a pallet in the hall, if such will content you; I can do no more."

Cugel gave a sigh of fretful dissatisfaction. "This fails to meet my expectations. I strongly desire a private chamber with a couch of good quality, a window overlooking the river, a heavy carpet to muffle the songs and slogans of the pot-room."

"I fear that you will be disappointed," said the landlord without emotion. "The single chamber of this description is already occupied, by that man with the yellow beard sitting yonder: a certain Lodermulch, also traveling to Erze Damath."

"Perhaps, on the plea of emergency, you might persuade him to vacate the chamber and occupy the pallet in my stead," suggested Cugel.

"I doubt if he is capable of such abnegation," the innkeeper replied. "But why not put the inquiry yourself? I, frankly, do not wish to broach the matter."

Cugel, surveying Lodermulch's strongly-marked features, his muscular arms and the somewhat disdainful manner in which he listened to the talk of the pilgrims, was inclined to join the innkeeper in his assessment of Lodermulch's character, and made no move to press the request. "It seems that I must occupy the pallet. Now, as to my supper: I require a fowl, suitably stuffed, trussed, roasted and garnished, accompanied by whatever side-dishes your kitchen affords."

"My kitchen is overtaxed and you must eat lentils with the pilgrims," said the landlord. "A single fowl is on hand, and this again has been reserved to the order of Lodermulch, for his evening repast."

Cugel shrugged in vexation. "No matter. I will wash the dust of travel from my face, and then take a goblet of wine."

"To the rear is flowing water and a trough occasionally

used for this purpose. I furnish unguents, pungent oils and hot cloths at extra charge."

"The water will suffice." Cugel walked to the rear of the inn, where he found a basin. After washing he looked about and noticed at some small distance a shed, stoutly constructed of timber. He started back into the inn, then halted and once more examined the shed. He crossed the intervening area, opened the door and looked within; then, engrossed in thought, he returned to the common room. The landlord served him a mug of mulled wine, which he took to an inconspicuous bench.

Lodermulch had been asked his opinion of the so-called Funambulous Evangels, who, refusing to place their feet upon the ground, went about their tasks by tightrope. In a curt voice Lodermulch exposed the fallacies of this particular doctrine. "They reckon the age of the earth at twenty-nine eons, rather than the customary twenty-three. They stipulate that for every square ell of soil two and one quarter million men have died and laid down their dust, thus creating a dank and ubiquitous mantle of lich-mold, upon which it is sacrilege to walk. The argument has a superficial plausibility, but consider: the dust of one desiccated corpse, spread over a square ell, affords a layer one thirty-third of an inch in depth. The total therefore represents almost one mile of compacted corpse-dust mantling the earth's surface, which is manifestly false."

A member of the sect, who, without access to his customary ropes, walked in cumbersome ceremonial shoes, made an excited expostulation. "You speak with neither logic nor comprehension! How can you be so absolute?"

Lodermulch raised his tufted eyebrows in surly displeasure. "Must I really expatiate? At the ocean's shore, does a cliff one mile in altitude follow the demarcation between land and sea? No. Everywhere is inequality. Headlands extend into the water; more often beaches of pure white sand are found. Nowhere are the massive buttresses of gray-white tuff upon which the doctrines of your sect depend."

"Inconsequential claptrap!" sputtered the Funambule.

"What is this?" demanded Lodermulch, expanding his massive chest. "I am not accustomed to derision!"

"No derision, but hard and cold refutal of your dogmatism! We claim that a proportion of the dust is blown into the ocean, a portion hangs suspended in the air, a portion seeps through crevices into underground caverns, and another portion is absorbed by trees, grasses and certain insects, so that little more than a half-mile of ancestral sediment covers the earth, upon which it is sacrilege to tread. Why are not the cliffs you mention everywhere visible? Because of that moistness expelled by innumerable men of the past! This has raised the ocean an exact equivalence, so that no brink or precipice can be noted; and herein lies your fallacy."

"Bah," muttered Lodermulch, turning away. "Somewhere there is a flaw in your concepts."

"By no means!" asserted the evangel, with that fervor which distinguished his kind. "Therefore, from respect to the dead, we walk aloft, on ropes and edges, and when we must travel, we use specially sanctified footgear."

During the conversation Cugel had departed the room. Now a moon-faced stripling wearing the smock of a porter approached the group. "You are the worthy Lodermulch?" he asked the person so designated.

Lodermulch squared about in his chair. "I am he."

"I bear a message, from one who has brought certain sums of money due you. He waits in a small shed behind the inn."

Lodermulch frowned incredulously. "You are certain that this person required Lodermulch, Provost of Barlig Township?"

"Indeed, sir, the name was specifically so."

"And what man bore the message?"

"He was a tall man, wearing a voluminous hood, and described himself as one of your intimates."

"Indeed," ruminated Lodermulch. "Tyzog, perhaps? Or conceivably Krednip. . . . Why would they not approach me directly? No doubt there is some good reason." He heaved his bulk erect. "I suppose I must investigate."

He stalked from the common room, circled the inn, and looked through the dim light toward the shed. "Ho there!" he called. "Tyzog? Krednip? Come forth!"

There was no response. Lodermulch went to peer into the shed. As soon as he had stepped within, Cugel came around from the rear, slammed shut the door, and threw bar and bolts.

Ignoring the muffled pounding and angry calls, Cugel returned into the inn. He sought out the innkeeper. "An alteration in arrangements: Lodermulch has been called away. He will require neither his chamber nor his roast fowl and has kindly urged both upon me!"

The innkeeper pulled at his beard, went to the door, and looked up and down the road. Slowly he returned. "Extraordinary! He has paid for both chamber and fowl, and made no representations regarding rebate."

"We arranged a settlement to our mutual satisfaction. To recompense you for extra effort, I now pay an additional three terces."

The innkeeper shrugged and took the coins. "It is all the same to me. Come, I will lead you to the chamber."

Cugel inspected the chamber and was well satisfied. Presently his supper was served. The roast fowl was beyond reproach, as were the additional dishes Lodermulch had ordered and which the landlord included with the meal.

Before retiring Cugel strolled behind the inn and satisfied himself that the bar at the door of the shed was in good order and that Lodermulch's hoarse calls were unlikely to attract attention. He rapped sharply on the door. "Peace, Lodermulch!" he called out sternly. "This is I, the innkeeper! Do not bellow so loudly; you will disturb my guests at their slumber."

Without waiting for reply, Cugel returned to the common room, where he fell into conversation with the leader of the pilgrim band. This was Garstang, a man spare and taut, with a waxen skin, a fragile skull, hooded eyes and a meticulous nose so thin as to be translucent when impinged across a light. Addressing him as a man of experience and erudition, Cugel inquired the route to Almery, but Garstang tended to believe the region sheerly imaginary.

Cugel asserted otherwise. "Almery is a region distinct; I vouch for this personally."

"Your knowledge, then, is more profound than my own," stated Garstang. "This river is the Asc; the land to this side is Sudun, across is Lelias. To the south lies Erze Damath, where you would be wise to travel, thence perhaps west across the Silver Desert and the Songan Sea, where you might make new inquiry."

"I will do as you suggest," said Cugel.

"We, devout Gilfigites all, are bound for Erze Damath and the Lustral Rites at the Black Obelisk," said Garstang. "Since the route lies through wastes, we are banded together against the erbs and gids. If you wish to join the group, to share both privileges and restrictions, you are welcome."

"The privileges are self-evident," said Cugel. "As to the restrictions?"

"Merely to obey the commands of the leader, which is to say, myself, and contribute a share of the expenses."

"I agree, without qualification," said Cugel.

"Excellent! We march on the morrow at dawn." Garstang pointed out certain other members of the group, which numbered fifty-seven. "There is Vitz, locutor to our little band, and there sits Casmyre, the theoretician. The man with iron teeth is Arlo, and he of the blue hat and silver buckle is Voynod, a wizard of no small repute. Absent from the room is the estimable though agnostic Lodermulch, as well as the unequivocally devout Subucule. Perhaps they seek to sway each other's convictions. The two who game with dice are Parso and Salanave. There is Hant, there Cary." Garstang named several others, citing their attributes. At last Cugel, pleading fatigue, repaired to his chamber. He relaxed upon the couch and at once fell asleep.

During the small hours he was subjected to a disturbance. Lodermulch, digging into the floor of the shed, then burrowing under the wall, had secured his freedom, and went at once to the inn. First he tried the door to Cugel's chamber, which Cugel had been at pains to lock.

"Who is there?" called Cugel.

"Open! It is I, Lodermulch. This is the chamber where I wish to sleep!"

"By no means," declared Cugel. "I paid a princely sum to secure a bed, and was even forced to wait while the landlord evicted a previous tenant. Be off with you now; I suspect that you are drunk; if you wish further revelry, rouse the wine-steward."

Lodermulch stamped away. Cugel lay back once more.

Presently he heard the thud of blows, and the landlord's cry as Lodermulch seized his beard. Lodermulch was eventually thrust from the inn, by the joint efforts of the innkeeper, his spouse, the porter, the pot-boy and others; whereupon Cugel gratefully returned to sleep.

Before dawn the pilgrims, together with Cugel, arose and took their breakfast. The innkeeper seemed somewhat sullen of mood, and displayed bruises, but he put no questions to Cugel, who in his turn initiated no conversation.

After breakfast the pilgrims assembled in the road, where they were joined by Lodermulch, who had spent the night pacing up and down the road.

Garstang made a count of the group, then blew a great blast on his whistle. The pilgrims marched forward, across the bridge, and set off along the south bank of the Asc toward Erze Damath.

2. The Raft on the River

For three days the pilgrims proceeded beside the Asc, at
night sleeping behind a barricade evoked by the wizard Voynod from a circlet of ivory slivers: a precaution of necessity,
for beyond the bars, barely visible by the rays of the fire,
were creatures anxious to join the company: deodands softly
pleading, erbs shifting posture back and forth from four feet
to two, comfortable in neither style. Once a gid attempted to
leap the barricade; on another occasion three hoons joined to
thrust against the posts—backing off, racing forward to strike
with grunts of effort, while from within the pilgrims watched
in fascination.

Cugel stepped close, to touch a flaming brand to one of
the heaving shapes, and elicited a scream of fury. A great gray
arm snatched through the gap; Cugel jumped back for his life.
The barricade held and presently the creatures fell to quarrel-
ing and departed.

On the evening of the third day the party came to the
confluence of the Asc with a great slow river which Garstang
identified as the Scamander. Nearby stood a forest of tall
baldamas, pines and spinth oaks. With the help of local wood-
cutters trees were felled, trimmed and conveyed to the water's
edge, where a raft was fabricated. With all the pilgrims aboard,
the raft was poled out into the current, where it drifted
downstream in ease and silence.

For five days the raft moved on the broad Scamander,
sometimes almost out of sight of the banks, sometimes gliding close beside the reeds which lined the shore. With nothing
better to do, the pilgrims engaged in lengthy disputations,
and the diversity of opinion upon every issue was remarkable.
As often as not the talk explored metaphysical arcana, or the
subtleties of Gilfigite principle.

Subucule, the most devout of the pilgrims, stated his
credo in detail. Essentially he professed the orthodox Gilfigite theosophy, in which Zo Zam, the eight-headed deity, after

creating cosmos, struck off his toe, which then became Gilfig, while the drops of blood dispersed to form the eight races of mankind. Roremaund, a skeptic, attacked the doctrine: "Who created this hypothetical 'creator' of yours? Another 'creator'? Far simpler merely to presuppose the end product: in this case, a blinking sun and a dying earth!" To which Subucule cited the Gilfigite Text in crushing refutal.

One named Bluner staunchly propounded his own creed. He believed the sun to be a cell in the corpus of a great deity, which had created the cosmos in a process analogous to the growth of a lichen along a rock.

Subucule considered the thesis over-elaborate: "If the sun were a cell what then becomes the nature of the earth?"

"An animalcule deriving nutriment," replied Bluner. "Such dependencies are known elsewhere and need not evoke astonishment."

"What then attacks the sun?" demanded Vitz in scorn. "Another animalcule similar to earth?"

Bluner began a detailed exposition of his organon, but before long was interrupted by Pralixus, a tall thin man with piercing green eyes. "Listen to me; I know all; my doctrine is simplicity itself. A vast number of conditions are possible, and there are an even greater number of impossibilities. Our cosmos is a possible condition: it exists. Why? Time is infinite, which is to say that every possible condition must come to pass. Since we reside in this particular possibility and know of no other, we arrogate to ourselves the quality of singleness. In truth, any universe which is possible sooner or later, not once but many times, will exist."

"I tend to a similar doctrine, though a devout Gilfigite," stated Casmyre the theoretician. "My philosophy presupposes a succession of creators, each absolute in his own right. To paraphrase the learned Pralixus, if a deity is possible, it must exist! Only impossible deities will not exist! The eight-headed Zo Zam who struck off his Divine Toe is possible, and hence exists, as is attested by the Gilfigite Texts!"

Subucule blinked, opened his mouth to speak, then closed it once more. Roremaund, the skeptic, turned away to inspect the waters of the Scamander.

Garstang, sitting to the side, smiled thoughtfully. "And you, Cugel the Clever, for once you are reticent. What is your belief?"

"It is somewhat inchoate," Cugel admitted. "I have assimilated a variety of viewpoints, each authoritative in its own right: from the priests at the Temple of Teleologues; from a bewitched bird who plucked messages from a box; from a fasting anchorite who drank a bottle of pink elixir which I offered him in jest. The resulting visions were contradictory but of great profundity. My world-scheme, hence, is syncretic."

"Interesting," said Garstang. "Lodermulch, what of you?"

"Ha," growled Lodermulch. "Notice this rent in my garment; I am at a loss to explain its presence! I am even more puzzled by the existence of the universe."

Others spoke. Voynod the wizard defined the known cosmos as the shadow of a region ruled by ghosts, themselves dependent for existence upon the psychic energies of men. The devout Subucule denounced this scheme as contrary to the Protocols of Gilfig.

The argument continued at length. Cugel and one or two others including Lodermulch became bored and instituted a game of chance, using dice and cards and counters. The stakes, originally nominal, began to grow. Lodermulch at first won scantily, then lost ever greater sums, while Cugel won stake after stake. Lodermulch presently flung down the dice and seizing Cugel's elbow shook it, to dislodge several additional dice from the cuff of his jacket. "Well then!" bawled Lodermulch, "what have we here? I thought to detect knavery, and here is justification! Return my money on the instant!"

"How can you say so?" demanded Cugel. "Where have you demonstrated chicanery? I carry dice—what of that? Am

I required to throw my property into the Scamander, before engaging in a game? You demean my reputation!"

"I care nothing for this," retorted Lodermulch. "I merely wish the return of my money."

"Impossible," said Cugel. "For all your bluster you have proved no malfeasance."

"Proof?" roared Lodermulch. "Need there be further? Notice these dice, all askew, some with identical markings on three sides, others rolling only with great effort, so heavy are they at one edge."

"Curios only," explained Cugel. He indicated Voynod the wizard, who had been watching. "Here is a man as keen of eye as he is agile of brain; ask if any illicit transaction was evident."

"None was evident," stated Voynod. "In my estimation Lodermulch has made an over-hasty accusation."

Garstang came forward, and heard the controversy. He spoke in a voice both judicious and conciliatory: "Trust is essential in a company such as ours, comrades and devout Gilfigites all. There can be no question of malice or deceit! Surely, Lodermulch, you have misjudged our friend Cugel!"

Lodermulch laughed harshly. "If this is conduct characteristic of the devout, I am fortunate not to have fallen in with ordinary folk!" With this remark he took himself to a corner of the raft, where he seated himself and fixed Cugel with a glance of menace and loathing.

Garstang shook his head in distress. "I fear Lodermulch has been offended. Perhaps, Cugel, if in a spirit of amity you were to return his gold—"

Cugel made a firm refusal. "It is a matter of principle. Lodermulch has assailed my most valuable possession, which is to say, my honor."

"Your nicety is commendable," said Garstang, "and Lodermulch has behaved tactlessly. Still, for the sake of good-fellowship—no? Well, I cannot argue the point. Ho hum. Always small troubles to fret us." Shaking his head, he departed.

Cugel gathered his winnings, together with the dice which Lodermulch had dislodged from his sleeve. "An unsettling incident," he told Voynod. "A boor, this Lodermulch! He has offended everyone; all have quit the game."

"Perhaps because all the money is in your possession," Voynod suggested.

Cugel examined his winnings with an air of surprise. "I never suspected that they were so substantial! Perhaps you will accept this sum to spare me the effort of carrying it?"

Voynod acquiesced and a share of the winnings changed hands.

Not long after, while the raft floated placidly along the river, the sun gave an alarming pulse. A purple film formed upon the surface like tarnish, then dissolved. Certain of the pilgrims ran back and forth in alarm, crying, "The sun goes dark! Prepare for the chill!"

Garstang, however, held up his hand in reassurance. "Calm, all! The quaver has departed, the sun is as before!"

"Think!" urged Subucule with great earnestness. "Would Gilfig allow this cataclysm, even while we travel to worship at the Black Obelisk?"

The group became quiet, though each had his personal interpretation of the event. Vitz, the locutor, saw an analogy to the blurring of vision, which might be cured by vigorous blinking. Voynod declared, "If all goes well at Erze Damath, I plan to dedicate the next four years of life to a scheme for replenishing the vigor of the sun!" Lodermulch merely made an offensive statement to the effect that for all of him the sun could go dark, with the pilgrims forced to grope their way to the Lustral Rites.

But the sun shone on as before. The raft drifted along the great Scamander, where the banks were now so low and devoid of vegetation as to seem distant dark lines. The day passed and the sun seemed to settle into the river itself, projecting a great maroon glare which gradually went dull and dark as the sun vanished.

In the twilight a fire was built, around which the pilgrims gathered to eat their supper. There was discussion of the sun's alarming flicker, and much speculation along eschatological lines. Subucule relinquished all responsibility for life, death, the future and past to Gilfig. Haxt, however, declared that he would feel easier if Gilfig had heretofore displayed a more expert control over the affairs of the world. For a period the talk became intense. Subucule accused Haxt of superficiality, while Haxt used such words as "credulity" and "blind abasement." Garstang intervened to point out that as yet all facts were not known, and that the Lustral Rites at the Black Obelisk might clarify the situation.

The next morning a great weir was noted ahead: a line of stout poles obstructing navigation of the river. At one area only was passage possible, and even this gap was closed by a heavy iron chain. The pilgrims allowed the raft to float close to this gap, then dropped the stone which served as an anchor. From a nearby hut appeared a zealot, long of hair and gaunt of limb, wearing tattered black robes and flourishing an iron staff. He sprang out along the weir to gaze threateningly down at those aboard the raft. "Go back, go back!" he shouted. "The passage of the river is under my control; I permit none to go by!"

Garstang stepped forward. "I beg your indulgence! We are a group of pilgrims bound for the Lustral Rites at Erze Damath. If necessary we will pay a fee to pass this weir, though we trust that in your generosity you will remit the toll."

The zealot gave a cry of harsh laughter and waved his iron staff. "My fee may not be remitted! I demand the life of the most evil of your company—unless one among you can to my satisfaction demonstrate his virtue!" And legs a-straddle, black robe flapping in the wind, he stood glaring down at the raft.

Among the pilgrims was a stir of uneasiness, and all looked furtively at one another. There was a mutter, which presently became a confusion of assertions and claims. Casmyre's strident tones at last rang forth. "It cannot be I who am most evil! My life has been clement and austere, and during the gambling I ignored an ignoble advantage."

Another called out, "I am even more virtuous, who eat only dry pulses for fear of taking life."

Another: "I am even of greater nicety, for I subsist solely upon the discarded husks of these same pulses, and bark which has fallen from trees, for fear of destroying even vegetative vitality."

Another: "My stomach refuses vegetable matter, but I uphold the same exalted ideals and allow only carrion to pass my lips."

Another: "I once swam on a lake of fire to notify an old women that the calamity she dreaded was unlikely to occur."

Cugel declared: "My life is incessant humility, and I am unswerving in my dedication to justice and equivalence, even though I fare the worse for my pains."

Voynod was no less staunch: "I am a wizard, true, but I devote my skill only to the amelioration of public woe."

Now it was Garstang's turn: "My virtue is of the quintessential sort, being distilled from the erudition of the ages. How can I be other than virtuous? I am dispassionate to the ordinary motives of mankind."

Finally all had spoken save Lodermuch, who stood to the side, a sour grin on his face. Voynod pointed a finger. "Speak, Lodermulch! Prove your virtue, or else be judged most evil, with the consequent forfeit of your life!"

Lodermulch laughed. He turned and made a great jump which carried him to an outlying member of the weir. He scrambled to the parapet, drew his sword and threatened the zealot. "We are all evil together, you as well as we, for enforcing this absurd condition. Relax the chain, or prepare to face my sword."

The zealot flung high his arms. "My condition is fulfilled; you, Lodermulch, have demonstrated your virtue. The raft may proceed. In addition, since you employ your sword in the defense of honor, I now bestow upon you this salve, which when applied to your blade enables it to slice steel or rock as easily as butter. Away, then, and may all profit by the Lustral devotions!"

Lodermulch accepted the salve and returned to the raft. The chain was relaxed and the raft slid without hindrance past the weir.

Garstang approached Lodermulch to voice measured approval for his act. He added caution: "In this case an impulsive, indeed almost insubordainte act redounded to the general benefit. If a similar circumstance arises in the future it would be well to take counsel with others of proved sagacity: myself, Casmyre, Voỹnod or Subucule."

Lodermulch grunted indifferently. "As you wish, so long as the delay involves me in no personal inconvenience." And Garstang was forced to be content with this.

The other pilgrims eyed Lodermulch with dissatisfaction, and drew themselves apart, so that Lodermulch sat by himself at the forward part of the raft.

Afternoon came, then sunset, evening and night; when morning arrived it was seen that Lodermulch had disappeared.

There was general puzzlement. Garstang made inquiries, but none could throw light upon the mystery, and there was no general consensus as to what in fact had occasioned the disappearance.

Strangely enough, the departure of the unpopular Lodermulch failed to restore the original cheer and fellowship to the group. Thereafter each of the pilgrims sat dourly silent, casting glances to left and right; there were no further games, nor philosophical discussions, and Garstang's announcement that Erze Damath lay a single day's journey ahead aroused no great enthusiasm.

3. Erze Damath

On the last night aboard the raft a semblance of the old
camaraderie returned. Vitz the locutor performed a number
of vocal exercises and Cugel demonstrated a high-kneed capering dance typical of the lobster fishermen of Kauchique,
where he had passed his youth. Voynod in his turn performed
a few simple metamorphoses, and then displayed a small
silver ring. He signaled Haxt. "Touch this with your tongue,
press it to your forehead, then look through."

"I see a procession!" exclaimed Haxt. "Men and women
by the hundreds, and thousands, marching past. My mother
and father walk before, then my grandparents—but who are
the others?"

"Your ancestors," declared Voynod, "each in his characteristic costume, back to the primordial homuncule from
which all of us are derived." He retrieved the ring, and
reaching into his pouch brought forth a dull blue and green
gem.

"Watch now, as I fling this jewel into the Scamander!"
and he tossed the gem off the side. It flickered through the
air and splashed into the dark water. "Now, I merely hold
forth my palm, and the gem returns!" And indeed, as the
company watched there was a wet sparkle across the firelight
and upon Voynod's palm rested the gem. "With this gem a
man need never fear penury. True, it is of no great value, but
he can sell it repeatedly. . . .

"What else shall I show you? This small amulet perhaps.
Frankly an erotic appurtenance, it arouses intense emotion in
that person toward whom the potency is directed. One must
be cautious in its use; and indeed, I have here an indispensable ancillary: a periapt in the shape of a ram's head, fashioned to the order of Emperor Dalmasmius the Tender, that
he might not injure the sensibilities of any of his ten thousand concubines. . . . What else can I display? Here: my

wand, which instantly affixes any object to any other. I keep it carefully sheathed so that I do not inadvertently weld trouser to buttock or pouch to fingertip. The object has many uses. What else? Let us see. . . . Ah, here! A horn of singular quality. When thrust into the mouth of a corpse, it stimulates the utterance of twenty final words. Inserted into the cadaver's ear it allows the transmission of information into the lifeless brain. . . . What have we here? Yes indeed: a small device which has brought much pleasure!" And Voynod displayed a doll which performed a heroic declamation, sang a somewhat raffish song and engaged in repartee with Cugel, who squatted close in front, watching all with great attentiveness.

At last Voynod tired of his display, and the pilgrims one by one reposed themselves to sleep.

Cugel lay awake, hands behind his head, staring up at the stars thinking of Voynod's unexpectedly large collection of thaumaturgical instruments and devices.

When satisfied that all were asleep, he arose to his feet and inspected the sleeping form of Voynod. The pouch was securely locked and tucked under Voynod's arm, much as Cugel has expected. Going to the little pantry where stores were kept, he secured a quantity of lard, which he mixed with flour to produce a white salve. From a fragment of heavy paper he folded a small box, which he filled with the salve. He then returned to his couch.

On the following morning he contrived that Voynod, as if by accident, should see him anointing his sword blade with the salve.

Voynod became instantly horrified. "It cannot be! I am astounded! Alas, poor Lodermulch!"

Cugel signaled him to silence. "What are you saying?" he muttered. "I merely protect my sword against rust."

Voynod shook his head with inexorable determination. "All is clear! For the sake of gain you have murdered

Lodermulch! I have no choice but to lodge an information with the thief-takers at Erze Damath!"

Cugel made an imploring gesture. "Do not be hasty! You have mistaken all; I am innocent!"

Voynod, a tall saturnine man with a purple flush under his eyes, a long chin and a tall pinched forehead, held up his hand. "I have never been one to tolerate homicide. The principle of equivalence must in this case apply, and a rigorous requital is necessary. At minimum, the evil-doer may never profit by his act!"

"You refer to the salve?" inquired Cugel delicately.

"Precisely," said Voynod. "Justice demands no less."

"You are a stern man," exclaimed Cugel in distress. "I have no choice but to submit to your judgment."

Voynod extended his hand. "The salve, then, and since you are obviously overcome by remorse I will say no more of the matter."

Cugel pursed his lips reflectively. "So be it. I have already anointed my sword. Therefore I will sacrifice the remainder of the salve in exchange for your erotic appurtenance and its ancillary, together with several lesser talismans."

"Do I hear correctly?" stormed Voynod. "Your arrogance transcends all! Such effectuants are beyond value!"

Cugel shrugged. "This salve is by no means an ordinary article of commerce."

After dispute Cugel relinquished the salve in return for a tube which projected blue concentrate to a distance of fifty paces, together with a scroll listing eighteen phases of the Laganetic Cycle; and with these items he was forced to be content.

Not long afterward the outlying ruins of Erze Damath appeared upon the western banks: ancient villas now toppled and forlorn among overgrown gardens.

The pilgrims plied poles to urge the raft toward the shore. In the distance appeared the tip of the Black Obelisk, at which all emitted a glad cry. The raft moved slantwise across the Scamander and was presently docked at one of the crumbling old jetties.

The pilgrims scrambled ashore, then gathered around Garstang, who addressed the group: "It is with vast satisfaction that I find myself discharged of responsibility. Behold! The holy city where Gilfig issued the Gneustic Dogma! Where he scourged Kazue and denounced Enxis the Witch! Not impossibly the sacred feet have trod this very soil!" Garstang made a dramatic gesture toward the ground, and the pilgrims, looking downward, shuffled their feet uneasily. "Be that as it may, we are here and each of us must feel relief. The way was tedious and not without peril. Fifty-nine set forth from Pholgus Valley. Bamish and Randol were taken by grues at Sagma Field; by the bridge across the Asc Cugel joined us; upon the Scamander we lost Lodermulch. Now we muster fifty-seven, comrades all, tried and true, and it is a sad thing to dissolve our association, which we all will remember forever!

"Two days hence the Lustral Rites begin. We are in good time. Those who have not disbursed all their funds gaming"—here Garstang turned a sharp glance toward Cugel—"may seek comfortable inns at which to house themselves. The impoverished must fare as best they can. Now our journey is at its end; we herewith disband and go our own ways, though all will necessarily meet two days hence at the Black Obelisk. Farewell until this time!"

The pilgrims now dispersed, some walking along the banks of the Scamander toward a nearby inn, others turning aside and proceeding into the city proper.

Cugel approached Voynod. "I am strange to this region, as you are aware; perhaps you can recommend an inn of large comfort at small cost."

"Indeed," said Voynod. "I am bound for just such an inn: the Old Dastric Empire Hostelry, which occupies the precincts of a former palace. Unless conditions have changed, sumptuous luxury and exquisite viands are offered at no great cost."

The prospect met with Cugel's approval; the two set out through the avenues of old Erze Damath, past clusters of stucco huts, then across a region where no buildings stood and the avenues created a vacant checkerboard, then into a district of great mansions still currently in use: these set back among intricate gardens. The folk of Erze Damath were handsome enough, if somewhat swarthier than the folk of Almery. The men wore only black: tight trousers and vests with black pompons; the women were splendid in gowns of yellow, red, orange and magenta, and their slippers gleamed with orange and black sequins. Blue and green were rare, being unlucky colors, and purple signified death.

The women displayed tall plumes in their hair, while the men wore jaunty black disks, their scalps protruding through a central hole. A resinous balsam seemed very much the fashion, and everyone Cugel met exuded a waft of aloes or myrrh or carcynth. All in all the folk of Erze Damath seemed no less cultivated than those of Kauchique, and rather more vital than the listless citizens of Azenomei.

Ahead appeared the Old Dastric Empire Hostelry, not far from the Black Obelisk itself. To the dissatisfaction of both Cugel and Voynod, the premises were completely occupied, and the attendant refused them admittance. "The Lustral Rites have attracted all manner of devout folk," he explained. "You will be fortunate to secure lodging of any kind."

So it proved: from inn to inn went Cugel and Voynod, to be turned away in every case. Finally, on the western outskirts of the city, at the very edge of the Silver Desert, they were received by a large tavern of somewhat disreputable appearance: the Inn of the Green Lamp.

"Until ten minutes ago I could not have housed you," stated the landlord, "but the thief-takers apprehended two persons who lodged here, naming them footpads and congenital rogues."

"I trust this is not the general tendency of your clientele?" inquired Voynod.

"Who is to say?" replied the innkeeper. "It is my business to provide food and drink and lodging, no more. Ruffians and deviants must eat, drink and sleep, no less than servants and zealots. All have passed on occasion through my doors, and, after all, what do I know of you?"

Dusk was falling and without further ado Cugel and Voynod housed themselves at the Sign of the Green Lamp. After refreshing themselves they repaired to the common room for their evening meal. This was a hall of considerable extent, with age-blackened beams, a floor of dark brown tile, and various posts and columns of scarred wood, each supporting a lamp. The clientele was various, as the landlord had intimated, displaying a dozen costumes and complexions. Desert-men lean as snakes, wearing leather smocks, sat on one hand; on the other were four with white faces and silky red top-knots who uttered never a word. Along a counter to the back sat a group of bravos in brown trousers, black capes and leather berets, each with a spherical jewel dangling by a gold chain from his ear.

Cugel and Voynod consumed a meal of fair quality, though somewhat rudely served, then sat drinking wine and considering how to pass the evening. Voynod decided to rehearse cries of passion and devotion frenzies to be exhibited at the Lustral Rites. Cugel thereupon besought him to lend his talisman of erotic stimulation. "The women of Erze Damath show to good advantage, and with the help of the talisman I will extend my knowledge of their capabilities."

"By no means," said Voynod, hugging his pouch close to his side. "My reasons need no amplification."

Cugel put on a sullen scowl. Voynod was a man whose grandiose personal conceptions seemed particularly far-fetched and distasteful, by reason of his unhealthy, gaunt and saturnine appearance.

Voynod drained his mug, with a meticulous frugality Cugel found additionally irritating, and rose to his feet. "I will now retire to my chamber."

As he turned away a bravo swaggering across the room jostled him. Voynod snapped an acrimonious instruction, which the bravo did not choose to ignore. "How dare you use such words to me! Draw and defend yourself, or I cut your nose from your face!" And the bravo snatched forth his blade.

"As you will," said Voynod. "One moment until I find my sword." With a wink at Cugel he anointed his blade with the salve, then turned to the bravo. "Prepare for death, my good fellow!" He leapt grandly forward. The bravo, noting Voynod's preparations, and understanding that he faced magic, stood numb with terror. With a flourish Voynod ran him through, and wiped his blade on the bravo's hat.

The dead man's companions at the counter started to their feet, but halted as Voynod with great aplomb turned to face them. "Take care, you dunghill cocks! Notice the fate of your fellow! He died by the power of my magic blade, which is of inexorable metal and cuts rock and steel like butter. Behold!" And Voynod struck out at a pillar. The blade, striking a iron bracket, broke into a dozen pieces. Voynod stood non-plussed, but the bravo's companions surged forward.

"What then of your magic blade? Our blades are ordinary steel but bite deep!" And in a moment Voynod was cut to bits.

The bravos now turned upon Cugel. "What of you? Do you wish to share the fate of your comrade?"

"By no means!" stated Cugel. "This man was but my servant, carrying my pouch. I am a magician; observe this tube! I will project blue concentrate at the first man to threaten me!"

The bravos shrugged and turned away. Cugel secured Voynod's pouch, then gestured to the landlord. "Be so good as to remove these corpses; then bring a further mug of spiced wine."

"What of your comrade's account?" demanded the landlord testily.

"I will settle it in full, have no fear."

The corpses were carried to the rear compound; Cugel consumed a last mug of wine, then retired to his chamber, where he spread the contents of Voynod's pouch upon the table. The money went into his purse; the talismans, amulets and instruments he packed into his own pouch; the salve he tossed aside. Content with the day's work, he reclined upon the couch, and was soon asleep.

On the following day Cugel roamed the city, climbing the tallest of the eight hills. The vista which spread before him was both bleak and magnificent. To right and left rolled the great Scamander. The avenues of the city marked off square blocks of ruins, empty wastes, the stucco huts of the poor and the palaces of the rich. Erze Damath was the largest city of Cugel's experience, far vaster than any of Almery or Ascolais, though now the greater part lay tumbled in moldering ruin.

Returning to the central section, Cugel sought out the booth of a professional geographer and after paying a fee inquired the most secure and expeditious route to Almery.

The sage gave no hasty nor ill-considered answer, but brought forth several charts and directories. After profound deliberation he turned to Cugel. "This is my counsel. Follow the Scamander north to the Asc, proceed along the Asc until you encounter a bridge of six piers. Here turn your face to the north, proceed across the Mountains of Magnatz, whereupon you will find before you that forest known as the Great Erm. Fare westward through this forest and approach the shore of the Northern Sea. Here you must build a coracle and entrust yourself to the force of wind and current. If by chance you should reach the Land of the Falling Wall, then it is a comparatively easy journey south to Almery."

Cugel made an impatient gesture. "In essence this is the way I came. Is there no other route?"

"Indeed there is. A rash man might choose to risk the Silver Desert, whereupon he would find the Songan Sea, across which lie the impassable wastes of a region contiguous to East Almery."

"Well then, this seems feasible. How may I cross the Silver Desert? Are there caravans?"

"To what purpose? There are none to buy the goods thus conveyed—only bandits who prefer to preempt the merchandise. A minimum force of forty men is necessary to intimidate the bandits."

Cugel departed the booth. At a nearby tavern he drank a flask of wine and considered how best to raise a force of forty men. The pilgrims, of course, numbered fifty-six—no, fifty-five, what with the death of Voynod. Still, such a band would serve very well. . . .

Cugel drank more wine and considered further.

At last he paid his score and turned his steps to the Black Obelisk. "Obelisk" perhaps was a misnomer, the object being a great fang of solid black stone rearing a hundred feet above the city. At the base five statues had been carved, each facing a different direction, each the Prime Adept of some particular creed. Gilfig faced to the south, his four hands presenting symbols, his feet resting upon the necks of ecstatic supplicants, with toes elongated and curled upward, to indicate elegance and delicacy.

Cugel sought information of a nearby attendant. "Who, in regard to the Black Obelisk, is Chief Hierarch, and where may he be found?"

"Precursor Hulm is that individual," said the attendant and indicated a splendid structure nearby. "Within that gem-encrusted structure his sanctum may be found."

Cugel proceeded to the building indicated and after many vehement declarations was ushered into the presence of Precursor Hulm: a man of middle years, somewhat stocky and round of face. Cugel gestured to the under-hierophant who so reluctantly had brought him hither. "Go; my message is for the Precursor alone."

The Precursor gave a signal; the hierophant departed.

Cugel hitched himself forward. "I may talk without fear of being overheard?"

"Such is the case."

"First of all," said Cugel, "know that I am a powerful wizard. Behold: a tube which projects blue concentrate! And here, a screed listing eighteen phases of the Laganetic Cycle! And this instrument: a horn which allows the dead to speak, and, used in another fashion, allows information to be conveyed into the dead brain! I possess other marvels galore!"

"Interesting indeed," murmured the Precursor.

"My second disclosure is this: at one time I served an incense-blender at the Temple of Teleologues in a far land, where I learned that each of the sacred images was constructed so that the priests, in case of urgency, might perform acts purporting to be those of the divinity itself."

"Why should this not be the case?" inquired the Precursor benignly. "The divinity, controlling every aspect of existence, persuades the priests to perform such acts."

Cugel assented to the proposition. "I therefore assume that the images carved into the Black Obelisk are somewhat similar?"

The Precursor smiled. "To which of the five do you specifically refer?"

"Specifically to the representation of Gilfig."

The Precursor's eyes went vague; he seemed to reflect.

Cugel indicated the various talismans and instruments. "In return for a service I will donate certain of these contrivances to the care of this office."

"What is the service?"

Cugel explained in detail, and the Precursor nodded thoughtfully. "Once more, if you will demonstrate your magic goods."

Cugel did so.

"These are all of your devices?"

Cugel reluctantly displayed the erotic stimulator and explained the function of the ancillary talisman. The Precursor nodded his head, briskly this time. "I believe that we can reach agreement; all is as omnipotent Gilfig desires."

"We are agreed, then?"

"We are agreed!"

The following morning the group of fifty-five pilgrims assembled at the Black Obelisk. They prostrated themselves before the image of Gilfig, and prepared to proceed with their devotions. Suddenly the eyes of the image flashed fire and the mouth opened. "Pilgrims!" came a brazen voice. "Go forth to do my bidding! Across the Silver Desert you must travel, to the shore of the Songan Sea! Here you will find a fane, before which you must abase yourselves. Go! Across the Silver Desert, with all dispatch!"

The voice quieted. Garstang spoke in a trembling voice. "We hear, O Gilfig! We obey!"

At this moment Cugel leapt forward. "I also have heard this marvel! I too will make the journey! Come, let us set forth!"

"Not so fast," said Garstang. "We cannot run skipping and bounding like dervishes. Supplies will be needed, as well as beasts of burden. To this end funds are required. Who then will subscribe?"

"I offer two hundred terces!" "And I, sixty terces, the sum of my wealth!" "I, who lost ninety terces gaming with Cugel, possess only forty terces, which I hereby contribute." So it went, and even Cugel turned sixty-five terces into the common fund.

"Good," said Garstang. "Tomorrow then I will make arrangements, and the following day, if all goes well, we depart Erze Damath by the Old West Gate!"

4. The Silver Desert and the Songan Sea

In the morning Garstang, with the assistance of Cugel and Casmyre, went forth to procure the necessary equipage. They were directed to an outfitting yard, situated on one of the now-vacant areas bounded by the boulevards of the old city. A wall of mud brick mingled with fragments of carved stone surrounded a compound, whence issued sounds: crying, calls, deep bellows, throaty growls, barks, screams and roars, and a strong multiphase odor, combined of ammonia, ensilage, a dozen sorts of dung, the taint of old meat, general acridity.

Passing through a portal, the travelers entered an office overlooking the central yard, where pens, cages and stockades held beasts of so great variety as to astound Cugel.

The yard-keeper came forward: a tall, yellow-skinned man, much scarred, lacking his nose and one ear. He wore a gown of gray leather belted at the waist and a tall conical black hat with flaring ear-flaps.

Garstang stated the purpose of the visit. "We are pilgrims who must journey across the Silver Desert, and wish to hire pack-beasts. We number fifty or more, and anticipate a journey of twenty days in each direction with perhaps five days spent at our devotions: let this information be a guide in your thinking. Naturally we expect only the staunchest, most industrious and amenable beasts at your disposal."

"All this is very well," stated the keeper, "but my price for hire is identical to my price for sale, so you might as well have the full benefit of your money, in the form of title to the beasts concerned in the transaction."

"And the price?" inquired Casmyre.

"This depends upon your choice; each beast commands a different value."

Garstang, who had been surveying the compound, shook his head ruefully. "I confess to puzzlement. Each beast is of a different sort, and none seem to fit any well-defined categories."

The keeper admitted that such was the case. "If you care to listen, I can explain all. The tale is of a continuing fascination, and will assist you in the management of your beasts."

"We will doubly profit to hear you, then," said Garstang gracefully, though Cugel was making motions of impatience.

The keeper went to a shelf and took forth a leather-bound folio. "In a past eon Mad King Kutt ordained a menagerie like none before, for his private amazement and the stupefaction of the world. His wizard, Follinense, therefore produced a group of beasts and teratoids unique, combining the wildest variety of plasms; to the result that you see."

"The menagerie has persisted so long?" asked Garstang in wonder.

"Indeed not. Nothing of Mad King Kutt is extant save the legend, and a casebook of the wizard Follinense"—here he tapped the leather folio—"which described his bizarre systemology. For instance—" He opened the folio. "Well . . . hmmm. Here is a statement, somewhat less explicit than others, in which he analyzes the half-men, little more than a brief set of notes:

> '*Gid: hybrid of man, gargoyle, whorl, leaping insect.*
> *Deodand: wolverine, basilisk, man.*
> *Erb: bear, man, lank-lizard, demon.*
> *Grue: man, ocular bat, the unusual hoon.*
> *Leukomorph: unknown.*
> *Bazil: felinodore, man, (wasp?).*'"

Casmyre clapped his hands in astonishment. "Did Follinense then create these creatures, to the subsequent disadvantage of humanity?"

"Surely not," said Garstang. "It seems more an exercise in idle musing. Twice he admits to wonder."

"Such is my opinion, in this present case," stated the keeper, "though elsewhere he is less dubious."

"How are these creatures before us then connected with the menagerie?" inquired Casmyre.

The keeper shrugged. "Another of the Mad King's jocularities. He loosed the entire assemblage upon the countryside, to the general disturbance. The creatures, endowed with an eclectic fecundity, became more rather than less bizarre, and now they roam the Plain of Oparona and Blanwalt Forest in great numbers."

"So then, what of us?" demanded Cugel. "We wish pack-animals, docile and frugal of habit, rather than freaks and curiosities, no matter how edifying."

"Certain of my ample stock are capable of this function," said the keeper with dignity. "These command the highest prices. On the other hand, for a single terce you may own a long-necked big-bellied creature of astounding voracity."

"The price is attractive," said Garstang with regret. "Unfortunately, we need beasts to carry food and water across the Silver Desert."

"In this case we must be more pointed." The keeper fell to studying his charges. "The tall beast on two legs is perhaps less ferocious than he appears. . . ."

Eventually a selection of beasts numbering fifteen was made, and a price agreed upon. The keeper brought them to the gate; Garstang, Cugel and Casmyre took possession and led the fifteen ill-matched creatures at a sedate pace through the streets of Erze Damath, to the West Gate. Here Cugel was left in charge, while Garstang and Casmyre went to purchase stores and other necessaries.

By nightfall all preparations were made, and on the following morning, when the first maroon ray of sunlight struck the Black Obelisk, the pilgrims set forth. The beasts carried panniers of food and bladders of water; the pilgrims all wore new shoes and broad-brimmed hats. Garstang had been unable to hire a guide, but had secured a chart from the geographer, though it indicated no more than a small circle labeled "Erze Damath" and a larger area marked "Songan Sea."

Cugel was given one of the beasts to lead, a twelve-legged creature twenty feet in length, with a small foolishly grinning child's head and tawny fur covering all. Cugel found the task irking, for the beast blew a reeking breath upon his neck and several times pressed so close as to tread on his heels.

Of the fifty-seven pilgrims who had disembarked from

the raft, forty-nine departed for the fane on the shores of the Songan Sea, and the number was almost at once reduced to forty-eight. A certain Tokharin, stepping off the trail to answer a call of nature, was stung by a monster scorpion, and ran northward in great leaps, screaming hoarsely, until presently he disappeared from view.

The day passed with no further incident. The land was a dry gray waste, scattered with flints, supporting only ironweed. To the south was a range of low hills, and Cugel thought to perceive one or two shapes standing motionless along the crest. At sunset the caravan halted; and Cugel, recalling the bandits who reputedly inhabited the area, persuaded Garstang to post two sentries: Lippelt and Mirch-Masen.

In the morning they were gone, leaving no trace, and the pilgrims were alarmed and oppressed. They stood in a nervous cluster looking in all directions. The desert lay flat and dim in the dark low light of dawn. To the south were a few hills, only their smooth top surfaces illuminated; elsewhere the land lay flat to the horizon.

Presently the caravan started off, and now there were but forty-six. Cugel, as before, was put in charge of the long many-legged beast, who now engaged in the practice of butting its grinning face into Cugel's shoulder blades.

The day passed without incident; miles ahead became miles behind. First marched Garstang, with a staff, then came Vitz and Casmyre, following by several others. Then came the pack-beasts, each with its particular silhouette: one low and sinuous; another tall and bifurcate, almost of human conformation, except for its head, which was small and squat like the shell of a horseshoe crab. Another, convex of back, seemed to bounce or prance on its six stiff legs; another was like a horse sheathed in white feathers. Behind the pack-beasts straggled the remaining pilgrims, with Bluner characteristically walking to the rear, in accordance with the exaggerated humility to which he was prone. At the camp that evening Cugel brought forth the expansible fence, once the property of Voynod, and enclosed the group in a stout stockade.

The following day the pilgrims crossed a range of low mountains, and here they suffered an attack by bandits, but it seemed no more than an exploratory skirmish, and the sole casualty was Haxt, who suffered a wound in the heel. But a more serious affair occurred two hours later. As they passed below a slope a boulder became dislodged, to roll through the caravan, killing a pack-beast, as well as Andle the Funambulous Evangel and Roremaund the Skeptic. During the night Haxt died also, evidently poisoned by the weapon which had wounded him.

With grave faces the pilgrims set forth, and almost at once were attacked from ambush by the bandits. Luckily the pilgrims were alert, and the bandits were routed with a dozen dead, while the pilgrims lost only Cray and Magasthen.

Now there was grumbling and long looks turned eastward toward Erze Damath. Garstang rallied the flagging spirits: "We are Gilfigites; Gilfig spoke! On the shores of the Songan Sea we will seek the sacred fane! Gilfig is all-wise and all-merciful; those who fall in his service are instantly transported to paradisiacal Gamamere! Pilgrims! To the west!"

Taking heart, the caravan once more set forth, and the day passed without further incident. During the night, however, three of the pack-beasts slipped their tethers and decamped, and Garstang was forced to announce short rations for all.

During the seventh day's march, Thilfox ate a handful of poison berries and died in spasms, whereupon his brother Vitz, the locutor, went raving mad and ran up the line of pack-beasts, blaspheming Gilfig and slashing water bladders with his knife until Cugel finally killed him.

Two days later the haggard band came upon a spring. In spite of Garstang's warning, Salanave and Arlo flung themselves down and drank in great gulps. Almost at once they clutched their bellies, gagged and choked, their lips the color of sand, and presently they were dead.

A week later fifteen men and four beasts came over a rise
to look out across the placid waters of the Songan Sea. Cugel
had survived, as well as Garstang, Casmyre and Subucule.
Before them lay a marsh, fed by a small stream. Cugel tested
the water with that amulet bestowed upon him by Iucounu,
and pronounced it safe. All drank to repletion, ate reeds
converted to a nutritious if insipid substance by the same
amulet, then slept.

Cugel, aroused by a sense of peril, jumped up, to note a
sinister stir among the reeds. He roused his fellows and all
readied their weapons; but whatever had caused the motion
took alarm and retired. The time was middle afternoon; the
pilgrims walked down to the bleak shore to take stock of the
situation. They looked north and south but found no trace of
the fane. Tempers flared; there was a quarrel which Garstang
was able to quell only by dint of the utmost persuasiveness.

Then Balch, who had wandered up the beach, returned in
great excitement: "A village!"

All set forth in hope and eagerness, but the village, when
the pilgrims approached, proved a poor thing indeed, a huddle
of reed huts inhabited by lizard people who bared their teeth
and lashed sinewy blue tails in defiance. The pilgrims moved
off down the beach and sat on hummocks watching the low
surf of the Songan Sea.

Garstang, frail and bent with the privations he had suffered, was the first to speak. He attempted to infuse his voice
with cheer. "We have arrived, we have triumphed over the
terrible Silver Desert! Now we need only locate the fane and
perform our devotions; we may then return to Erze Damath
and a future of assured bliss!"

"All very well," grumbled Balch, "but where may the
fane be found? To right and left is the same bleak beach!"

"We must put our trust in the guidance of Gilfig!" declared Subucule. He scratched an arrow upon a bit of wood,
and touched it with his holy ribbon. He called, "Gilfig, O
Gilfig! Guide us to the fane! I hereby toss high a marked

pointer!" And he flung the chip high into the air. When it alighted, the arrow pointed south. "South we must fare!" cried Garstang. "South to the fane!"

But Balch and certain others refused to respond. "Do you not see that we are fatigued to the point of death? In my opinion Gilfig should have guided our steps to the fane, instead of abandoning us to uncertainty!"

"Gilfig has guided us indeed!" responded Subucule. "Did you not notice the direction of the arrow?"

Balch gave a croak of sardonic laughter. "Any stick thrown high must come down, and it will point south as easily as north."

Subucule drew back in horror. "You blaspheme Gilfig!"

"Not at all; I am not sure that Gilfig heard your instruction, or perhaps you gave him insufficient time to react. Toss up the stick one hundred times; if it points south on each occasion, I will march south in haste."

"Very well," said Subucule. He once again called upon Gilfig and threw up the chip, but when it struck the ground the arrow pointed north.

Balch said nothing. Subucule blinked, then grew red in the face. "Gilfig has no time for games. He directed us once, and deemed it sufficient."

"I am unconvinced," said Balch.

"And I."

"And I."

Garstand held up his arms imploringly. "We have come far; we have toiled together, rejoiced together, fought and suffered together—let us not now fall in dissidence!"

Balch and the others only shrugged. "We will not plunge blindly south."

"What will you do, then? Go north? Or return to Erze Damath?"

"Erze Damath? Without food and only four pack-beasts? Bah!"

"Then let us fare south in search of the fane."

Balch gave another mulish shrug, at which Subucule became angry. "So be it! Those who fare south to this side, those who cast in with Balch to that!"

Garstang, Cugel and Casmyre joined Subucule; the others stayed with Balch, a group numbering eleven, and now they fell to whispering among themselves, while the four faithful pilgrims watched in apprehension.

The eleven jumped to their feet. "Farewell."

"Where do you go?" asked Garstang.

"No matter. Seek your fane if you must; we go about our own affairs." With the briefest of farewells they marched to the village of the lizard folk, where they slaughtered the males, filed the teeth of the females, dressed them in garments of reeds, and installed themselves as lords of the village.

Garstang, Subucule, Casmyre and Cugel meanwhile traveled south along the shore. At nightfall they pitched camp and dined upon molluscs and crabs. In the morning they found that the four remaining pack-beasts had departed and now they were alone.

"It is the will of Gilfig," said Subucule. "We need only find the fane and die!"

"Courage!" muttered Garstang. "Let us not give way to despair!"

"What else is left? Will we ever see Pholgus Valley again?"

"Who knows? Let us first perform our devotions at the fane."

With that they proceeded, and marched the remainder of the day. By nightfall they were too tired to do more than slump to the sand of the beach.

The sea spread before them, flat as a table, so calm that the setting sun cast only its exact image rather than a trail. Clams and crabs once more provided a meager supper, after which they composed themselves to sleep on the beach.

Somewhat after the first hours of night Cugel was awakened by a sound of music. Starting up, he looked across the water to find that a ghostly city had come into existence.

Slender towers reared into the sky, lit by glittering motes of white light which drifted slowly up and down, back and forth. On the promenades sauntered the gayest of crowds, wearing pale luminous garments and blowing horns of delicate sound. A barge piled with silken cushions, moved by an enormous sail of cornflower silk, drifted past. Lamps at the bow and stern-post illuminated a deck thronged with merrymakers: some singing and playing lutes, others drinking from goblets.

Cugel ached to share their joy. He struggled to his knees, and called out. The merrymakers put down their instruments and stared at him, but now the barge had drifted past, tugged by the great blue sail. Presently the city flickered and vanished, leaving only the dark night sky.

Cugel stared into the night, his throat aching with a sorrow he had never known before. To his surprise he found himself standing at the edge of the water. Nearby were Subucule, Garstang and Casmyre. All gazed at each other through the dark, but exchanged no words. All returned up the beach, where presently they fell asleep in the sand.

Throughout the next day there was little conversation, and even a mutual avoidance, as if each of the four wished to be alone with his thoughts. From time to time one or the other looked half-heartedly toward the south, but no one seemed in a mood to leave the spot, and no one spoke of departure.

The day passed while the pilgrims rested in a half-torpor. Sunset came, and night; but none of the group sought to sleep.

During the middle evening the ghost city reappeared, and tonight a fête was in progress. Fireworks of a wonderful intricacy bloomed in the sky: laces, nets, starbursts of red and green and blue and silver. Along the promenade came a parade, with ghost-maidens dressed in iridescent garments, ghost-musicians in voluminous garments of red and orange, and capering ghost-harlequins. For hours the sound of revelry drifted across the water, and Cugel went out to stand knee-deep, and here he watched until the fête quieted and the city dimmed. As he turned away, the others followed him back up the shore.

On the following day all were weak from hunger and thirst. In a croaking voice Cugel muttered that they must proceed. Garstang nodded and said huskily, "To the fane, the fane of Gilfig!"

Subucule nodded. The cheeks of his once plump face were haggard; his eyes were filmed and clouded. "Yes," he wheezed. "We have rested; on we must go!"

Casmyre nodded dully. "To the fane!"

But none set forth to the south. Cugel wandered up the fore-shore and seated himself to wait for nightfall. Looking to his right, he saw a human skeleton resting in a posture not dissimilar to his own. Shuddering, Cugel turned to the left, and here was a second skeleton, this one broken by time and the seasons, and beyond yet another, this a mere heap of bones.

Cugel rose to his feet and ran tottering to the others. "Quick!" he called. "While strength yet remains to us! To the south! Come, before we die, like those whose bones rest above!"

"Yes, yes," mumbled Garstang. "To the fane." And he heaved himself to his feet. "Come!" he called to the others. "We fare south!"

Subucule raised himself erect, but Casmyre, after a listless attempt, fell back. "Here I stay," he said. "When you reach the fane, intercede for me with Gilfig; explain that the entrancement overcame the strength of my body."

Garstang wished to remain and plead, but Cugel pointed to the setting sun. "If we wait till darkness, we are lost! Tomorrow our strength will be gone!"

Subucule took Garstang's arm. "We must be away, before nightfall."

Garstang made a final plea to Casmyre. "My friend and fellow, gather your strength. Together we have come, from far Pholgus Valley, by raft down the Scamander, and across the dreadful desert! Must we part before attaining the fane?"

"Come, to the fane!" croaked Cugel.

But Casmyre turned his face away. Cugel and Subucule led Garstang away, with tears coursing down his withered cheeks; and they staggered south along the beach, averting their eyes from the clear smooth face of the sea.

The old sun set and cast up a fan of color. A high scatter of cloud-flakes glowed halcyon yellow on a strange bronze-brown sky. The city now appeared, and never had it seemed more magnificent, with spires catching the light of sunset. Along the promenade walked youths and maidens with flowers in their hair, and sometimes they paused to stare at the three who walked along the beach. Sunset faded; white lights shone from the city, and music wafted across the water. For a long time it followed the three pilgrims, at last fading into the distance and dying. The sea lay blank to the west, reflecting a few last umber and orange glimmers.

About this time the pilgrims found a stream of fresh water, with berries and wild plums growing nearby, and here they rested the night. In the morning Cugel trapped a fish and caught crabs along the beach. Strengthened, the three continued south, always seeking ahead for the fane, which now Cugel had almost come to expect, so intense was the feeling of Garstang and Subucule. Indeed, as the days passed, it was the devout Subucule who began to despair, to question the sincerity of Gilfig's command, to doubt the essential virtue of Gilfig himself. "What is gained by this agonizing pilgrimage? Does Gilfig doubt our devotion? Surely we proved ourselves by attendance at the Lustral Rites; why has he sent us so far?"

"The ways of Gilfig are inscrutable," said Garstang. "We have come so far; we must seek on and on and on!"

Subucule stopped short, to look back the way they had come. "Here is my proposal. At this spot let us erect an altar of stones, which becomes our fane; let us then perform a rite.

With Gilfig's requirement satisfied, we may turn our faces to the north, to the village where our fellows reside. Here, happily we may recapture the pack-beasts, replenish our stores, and set forth across the dessert, perhaps to arrive once more at Erze Damath."

Garstang hesitated. "There is much to recommend your proposal. And yet—"

"A boat!" cried Cugel. He pointed to the sea where a half-mile offshore floated a fishing boat propelled by a square sail hanging from a long limber yard. It passed behind a headland which rose a mile south of where the pilgrims stood, and now Cugel indicated a village along the shore.

"Excellent!" declared Garstang. "These folk may be fellow Gilfigites, and this village the site of the fane! Let us proceed!"

Subucule still was reluctant. "Could knowledge of the sacred texts have penetrated so far?"

"Caution is the watchword," said Cugel. "We must reconnoiter with great care." And he led the way through a forest of tamarisk and larch, to where they could look down into the village. The huts were rudely constructed of black stone and housed a folk of ferocious aspect. Black hair in spikes surrounded the round clay-colored faces; coarse black bristles grew off the burly shoulders like epaulettes. Fangs protruded from the mouths of male and female alike and all spoke in harsh growling shouts. Cugel, Garstang and Subucule drew back with the utmost caution, and, hidden among the trees, conferred in low voices.

Garstang at last was discouraged and found nothing more to hope for. "I am exhausted, spiritually as well as physically; perhaps here is where I die."

Subucule looked to the north. "I return to take my chances on the Silver Desert. If all goes well, I will arrive once more at Erze Damath, or even Pholgus Valley."

Garstang turned to Cugel. "And what of you, since the fane of Gilfig is nowhere to be found?"

Cugel pointed to a dock at which a number of boats were

moored. "My destination is Almery, across the Songan Sea. I propose to commandeer a boat and sail to the west."

"I then bid you farewell," said Subucule. "Garstang, will you come?"

Garstang shook his head. "It is too far. I would surely die on the desert. I will cross the sea with Cugel and take the Word of Gilfig to the folk of Almery."

"Farewell, then, to you as well," said Subucule. Then he turned swiftly, to hide the emotion on his face, and started north.

Cugel and Garstang watched the sturdy form recede into the distance and disappear. Then they turned to a consideration of the dock. Garstang was dubious. "The boats seem seaworthy enough, but to 'commandeer' is to steal: an act specifically discountenanced by Gilfig."

"No difficulty exists," said Cugel. "I will place gold coins upon the dock, to a fair valuation of the boat."

Garstang gave a dubious assent. "What then of food and water?"

"After securing the boat, we will proceed along the coast until we are able to secure supplies, after which we sail due west."

To this Garstang assented and the two fell to examining the boats, comparing one against the other. The final selection was a staunch craft some ten or twelve paces long, of ample beam, with a small cabin.

At dusk they stole down to the dock. All was quiet: the fishermen had returned to the village. Garstang boarded the craft and reported all in good order. Cugel began casting off the lines, when from the end of the dock came a savage outcry and a dozen of the burly villagers came lumbering forth.

"We are lost!" cried Cugel. "Run for your life, or better, swim!"

"Impossible," declared Garstang. "If this is death, I will meet it with what dignity I am able!" And he climbed up on the dock.

In short order they were surrounded by folk of all ages, attracted by the commotion. One, an elder of the village, inquired in a stern voice, "What do you here, skulking on our dock, and preparing to steal a boat?"

"Our motive is simplicity itself," said Cugel. "We wish to cross the sea."

"What?" roared the elder. "How is that possible? The boat carries neither food nor water, and is poorly equipped. Why did you not approach us and make your needs known?"

Cugel blinked and exchanged a glance with Garstang. He shrugged. "I will be candid. Your appearance caused us such alarm that we did not dare."

The remark evoked mingled amusement and surprise in the crowd. The spokesman said, "All of us are puzzled; explain if you will."

"Very well," said Cugel. "May I be absolutely frank?"

"By all means!"

"Certain aspects of your appearance impress us as feral and barbarous: your protruding fangs, the black mane which surrounds your faces, the cacophony of your speech—to name only a few items."

The villagers laughed incredulously. "What nonsense!" they cried. "Our teeth are long that we may tear the coarse fish on which we subsist. We wear our hair thus to repel a certain noxious insect, and since we are all rather deaf, we possibly tend to shout. Essentially we are a gentle and kindly folk."

"Exactly," said the elder, "and in order to demonstrate this, tomorrow we shall provision our best boat and send you forth with hopes and good wishes. Tonight there shall be a feast in your honor!"

"Here is a village of true saintliness," declared Garstang. "Are you by chance worshippers of Gilfig?"

"No; we prostrate ourselves before the fish-god Yob, who seems as efficacious as any. But come, let us ascend to the village. We must make preparations for the feast."

They climbed steps hewn in the rock of the cliff, which gave upon an area illuminated by a dozen flaring torches. The elder indicated a hut more commodious than the others: "This is where you shall rest the night; I will sleep elsewhere."

Garstang again was moved to comment upon the benevolence of the fisher-folk, at which the elder bowed his head. "We try to achieve a spiritual unity. Indeed, we symbolize this ideal in the main dish of our ceremonial feasts." He turned, clapping his hands. "Let us prepare!"

A great cauldron was hung over a tripod; a block and a cleaver were arranged, and now each of the villagers, marching past the block, chopped off a finger and cast it into the pot.

The elder explained. "By this simple rite, which naturally you are expected to join, we demonstrate our common heritage and our mutual dependence. Come, let us step into the line." And Cugel and Garstang had no choice but to excise fingers and cast them into the pot with the others.

The feast continued long into the night. In the morning the villagers were as good as their word. An especially seaworthy boat was provided and loaded with stores, including food left over from the previous night's feast.

The villagers gathered on the dock. Cugel and Garstang voiced their gratitude, then Cugel hoisted the sail and Garstang threw off the mooring lines. A wind filled the sail and the boat moved out on the face of the Songan Sea. Gradually the shore became one with the murk of distance, and the two were alone, with only the black metallic shimmer of the water to all sides.

Noon came, and the boat moved in an elemental emptiness: water below, air above; silence in all directions. The afternoon was long and torpid, unreal as a dream; and the melancholy grandeur of sunset was followed by a dusk the color of watered wine.

The wind seemed to freshen and all night they steered west. At dawn the wind died and with sails flapping idly both Cugel and Garstang slept.

Eight times the cycle was repeated. On the morning of
the ninth day a low coastline was sighted ahead. During the
middle afternoon they drove the prow of their boat through
gentle surf up on a wide white beach. "This then is Almery?"
asked Garstang.

"So I believe," said Cugel, "but which quarter I am
uncertain. Azenomei may lie to north, west or south. If the
forest yonder is that which shrouds East Almery, we would
do well to pass to the side, as it bears an evil reputation."

Garstang pointed down the shore. "Notice: another village. If the folk here are like those across the sea, they will
help us on our way. Come, let us make our wants known."

Cugel hung back. "It might be wise to reconnoiter, as
before."

"To what end?" asked Garstang. "On that occasion we
were only misled and confused." He led the way down the
beach toward the village. As they approached they could see
folk moving across the central plaza: a graceful golden-haired
people, who spoke to each other in voices like music.

Garstang advanced joyfully, expecting a welcome even
more expansive than that they had received on the other
shore; but the villagers ran forward and caught them under
nets. "Why do you do this?" called Garstang. "We are strangers and intend no harm!"

"You are strangers; just so," spoke the tallest of the
golden-haired villagers. "We worship that inexorable god
known as Dangott. Strangers are automatically heretics, and
so are fed to the sacred apes." With that they began to drag
Cugel and Garstang over the sharp stones of the fore-shore
while the beautiful children of the village danced joyously to
either side.

Cugel managed to bring forth the tube he had secured
from Voynod and expelled blue concentrate at the villagers.
Aghast, they toppled to the ground and Cugel was able to
extricate himself from the net. Drawing his sword, he leapt
forward to cut Garstang free, but now the villagers rallied.

Cugel once more employed his tube, and the villagers fled in dismal agony.

"Go, Cugel," spoke Garstang. "I am an old man, of little vitality. Take to your heels; seek safety, with all my good wishes."

"This normally would be my impulse," Cugel conceded. "But these people have stimulated me to quixotic folly; so clamber from the net; we retreat together." Once more he wrought dismay with the blue projection, while Garstang freed himself, and the two fled along the beach.

The villagers pursued with harpoons. Their first cast pierced Garstang through the back. He fell without a sound. Cugel swung about and aimed the tube, but the spell was exhausted and only a limpid exudation appeared. The villagers drew back their arms to hurl a second volley; Cugel shouted a curse, dodged and ducked, and the harpoons plunged past him into the sand of the beach.

Cugel shook his fist a final time, then took to his heels and fled into the forest.

The Secret

UNBEAMS SLANTED through chinks in the wall of the hut; from the lagoon came shouts and splashing of the village children. Rona ta Inga at last opened his eyes. He had slept far past his usual hour of arising, far into the morning. He stretched his legs, cupped hands behind his head, stared absently up at the ceiling of thatch. In actuality he had awakened at the usual hour, to drift off again into a dreaming doze—a habit to which lately he had become prone. Only lately. Inga frowned and sat up with a jerk. What did this mean? Was it a si n? Per-haps he should inquire from Takti-Tai. . . . But it was all so ridiculous. He had slept late for the most ordinary of reasons: he enjoyed lazing and drowsing and dreaming.

On the mat beside him were crumpled flowers, where Mai-Mio had lain. Inga gathered the blossoms and laid them on the shelf which held his scant possessions. An enchanting creature, this Mai-Mio. She laughed no more and no less than other girls; her eyes were like other eyes, her mouth like all mouths; but her quaint and charming mannerisms made her absolutely unique: the single Mai-Mio in all the universe. Inga had loved many maidens. All in some way were singular, but Mai-Mio only recently had become a woman—even now from a distance she might be mistaken for a boy—while Inga was

249

older by at least five or six seasons. He was not quite sure. It
mattered little, in any event. It mattered very little, he told
himself again, quite emphatically. This was his village, his
island; he had no desire to leave. Ever!

The children came up the beach from the lagoon. Two or
three darted under his hut, swinging on one of the poles,
chanting nonsense-words. The hut trembled; the outcry
jarred upon Inga's nerves. He shouted in irritation. The children became instantly silent, in awe and astonishment, and
trotted away looking over their shoulders.

Inga frowned; for the second time this morning he felt
dissatisfied with himself. He would gain an unenviable reputation if he kept on in such a fashion. What had come over
him? He was the same Inga that he was yesterday . . . except
for the fact that a day had elapsed and he was a day older.

He went out on the porch before his hut, stretched in the
sunlight. To right and left were forty or fifty other such huts
as his own, with intervening trees; ahead lay the lagoon blue
and sparkling in the sunlight. Inga jumped to the ground,
walked to the lagoon, swam, dived far down among the glittering pebbles and ocean growths which covered the lagoon
floor. Emerging he felt relaxed and at peace—once more himself: Rona ta Inga, as he had always been, and always would
be!

Squatting on his porch he breakfasted on fruit and cold
baked fish from last night's feast and considered the day
ahead. There was no urgency, no duty to fulfil, no need to
satisfy. He could join the party of young bucks now on their
way into the forest hoping to snare fowl. He could fashion a
brooch of carved shell and goana-nut for Mai-Mio. He could
lounge and gossip; he could fish. Or he could visit his best
friend Takti-Tai—who was building a boat. Inga rose to his
feet. He would fish. He walked along the beach to his canoe,
checked equipment, pushed off, paddled across the lagoon to
the opening in the reef. The winds blew to the west as always.

Leaving the lagoon Inga turned a swift glance downwind—an almost furtive glance—then bent his neck into the wind and paddled east.

Within the hour he had caught six fine fish, and drifted back along the reef to the lagoon entrance. Everyone was swimming when he returned. Maidens, young men, children. Mai-Mio paddled to the canoe, hooked her arms over the gunwales, grinned up at him, water glistening on her cheeks. "Rona ta Inga! Did you catch fish? Or am I bad luck?"

"See for yourself."

She looked. "Five—no, six! All fat silver-fins! I am good luck! May I sleep often in your hut?"

"So long as I catch fish the following day."

She dropped back into the water, splashed him, sank out of sight. Through the undulating surface Inga could see her slender brown form skimming off across the bottom. He beached the canoe, wrapped the fish in big sipi-leaves and stored them in a cool cistern, then ran down to the lagoon to join the swimming.

Later he and Mai-Mio sat in the shade; she plaiting a decorative cord of colored bark which later she would weave into a basket, he leaning back, looking across the water. Artlessly Mai-Mio chattered—of the new song Ama ta Lalau had composed, of the odd fish she had seen while swimming underwater, of the change which had come over Takti-Tai since he had started building his boat.

Inga made an absent-minded sound, but said nothing.

"We have formed a band," Mai-Mio confided. "There are six of us: Ipa, Tuiti, Hali-Sai-Iano, Zoma, Oiu-Ngo and myself. We have pledged never to leave the island. Never, never, never. There is too much joy here. Never will we sail west—never. Whatever the secret we do not wish to know."

Inga smiled, a rather wistful smile. "There is much wisdom in the pledge you have made."

She stroked his arm. "Why do you not join us in our

pledge? True, we are six girls—but a pledge is a pledge."

"True."

"Do you want to sail west?"

"No."

Mai-Mio excitedly rose to her knees. "I will call together
the band, and all of us, all together: we will recite the pledge
again, never will we leave our island! And to think, you are
the oldest of all at the village!"

"Takti-Tai is older," said Inga.

"But Takti-Tai is building his boat! He hardly counts any
more!"

"Vai-Ona is as old as I. Almost as old."

"Do you know something? Whenever Vai Ona goes out to
fish, he always looks to the west. He wonders."

"Everyone wonders."

"Not I!" Mai-Mio jumped to her feet. "Not I—not any of
the band. Never, never, never—never will we leave the island!
We have pledged ourselves!" She reached down, patted Inga's
cheek, ran off to where a group of her friends were sharing a
basket of fruit.

Inga sat quietly for five minutes. Then he made an impatient gesture, rose and walked along the shore to the platform
where Takti-Tai worked on his boat. This was a catamaran
with a broad deck, a shelter of woven withe thatched with
sipi-leaf, a stout mast. In silence Inga helped Takti-Tai shape
the mast, scraping a tall well-seasoned pa-siao-tui sapling with
sharp shells. Inga presently paused, laid aside the shell. He
said, "Long ago there were four of us. You, me, Akara and
Zan. Remember?"

Takti-Tai nodded.

"We pledged never to leave the island. We swore never to
weaken, we spilled blood to seal the pact. Never would we
sail west."

"I remember."

"Now you sail," said Inga. "I will be the last of the group."

Takti-Tai paused in his scraping, looked at Inga, as if he

would speak, then bent once more over the mast. Inga presently returned up the beach to his hut, where squatting on the porch he carved at the brooch for Mai-Mio.

A youth presently came to sit beside him. Inga, who had no particular wish for companionship, continued with his carving. But the youth, absorbed in his own problems, failed to notice. "Advise me, Rona ta Inga. You are the oldest of the village and very sage." Inga raised his eyebrows, then scowled, but said nothing.

"I love Hali Sai Iano, I long for her desperately, but she laughs at me and runs off to throw her arms about the neck of Hopu. What should I do?"

"The situation is quite simple," said Inga. "She prefers Hopu. You need merely select another girl. What of Talau Io? She is pretty and affectionate, and seems to like you."

The youth vented a sigh. "Very well. I will do as you suggest. After all one girl is much like another." He departed, unaware of the sardonic look Inga directed at his back. He asked himself, why do they come to me for advice? I am only two or three, or at most four or five, seasons their senior. It is as if they think me the fount and source of all sagacity!

During the evening a baby was born. The mother was Omei Ni Io, who for almost a season had slept in Inga's hut. Since it was a boy-child she named it Inga ta Omei. There was a naming ceremony at which Inga presided. The singing and dancing lasted until late, and if it were not for the fact that the child was his own, with his name, Inga would have crept off early to his hut. He had attended many naming ceremonies.

A week later Takti-Tai sailed west, and there was a ceremony of a different sort. Everyone came to the beach to touch the hull of the boat and bless it with water. Tears ran freely down all cheeks, including Takti-Tai's. For the last time he looked around the lagoon, into the faces of those he would be leaving. Then he turned, signalled; the young men pushed the boat away from the beach, then jumping into the water, towed it across the lagoon, guided it out into the

ocean. Takti-Tai cut brails, tightened halyards; the big square
sail billowed in the wind. The boat surged west. Takti-Tai
stood on the platform, gave a final flourish of the hand, and
those on the beach waved farewell. The boat moved out into
the afternoon, and when the sun sank, it could be seen no
more.

During the evening meal the talk was quiet; everyone
stared into the fire. Mai-Mio finally jumped to her feet. "Not
I," she chanted. "Not I—ever, ever, ever!"

"Nor I," shouted Ama ta Lalau, who of all the youths
was the most proficient musician. He reached for the guitar
which he had carved from a black soa-gum trunk, struck
chords, began to sing.

Inga watched quietly. He was now the oldest on the
island, and it seemed as if the others were treating him with a
new respect. Ridiculous! What nonsense! So little older was
he that it made no difference whatever! But he noticed that
Mai-Mio was laughingly attentive to Ama ta Lalau, who
responded to the flirtation with great gallantry. Inga watched
with a heavy feeling around the heart, and presently went off
to his hut. That night, for the first time in weeks, Mai-Mio did
not sleep beside him. No matter, Inga told himself: one girl is
much like another.

The following day he wandered up the beach to the platform where Takti-Tai had built his boat. The area was clean
and tidy, and tools were hung carefully in a nearby shed. In
the forest beyond grew fine makara trees, from which the
staunchest hulls were fashioned.

Inga turned away. He took his canoe out to catch fish,
and leaving the lagoon looked to the west. There was nothing
to see but empty horizon, precisely like the horizon to east,
to north and to south—except that the western horizon concealed the secret. And the rest of the day he felt uneasy.
During the evening meal he looked from face to face. None
were the faces of his dear friends; they all had built their

boats and had sailed. His friends had departed; his friends knew the secret.

The next morning, without making a conscious decision, Inga sharpened the tools and felled two fine makara trees. He was not precisely building a boat—so he assured himself—but it did no harm for wood to season.

Nevertheless the following day he trimmed the trees, cut the trunk to length, and the next day assembled all the young men to help carry the trunks to the platform. No one seemed surprised; everyone knew that Rona ta Inga was building his boat. Mai-Mio had now frankly taken up with Ama ta Lalau and as Inga worked on his boat he watched them play in the water, not without a lump of bitterness in his throat. Yes, he told himself, it would be pleasure indeed to join his true friends—the youths and maidens he had known since he dropped his milk-name, whom he had sported with, who now were departed, and for whom he felt an aching loneliness. Diligently he hollowed the hulls, burning, scraping, chiselling. Then the platform was secured, the little shelter woven and thatched to protect him from rain. He scraped a mast from a flawless pa-siao-tui sapling, stepped and stayed it. He gathered bast, wove a coarse but sturdy sail, hung it to stretch and season. Then he began to provision the boat. He gathered nut-meats, dried fruits, smoked fish wrapped in sipi-leaf. He filled blow-fish bladders with water. How long was the trip to the west? No one knew. Best not to go hungry, best to stock the boat well: once down the wind there was no turning back.

One day he was ready. It was a day much like all the other days of his life. The sun shone warm and bright, the lagoon glittered and rippled up and down the beach in little gushes of play-surf. Rona ta Inga's throat felt tense and stiff; he could hardly trust his voice. The young folk came to line the beach; all blessed the boat with water. Inga gazed into each face, then along the line of huts, the trees, the beaches, the scenes he loved with such intensity. . . . Already they seemed remote. Tears were coursing his cheeks. He held up his hand, turned away. He felt the boat leave the beach, float free on the water. Swimmers thrust him out into the ocean. For the last time he turned to look back at the village, fighting a sudden maddening urge to jump from the boat, to swim back to the village. He hoisted the sail, the wind thrust deep into the hollow. Water surged under the hulls and he was coasting west, with the island astern.

Up the blue swells, down into the long troughs, the wake gurgling, the bow rising and falling. The long afternoon waned and became golden; sunset burned and ebbed and became a halcyon dusk. The stars appeared, and Inga, sitting silently by his rudder, held the sail full to the wind. At midnight he lowered the sail and slept, the boat drifting quietly.

In the morning he was completely alone, the horizons blank. He raised the sail and scudded west, and so passed the day, and the next, and others. And Inga became thankful that he had provisioned the boat with generosity. On the sixth day he seemed to notice that a chill had come into the wind; on the eighth day he sailed under a high overcast, the like of which he had never seen before. The ocean changed from blue to a gray which presently took on a green tinge, and now the water was cold. The wind blew with great force, bellying his bast sail, and Inga huddled in the shelter to avoid the harsh spray. On the morning of the ninth day he thought to see a dim dark shape loom ahead, which at noon became a line of tall cliffs with surf beating against jagged rocks, roaring back and forth across coarse shingle. In mid-afternoon he ran his boat up on one of the shingle beaches, jumped gingerly ashore. Shivering in the whooping gusts, he took stock of the situation. There was no living thing to be seen along the foreshore but three or four gray gulls. A hundred yards to his right lay a battered hulk of another boat, and beyond was a tangle of wood and fiber which might have been still another.

Inga carried ashore what provisions remained, bundled

them together, and by a faint trail climbed the cliffs. He came out on an expanse of rolling gray-green downs. Two or three miles inland rose a line of low hills, toward which the trail seemed to lead.

Inga looked right and left; again there was no living creature in sight other than gulls. Shouldering his bundle he set forth along the trail.

Nearing the hills he came upon a hut of turf and stone, beside a patch of cultivated soil. A man and a woman worked in the field. Inga peered closer. What manner of creatures were these? They resembled human beings; they had arms and legs and faces—but how seamed and seared and gray they were! How shrunken were their hands, how bent and hobbled as they worked! He walked quickly by, and they did not appear to notice him.

Now Inga hastened, as the end of the day was drawing on and the hills loomed before him. The trail led along a valley grown with gnarled oak and low purple-green shrubs, then slanted up the hillside through a stony gap, where the wind generated whistling musical sounds. From the gap Inga looked out over a flat valley. He saw copses of low trees, plots of tilled land, a group of huts. Slowly he walked down the trail. In a nearby field a man raised his head. Inga paused, thinking to recognize him. Was this not Akara ta Oma who had sailed west ten or twelve seasons back? It seemed impossible. This man was fat, the hair had almost departed his head, his cheeks hung loose at the jawline. No, this could not be lithe Akara ta Oma! Hurriedly Inga turned away, and presently entered the village. Before a nearby hut stood one whom he recognized with joy. "Takti-Tai!"

Takti-Tai nodded. "Rona ta Inga. I know you'd be coming soon."

"I'm delighted to see you! But let us leave this terrible place; let us return to the island!"

Takti-Tai smiled a little, shook his head.

Inga protested heatedly, "Don't tell me you prefer this

dismal land? Come! My boat is still seaworthy. If somehow
we can back it off the beach, gain the open sea . . ."

The wind sang down over the mountains, strummed
through the trees. Inga's words died in his throat. It was
clearly impossible to work the boat off the foreshore.

"Not only the wind," said Takti-Tai. "We could not go
back now. We know the secret."

Inga stared in wonderment. "The secret? Not I."

"Come. Now you will learn."

Takti-Tai took him through the village to a structure of
stone with a high-gabled roof shingled with slate. "Enter, and
you will know the secret."

Hesitantly Rona ta Inga entered the stone structure. On a
stone table lay a still figure surrounded by six tall candles.
Inga stared at the shrunken white face, at the white sheet
which lay motionless over the narrow chest. "Who is this? A
man? How thin he is. Does he sleep? Why do you show me
such a thing?"

"This is the secret," said Takti-Tai. "It is called 'death'."

Liane the Wayfarer

THROUGH the dim forest came Liane the Way-farer, passing along the shadowed glades with a prancing lightfooted gait. He whistled, he carol-ed, he was plainly in high spirits. Around his finger he twirled a bit of wrought bronze—a circlet graved with angular crabbed characters, now stained black.

By excellent chance he had found it, banded around the root of an ancient yew. Hacking it free, he had seen the char-acters on the inner surface—rude forceful symbols, doubtless the cast of a powerful antique rune . . . Best take it to a magi-cian and have it tested for sorcery.

Liane made a wry mouth. There were objections to the course. Sometimes it seemed as if all living creatures conspired to exasperate him. Only this morning, the spice merchant—what a tumult he had made dying! How carelessly he had spewed blood on Liane's cock comb sandals! Still, thought Liane, every unpleasantness carried with it compensation. While digging the grave he had found the bronze ring.

And Liane's spirits soared; he laughed in pure joy. He bounded, he leapt. His green cape flapped behind him, the red feather in his cap winked and blinked . . . But still—Liane slowed his step—he was no whit closer to the mystery of the magic, if magic the ring possessed.

Experiment, that was the word!

He stopped where the ruby sunlight slanted down without hindrance from the high foliage, examined the ring, traced the glyphs with his fingernail. He peered through. A faint film, a flicker? He held it at arm's length. It was clearly a coronet. He whipped off his cap, set the band on his brow, rolled his great golden eyes, preened himself . . . Odd. It slipped down on his ears. It tipped across his eyes. Darkness. Frantically Liane clawed it off . . . A bronze ring, a hand's-breadth in diameter. Queer.

He tried again. It slipped down over his head, his shoulders. His head was in the darkness of a strange separate space. Looking down, he saw the level of the outside light dropping as he dropped the ring.

Slowly down . . . Now it was around his ankles—and in sudden panic, Liane snatched the ring up over his body, emerged blinking into the maroon light of the forest.

He saw a blue-white green-white flicker against the foliage. It was a Twk-man, mounted on a dragon-fly, and light glinted from the dragon-fly's wings.

Liane called sharply, "Here, sir! Here sir!"

The Twk-man perched his mount on a twig. "Well, Liane, what do you wish?"

"Watch now, and remember what you see." Liane pulled the ring over his head, dropped it to his feet, lifted it back. He looked up to the Twk-man, who was chewing a leaf. "And what did you see?"

"I saw Liane vanish from mortal sight—except for the red curled toes of his sandals. All else was as air."

"Ha!" cried Liane. "Think of it! Have you ever seen the like?"

The Twk-man asked carelessly, "Do you have salt? I would have salt."

Liane cut his exultations short, eyed the Twk-man closely. "What news do you bring me?"

"Three erbs killed Florejin and Dream-builder, and burst

all his bubbles. The air above the manse was colored for many minutes with the flitting fragments."

"A gram."

"Lord Kandive the Golden has built a barge of carven mowood ten lengths high, and it floats on the River Scaum for the Regatta, full of treasure."

"Two grams."

"A golden witch named Lith has come to live on Thamber Meadow. She is quiet and very beautiful."

"Three grams."

"Enough," said the Twk-man, and leaned forward to watch while Liane weighed out the salt in a tiny balance. He packed it in small panniers hanging on each side of the ribbed thorax, then twitched the insect into the air and flicked off through the forest vaults.

Once more Liane tried his bronze ring, and this time brought it entirely past his feet, stepped out of it and brought the ring up into the darkness beside him. What a wonderful sanctuary! A hole whose opening could be hidden inside the hole itself! Down with the ring to his feet, step through, bring it up his slender frame and over his shoulders, out into the forest with a small bronze ring in his hand.

Ho! and off to Thamber Meadow to see the beautiful golden witch.

Her hut was a simple affair of woven reeds—a low dome with two round windows and a low door. He saw Lith at the pond bare-legged among the water shoots, catching frogs for her supper. A white kirtle was gathered up tight around her thighs; stock-still she stood and the dark water rippled rings away from her slender knees.

She was more beautiful than Liane could have imagined, as if one of Florejin's wasted bubbles had burst here on the water. Her skin was pale creamed stirred gold, her hair a denser, wetter gold. Her eyes were like Liane's own, great golden orbs, and hers were wide apart, tilted slightly.

Liane strode forward and planted himself on the bank.

She looked up startled, her ripe mouth half-open.

"Behold, golden witch, here is Liane. He has come to welcome you to Thamber; and he offers you his friendship, his love . . ."

Lith bent, scooped a handful of slime from the bank and flung it into his face.

Shouting the most violent curses, Liane wiped his eyes free, but the door to the hut had slammed shut.

Liane strode to the door and pounded it with his fist.

"Open and show your witch's face, or I burn the hut!"

The door opened, and the girl looked forth, smiling. "What now?"

Liane entered the hut and lunged for the girl, but twenty thin shafts darted out, twenty points pricking his chest. He halted, eyebrows raised, mouth twitching.

"Down steel," said Lith. The blades snapped from view. "So easily could I seek your vitality," said Lith, "had I willed."

Liane frowned and rubbed his chin as if pondering. "You understand," he said earnestly, "what a witless thing you do. Liane is feared by those who fear fear, loved by those who love love. And you—" his eyes swam the golden glory of her body— "you are ripe as a sweet fruit, you are eager, you glisten and tremble with love. You please Liane, and he will spend much warmness on you."

"No, no," said Lith, with a slow smile. "You are too hasty."

Liane looked at her in surprise. "Indeed?"

"I am Lith," said she. "I am what you say I am. I ferment, I burn, I seethe. Yet I may have no lover but him who has served me. He must be brave, swift, cunning."

"I am he," said Liane. He chewed at his lip. "It is not usually thus. I detest this indecision." He took a step forward. "Come, let us—"

She backed away. "No, no. You forget. How have you served me, how have you gained the right to my love?"

"Absurdity!" stormed Liane. "Look at me! Note my

perfect grace, the beauty of my form and feature, my great eyes, as golden as your own, my manifest will and power . . . It is you who should serve me. That is how I will have it." He sank upon a low divan. "Woman, give me wine."

She shook her head. "In my small domed hut I cannot be forced. Perhaps outside on Thamber Meadow—but in here, among my blue and red tassels, with twenty blades of steel at my call, you must obey me. . . . So choose. Either arise and go, never to return, or else agree to serve me on one small mission, and then have me and all my ardor."

Liane sat straight and stiff. An odd creature, the golden witch. But, indeed, she was worth some exertion, and he would make her pay for her impudence.

"Very well, then," he said blandly. "I will serve you. What do you wish? Jewels? I can suffocate you in pearls, blind you with diamonds. I have two emeralds the size of your fist, and they are green oceans, where the gaze is trapped and wanders forever among vertical green prisms . . ."

"No, no jewels—"

"An enemy, perhaps. Ah, so simple. Liane will kill you ten men. Two steps forward, thrust—*thus*!" He lunged. "And souls go thrilling up like bubbles in a beaker of mead."

"No. I want no killing."

He sat back, frowning. "What, then?"

She stepped to the back of the room and pulled at a drape. It swung aside, displaying a golden tapestry. The scene was a valley bounded by two steep mountains, a broad valley where a placid river ran, past a quiet village and so into a grove of trees. Golden was the river, golden the mountains, golden the trees—golds so various, so rich, so subtle that the effect was like a many-colored landscape. But the tapestry had been rudely hacked in half.

Liane was entranced. "Exquisite, exquisite . . ."

Lith said, "It is the Magic Valley of Ariventa so depicted. The other half has been stolen from me, and its recovery is the service I wish of you."

"Where is the other half?" demanded Liane. "Whↄ is the dastard?"

Now she watched him closely. "Have you ever heard of Chun? Chun the Unavoidable?"

Liane considered. "No.".

"He stole the half to my tapestry, and hung it in a marble hall, and this hall is in the ruins to the north of Kaiin."

"Ha!" muttered Liane.

"The hall is by the Place of Whispers, and is marked by a leaning column with a black medallion of a phoenix and a two-headed lizard."

"I go," said Liane. He rose. "One day to Kaiin, one day to steal, one day to return. Three days."

Lith followed him to the door. "Beware of Chun the Unavoidable," she whispered.

And Liane strode away whistling, the red feather bobbing in his green cap. Lith watched him, then turned and slowly approached the golden tapestry. "Golden Ariventa," she whispered, "my heart cries and hurts with longing for you . . ."

The Derna is a swifter, thinner river than the Scaum, its bosomy sister to the south. And where the Scaum wallows through a broad dale, purple with horse-blossom, pocked white and gray with crumbling castles, the Derna has sheered a steep canyon, overhung by forested bluffs.

An ancient flint road long ago followed the course of the Derna, but now the exaggeration of the meandering had cut into the pavement, so that Liane, treading the road to Kaiin, was occasionally forced to leave the road and make a detour through banks of thorn and the tubegrass which whistled in the breeze.

The red sun, drifting across the universe like an old man creeping to his death-bed, hung low to the horizon when Liane breasted Porphiron Scar, looked across white-walled Kaiin and the blue bay of Sanreale beyond.

Directly below was the market-place, a medley of stalls

selling fruit, slabs of pale meat, molluscs from the slime banks, dull flagons of wine. And the quiet people of Kaiin moved among the stalls, buying their sustenance, carrying it loosely to their stone chambers.

Beyond the market-place rose a bank of ruined columns, like broken teeth—legs to the arena built two hundred feet from the ground by Mad King Shin; beyond, in a grove of bay trees, the glossy dome of the palace was visible, where Kandive the Golden ruled Kaiin and as much of Ascolais as one could see from a vantage on Porphiron Scar.

The Derna, no longer a flow of clear water, poured through a network of dank canals and subterranean tubes, and finally seeped past rotting wharves into the Bay of Sanreale.

A bed for the night, thought Liane; then to his business in the morning.

He leapt down the zig-zag steps—back, forth, back, forth —and came out into the market-place. And now he put on a grave demeanor. Liane the Wayfarer was not unknown in Kaiin, and many were ill-minded enough to work him harm.

He moved sedately in the shade of the Pannone Wall, turned through a narrow cobbled street, bordered by old wooden houses glowing the rich brown of old stump-water in the rays of the setting sun, and so came to a small square and the high stone face of the Magician's Inn.

The host, a small fat man, sad of eye, with a small fat nose the identical shape of the body, was scraping ashes from the hearth. He straightened his back and hurried behind the counter of his little alcove.

Liane said, "A chamber, well-aired, and a supper of mushrooms, wine and oysters."

The innkeeper bowed humbly.

"Indeed, sir—and how will you pay?"

Liane flung down a leather sack, taken this very morning. The innkeeper raised his eyebrows in pleasure at the fragrance.

"The ground buds of the spase-bush, brought from a far land," said Liane.

"Excellent, excellent ... Your chamber, sir, and your supper at once."

As Liane ate, several other guests of the house appeared and sat before the fire with wine, and the talk grew large, and dwelt on wizards of the past and the great days of magic.

"Great Phandaal knew a lore now forgot," said one old man with hair dyed orange. "He tied white and black strips to the legs of sparrows and sent them veering to his direction. And where they wove their magic woof, great trees appeared, laden with flowers, fruit, nuts, or bulbs or rare liqueurs. It is said that thus he wove Great Da Forest on the shores of Sanra Water."

"Ha," said a dour man in a garment of dark blue, brown and black, "this I can do." He brought forth a bit of string, flicked it, whirled it, spoke a quiet word, and the vitality of the pattern fused the string into a tongue of red and yellow fire, which danced, curled, darted back and forth along the table till the dour man killed it with a gesture.

"And this I can do," said a hooded figure in a black cape sprinkled with silver circles. He brought forth a small tray, laid it on the table and sprinkled therein a pinch of ashes from the hearth. He brought forth a whistle and blew a clear tone, and up from the tray came glittering motes, flashing the prismatic colors red, blue, green, yellow. They floated up a foot and burst in coruscations of brilliant colors, each a beautiful star-shaped pattern, and each burst sounded a tiny repetition of the original tone—the clearest, purest sound in the world. The motes became fewer, the magician blew a different tone, and again the motes floated up to burst in glorious ornamental spangles. Another time—another swarm of motes. At last the magician replaced his whistle, wiped off the tray, tucked it inside his cloak and lapsed back to silence.

Now the other wizards surged forward, and soon the air above the table swarmed with visions, quivered with spells. One showed the group nine new colors of ineffable charm and radiance; another caused a mouth to form on the landlord's forehead and revile the crowd, much to the landlord's discomfiture, since it was his own voice. Another displayed a green glass bottle from which the face of a demon peered and grimaced; another a ball of pure crystal which rolled back and forward to the command of the sorcerer who owned it, and who claimed it to be an earring of the fabled master Sankaferrin.

Liane had attentively watched all, crowing in delight at the bottled imp, and trying to cozen the obedient crystal from its owner, without success.

And Liane became pettish, complaining that the world was full of rock-hearted men, but the sorcerer with the crystal earring remained indifferent, and even when Liane spread out twelve packets of rare spice he refused to part with his toy.

Liane pleaded, "I wish only to please the witch Lith."

"Please her with the spice, then."

Liane said ingenuously, "Indeed, she has but one wish, a bit of tapestry which I must steal from Chun the Unavoidable."

And he looked from face to suddenly silent face.

"What causes such immediate sobriety? Ho, Landlord, more wine!"

The sorcerer with the earring said, "If the floor swam ankle deep with wine—the rich red wine of Tanvilkat—the leaden print of the name would still ride the air."

"Ha," laughed Liane, "let only a taste of that wine pass your lips, and the fumes would erase all memory."

"See his eyes," came a whisper. "Great and golden."

"And quick to see," spoke Liane. "And these legs—quick to run, fleet as starlight on the waves. And this arm—quick to stab with steel. And my magic—which will set me to a refuge that is out of all cognizance." He gulped wine from a beaker. "Now behold. This is magic from antique days." He set the bronze band over his head, stepped through, brought it up inside the darkness. When he deemed that sufficient time had elapsed, he stepped through once more.

The fire glowed, the landlord stood in his alcove, Liane's wine was at hand. But of the assembled magicians there was no trace.

Liane looked about in puzzlement. "And where are my wizardly friends?"

The landlord turned his head. "They took to their chambers; the name you spoke weighed on their souls."

And Liane drank his wine in frowning silence.

Next morning he left the inn and picked a roundabout way to the Old Town—a gray wilderness of tumbled pillars, weathered blocks of sandstone, slumped pediments with crumbled inscriptions, flagged terraces overgrown with rusty moss. Lizards, snakes, insects crawled the ruins; no other life did he see.

Threading a way through the rubble, he almost stumbled on a corpse—the body of a youth, one who stared at the sky with empty eye-sockets.

Liane felt a presence. He leapt back, rapier half-bared. A stooped old man stood watching him. He spoke in a feeble, quavering voice: "And what will you have in the Old Town?"

Liane replaced his rapier. "I seek the Place of Whispers. Perhaps you will direct me."

The old man made a croaking sound at the back of his throat. "Another? Another? When will it cease . . ." He motioned to the corpse. "This one came yesterday seeking the Place of Whispers. He would steal from Chun the Unavoidable. See him now." He turned away. "Come with me." He disappeared over a tumble of rock.

Liane followed. The old man stood by another corpse with eye-sockets bereft and bloody. "This one came four days ago, and he met Chun the Unavoidable . . . And over there behind the arch is still another, a great warrior in cloison armor. And there—and there—" he pointed, pointed. "And there—and there—like crushed flies."

He turned his water-blue gaze back to Liane. "Return, young man, return—lest your body lie here in its green cloak to rot on the flagstones."

Liane drew his rapier and flourished it. "I am Liane the Wayfarer; let them who offend me have fear. And where is the Place of Whispers?"

"If you must know," said the old man, "it is beyond that broken obelisk. But you go to your peril."

"I am Liane the Wayfarer. Peril goes with me."

The old man stood like a piece of weathered statuary as Liane strode off.

And Liane asked himself, suppose this old man were an agent of Chun, and at this minute were on his way to warn him? . . . Best to take all precautions. He leapt up on a high entablature and ran crouching back to where he had left the ancient.

Here he came, muttering to himself, leaning on his staff. Liane dropped a block of granite as large as his head. A thud, a croak, a gasp—and Liane went his way.

He strode past the broken obelisk, into a wide court—the Place of Whispers. Directly opposite was a long wide hall, marked by a leaning column with a big black medallion, the sign of a phoenix and a two-headed lizard.

Liane merged himself with the shadow of a wall, and stood watching like a wolf, alert for any flicker of motion.

All was quiet. The sunlight invested the ruins with dreary splendor. To all sides, as far as the eye could reach, was broken stone, a wasteland leached by a thousand rains, until now the sense of man had departed and the stone was one with the natural earth.

The sun moved across the dark-blue sky. Liane presently stole from his vantage-point and circled the hall. No sight nor sign did he see.

He approached the building from the rear and pressed his ear to the stone. It was dead, without vibration. Around the side—watching up, down, to all sides; a breach in the wall. Liane peered inside. At the back hung half a golden tapestry. Otherwise the hall was empty.

Liane looked up, down, this side, that. There was nothing in sight. He continued around the hall.

He came to another broken place. He looked within. To the rear hung the golden tapestry. Nothing else, to right or left, no sight or sound.

Liane continued to the front of the hall and sought into the eaves: dead as dust.

He had a clear view of the room. Bare, barren, except for the bit of golden tapestry.

Liane entered, striding with long soft steps. He halted in the middle of the floor. Light came to him from all sides except the rear wall. There were a dozen openings from which to flee and no sound except the dull thudding of his heart.

He took two steps forward. The tapestry was almost at his fingertips.

He stepped forward and swiftly jerked the tapestry down from the wall.

And behind it was Chun the Unavoidable.

Liane screamed. He turned on paralyzed legs and they were leaden, like legs in a dream which refused to run.

Chun dropped out of the wall and advanced. Over his shiny black back he wore a robe of eyeballs threaded on silk.

Liane was running, fleetly now. He sprang, he soared. The tips of his toes scarcely touched the ground. Out the hall, across the square, into the wilderness of broken statues and fallen columns. And behind came Chun, running like a dog.

Liane sped along the crest of a wall and sprang a great gap to a shattered fountain. Behind came Chun.

Liane darted up a narrow alley, climbed over a pile of refuse, over a roof, down into a court. Behind came Chun.

Liane sped down a wide avenue lined with a few stunted old cypress trees, and he heard Chun close at his heels. He turned into an archway, pulled his bronze ring over his head, down to his feet. He stepped through, brought the ring up inside the darkness. Sanctuary. He was alone in a dark magic silence, dead space . . .

He felt a stir behind him, a breath of air. At his elbow a voice said, "I am Chun the Unavoidable."

Lith sat on her couch near the candles, weaving a cap from frogskins. The door to her hut was barred, the windows shuttered. Outside, Thamber Meadow drowsed in darkness.

A scrape at her door, a creak as the lock was tested. Lith became rigid and stared at the door.

A voice said, "Tonight, O Lith, tonight it is two long bright threads for you. Two because the eyes were so great, so large, so golden . . ."

Lith sat quiet. She waited an hour; then, creeping to the door, she listened. The sense of presence was absent. A frog croaked nearby.

She eased the door ajar, found the threads and closed the door. She ran to her golden tapestry and fitted the threads into the ravelled warp.

And she stared at the golden valley, sick with longing for Ariventa, and tears blurred out the peaceful river, the quiet golden forest. "The cloth slowly grows wider . . . One day it will be done, and I will come home . . ."